FAE GODS
FAE GODS TRILOGY

KATHY HAAN

Edited by
JESSICA RYN

This is a work of fiction. Names, characters, places, and incidents either are the product of the author's imagination or are used fictitiously. Any resemblance to actual persons, living or dead, events, or locales is entirely coincidental.

Copyright © 2023 by Kathy Haan

All rights reserved.

No part of this book may be reproduced in any form or by any electronic or mechanical means, including information storage and retrieval systems, without written permission from the author, except for the use of brief quotations in a book review. For more information, email kathy@idyllicpursuit.com.

ISBN 978-1-960256-90-4 (eBook)

ISBN 978-1-960256-02-7 (paperback)

First edition April 2023

Book cover design by Atra Luna Design

Published by Thousand Lives Press, LLC

To the woman whose spirit yearns,
But whose heart is trapped in chains.
May these stories of Fae Gods and turns,
Bring some magic to ease your pains.

In a world where love can be unyielding,
And the weight of life can make us break,
May these tales be a form of shielding,
And offer solace for your sake.

Let the verses flow and remind you,
That your dreams are vibrant and bright,
And though the pressures may bind you,
You can still find your way to the light.

xoxo
Kathy Haan

CHAPTER ONE

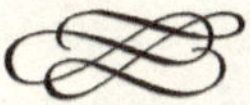

VOX

She's completely unaware of how magnificent she is, but I see it there inside her: a spark of something extraordinary hidden just beneath the surface.

Jocelyn tucks her long, tanned legs under her on the cream-colored couch that she'd paid a small fortune for, and the giant wrinkled dog sprawls on the floor beside her. He's called Rolls, a gentle beast that likely outweighs her. With her phone resting on her braless chest, Jocelyn's lost in the mindless scrolling that consumes her evenings.

Today, she's had her hair dyed, a subtle change that leaves it a touch sleeker than usual, dusting her shoulders with soft flaxen waves. It's beautiful, but I can't help but miss the sight of the column of her neck when she wears it up, and that delicate bob of her throat when she swallows. We're not allowed to touch her, but I'm privy to every aspect of her life. For thirty-six years, our kind have kept watch and witnessed every special moment, each mundane task, and every dream crushed beneath the heel of an inattentive husband.

Jocelyn met Alexander at a college graduation party, and they were married not long after. But the reality of her soul-sucking marriage sets in with every missed anniversary, forgotten date night, and rushed pleasantries when he gets home from a long day at the office. She's a great wife, though he takes advantage of her kind nature. She's turned this enormous mausoleum of a house into a home and sits alone most days and nights. No cleaners or staff touch the place, though they can afford it. Jocelyn prefers to do it herself.

Supper is on the table every evening by seven. She cleans up on her own while the husband knocks back a whiskey in front of the game, and by ten, he crawls in bed to fuck her for twenty-seven seconds before rolling over and passing out.

Occasionally, he'll offer to help get her off, but she's too kind to him about it. He's never once given her an orgasm, but she fakes it every time. She's got a deep nightstand drawer full of toys she's either bought at toy parties or ordered discreetly on her phone after yet another night of dissatisfying sex in an attempt to spice things up in their sex lives.

It's not her fault, though. Alex doesn't seem to know enough about what makes her curl her toes because he just doesn't care enough to. She's like a pretty, decorated doll, tucked away on a shelf to be used and then tossed haphazardly into a box when his needs are met. But ever the doting wife, she drags herself out of that chest every night and repeats the same process day after day.

An incoming text buzzes on her phone, and I peek over her shoulder to read it.

> Won't be home until 8. Can you make calzones?

A deep sigh escapes her full, painted lips. I don't know why he asks her to make these when all he does is compare them to his mother's. But I've tasted both Jocelyn's cooking and hers—letting Rolls take the blame for the missing food—and Jocelyn's beats the mother-in-law's from-a-can dough recipe by a landslide. I may be immortal, but I still need to eat and sleep, just like mortals do, otherwise, I'm miserable.

By the time she finishes folding the dough over the ingredients and pinching the sides, she's got an hour left before he comes home, granting her plenty of time to kill before she needs to put the calzones in the oven.

Wrapping the blush-pink scrunchy at her wrist around her hair—*ah, yes, there's her neck*—she trudges up the stairs, Rolls right on her heel. Her bare feet leave brief marks on the shiny floor before they evaporate. She's got a slinky maxi dress on that sits just below the knees, and it hugs her curvy figure.

Oh?

She just shut Rolls out of her bedroom.

I know what that means.

I run my hand down the door jamb, the wood smooth and cool, almost airy to the touch. There's a buffer, as if my hand is suspended in a vacuum for a moment, and then it passes through, touching the door and coming back out the other side. I feel it with both hands this time, then try to go through with my head.

There's a fuzzy feeling every time my body grazes a surface. Passing through doors is a little uncomfortable, but as I do, I'm greeted by the sight of Joss leaning over the edge of her bed, digging into the drawer of goodies. She pulls out a little grey cinch bag and removes the palm-sized red rose toy with a suction on the end. Reclining on the giant mound of pillows, she hikes up her dress, so it falls to where her hips meet her thick thighs.

In college, she'd once confided in her friend, Dacia, about how turned on she got when her boyfriend watched her get off, or when one of her boyfriend's buddies watched them fuck. So, when I position myself in my usual spot—the chaise lounge in front of the bed—I do so knowing she'd love it if she knew I was here.

Jocelyn had bought the sofa to use during sex, but most of the time it holds Alex's clothes until she can tidy up after him.

My attention narrows to the sliver of black between her legs. She's got a pair of cotton panties on, a damp spot at the crotch. Through the top of her dress, she kneads her nipples, tugging on them and twisting them. Her other hand thumbs the on switch of her toy and she tucks it into her underwear, holding it in place. She never starts at the highest setting, but within minutes she's got it on level three, and its constant buzz is usually enough to give her release not long after.

But when she digs out her laptop from its resting place on the side of the bed, I know I'm in for a longer show. She'll edge herself for as long as she can. She likes to bring herself just to the brink before easing off, over and over. Then, when she senses the battery getting low or her time running short, she works a little harder at leaping off the precipice.

I inch my way closer to her, lying in Alex's spot on the bed to get a better look at what she's typing into the search window. She's using the browser's incognito setting. Alex doesn't have any idea that she has to take things into her own hands every day.

monster hentai gif

My cock twitches, aching to be let out. I love her taste in porn. You can take the fae out of the realm, but you can't take the fae out of their nature. She's got a thing for being dominated and loves to watch voyeur clips, though you'd never know it based on the vanilla guy she married. His idea of kinky is sex with the lights on.

No, she wants to be pinned down and properly worshipped before she's fucked. Ideally, by a mythical creature twice her size with a cock the size of her forearm—while others watch.

She finds a gif of a cartoon human being used like a fuck toy by a giant elf of some sort. He looks more fae, but green. Compared to the creature, the human is tiny, impaled like one of those cock sleeves.

A wry grin curls my lips. That's about what we'd look like together, though I'm not quite that large and I'm not green. I've got the pointy ears and muscles, though, but far better looks.

I'm hard, but I can't help it. Watching her at the computer never fails to get me going. She's got those big green eyes and that soft skin, and all I can think of is how it would feel to be inside her. I unzip my jeans, and my cock springs free, aching and weeping for relief.

Sometimes, when I lie here next to her, I pretend she's my mate, and I'm pleasuring her, making her fall apart beneath me. I'm certain the others do too, but we never talk about it. Our charge is off-limits.

And I don't have a mate. Neither of us do.

Jocelyn has royal fae in her lineage. We're duty bound to keep watch over her, and we do it without question or complaint, though she doesn't know about supernatural creatures. Maybe it's why her subconscious loves the porn she does. If she knew, she wouldn't be wasting her life away with a commoner like Alex. Instead, she would find a partner from her own kind who could provide the love and protection someone of royal lineage deserves.

Jocelyn doesn't find a gif she likes, so she searches for a video. Risky move on her part, knowing Alex is often home around this time. If he catches her, she risks alienating him further and damaging their fragile relationship even more. Not that we'd mind.

We don't like him.

Locating the hentai video she watches often about a woman developing Stockholm syndrome for her captors, she parts her thighs and focuses on the vibrating rose between them. It's not the video I'm interested in, but the roll of her hips as she drags her fingers through her folds and gasps into the night. The scent she gives off captivates me—a sweet, intoxicating perfume of desire that taints the air around her.

Tugging on my cock, I whisper softly, as if speaking directly to her: "That's my girl; fuck those fingers. Imagine that's me licking your clit, tasting the slickness between your legs."

She can't hear or see me thanks to magic we put in place every day, but I savor her pleasure until I reach my own. I come with a deep groan as the orgasmic waves rip through me. Using magic to clean up the mess coating my bare stomach, I watch the rise and fall of her chest as her breathing slows, and she becomes calm again.

In this moment of unity between us, all I want to do is imagine myself wrapping my arms around Jocelyn and protecting her from all the dangers life throws her way.

We may never be together in reality, but for now at least, this shared moment between us holds something special for me to treasure long after we've parted ways for the night.

Using the en suite bathroom, she cleans off her toy and puts it back in its designated box before returning to bed.

For a moment, she's at peace. In that fleeting second, serenity embraces her. Her eyes close gently, her body sinking into the plush mattress as she surrenders to slumber. Casting a glance at the clock, I grant her a mere fifteen minutes of reprieve before I slip through the door to find Rolls, his massive form sprawled in the corner, soft snores escaping his snout. Shifting forms to make myself visible, I bestow a gentle pat upon him, startling him enough to elicit a surprised yelp. Rising to his feet with a languid stretch, he throws me a drowsy, disgruntled look as he trails behind me to her door.

Casting him an anticipatory gaze, I extend my hand, motioning for him to perform his task. In response, Rolls regards my pocket with interest. Releasing an exasperated sigh, I retrieve a treat, concealing it within my closed fist. Rolls barks and nudges my hand with his nose. Grinning with satisfaction, I reveal the treat, offering it to him while rubbing his ears affectionately.

Just as Joss wrenches the door open, I fade back into invisibility.

Dinner is prepared and in the oven just as Alex arrives home, perfectly timed with the food's completion. He casts his jacket onto the bench near the front door before placing a peck upon Jocelyn's forehead.

With only half an inch difference between their heights, he doesn't need to stoop, yet he persists in kissing her there. For years, the gesture has puzzled me.

Humans.

"What did you do all day?" He surveys the spotless home.

Jocelyn bends to retrieve his discarded jacket, draping it over her arm. "I got my hair done." She strides to the hallway closet to hang it up on his behalf. It should be him attending to her every need.

"What did you do to it?"

Although he can't see her expression, I can. The way her features diminish, as though he'd let all the wind out of her sails.

"Oh, just a trim and a touch-up." She puts on her cheery voice and reorganizes the shoes he's kicked off in the middle of the entry.

One-by-one, he toes his socks off, leaving a trail of his clothes until he reaches the dining table in just his undershirt and briefs. She shuffles behind him, picking up after this man child.

Tossing his clothes into the laundry chute in the hallway, she hurries to the kitchen to take the food out of the oven when the timer goes off. She plates it along with the vegetables he won't eat but will feed to Rolls when she isn't looking.

The dog still hates him.

"I talked to my parents today." Jocelyn places Alex's food in front of him because he's incapable of serving himself. "They called from a payphone somewhere in Kathmandu. Can you believe there are still payphones around?"

He's busy scrolling through his phone and didn't hear what she said, though he responds anyway. "That's a bummer."

He's not even listening to her. Fucking asshole.

Jocelyn lowers herself into her seat, deflated, as she pours herself a glass of wine and doesn't bother offering Alex any. *'Atta girl.*

She takes a big gulp, dots her mouth with a napkin, and cuts her calzone with a fork and knife. After she skewers a piece, she shoves one into her mouth, chewing and swallowing as she simmers in her discontent with him.

Alex scoops up his plate with one hand, phone scrolling in the other, as he scoots out of his chair and brings it to the living room. He plops into his leather recliner, sets the plate on his slightly rounded stomach, and reclines.

"Be a sweetheart and bring me a drink," he calls out, his focus now on the college football game blaring from the TV.

Joss reluctantly rises from her seat to fetch him his whiskey. *There are days when I secretly wish she'd just poison him and wash her hands of the whole ordeal. In that case, we'd have no choice but to bring her to the fae realm where she truly belongs. But, of course, she doesn't, opting instead to indulge him like the overgrown child he is.*

Later, when he retires to their room, Jocelyn is asleep. She lies motionless on the bed, her hair cascading over their expensive pillows and sheets. Perched on the dresser next to her side of the bed, I watch as he tugs her to his front and wraps his arms around her athletic frame. She stirs when he gropes her breast and wakes fully when his hands trail down her stomach and beneath her panties.

He kisses her neck, rutting against her hip. He slides her underwear down and falls onto his back, rolling her on top of him.

This lazy asshole is never on top. He has no idea how desperately she wants to be taken. If I weren't so angry at him, I'd be jealous.

Mechanically, she removes her tank top, spilling her breasts into his greedy, unworthy hands. He groans when she lowers herself onto his average—for a human, tiny for a fae—length. She doesn't have to ride him long as he shoots himself into her in under a minute.

Small mercies for birth control. We don't want her procreating with this ... peasant.

Jocelyn hops off him and cleans herself in the bathroom while Alex takes a tissue to his junk. She doesn't have her usual smile on her face when she rejoins him in the bedroom. He wouldn't notice, though, because he's already got an arm slung over his eyes, ready to pass out.

Has she finally had enough of his shit?

"Alex," she whispers. She sits on the edge of her side of the bed, her legs dangling off the elevated mattress. "I booked the honeymoon suite for next week."

"Huh," he grumbles, the word muffled and heavy with the weight of exhaustion.

Tell him you're leaving, baby girl.

My fellow guardians, Remy and Niko, file into the room and stand silently beside me just as she speaks, their expressions tense and attentive.

"For our trip." She pulls her shirt on, the nightgown fabric clinging to her skin. "It's got this beautiful—"

"What trip?" he interrupts, uncovering his eyes and squinting her way.

"Our vacation?" She turns to face him, worry evident on her face. "Maldives? We're staying over the water for ten days. No internet, no cell reception, just us. We've been planning this for months—surely, you haven't forgotten?"

"When is it?"

"We leave on Thursday." Her voice is quiet, as though spoken on the final dredges of a breath.

He slides a hand over his face, groaning. "Babe, I'm sorry, I can't. I've got the investment lawyers coming for their due diligence meeting and they're going to be there for at least three weeks." His arm covers his eyes again, conversation over. "You can go, and I'll catch the next one."

The room is quiet, only the gentle hum of Jocelyn's fan as background noise. But I hear the slow intake of breath she takes as she builds up the courage to reveal something big.

"This isn't working," she says, her voice barely above a whisper, the pain evident in her eyes.

"I'll have someone fix it later," he mutters and flops over, completely oblivious to the depth of her feelings. "I've told you we can just hire people to clean and fix things, Jossy."

"This. Us. We aren't working, Alex," she clarifies, each word punctuated by the fierce determination that lights a fire within her.

Remy, Niko, and I exchange glances, the unspoken communication between us clear as day. "This is huge," I whisper, even though we know Jocelyn and Alex can't hear us.

"What are you going on about?" Alex rises onto his shoulder, his brow furrowing as he struggles to understand her distress. "We work great."

But as I watch Jocelyn's face, her eyes glistening with unshed tears and her lips trembling with suppressed emotion, I know that she's finally reaching her breaking point. And maybe, just maybe, this will be the catalyst that sets her free.

I'd wanted to kill this asshole the moment he made a pass at her at a party. That was almost fifteen years ago.

"What's my favorite position?" she asks, her voice trembling yet resolute.

"Huh?"

"What's my favorite position?" she repeats, turning to face him, her gaze challenging.

"Reverse cowgirl."

"Wrong." She shakes her head, a bitter smile touching her lips. "It's doggy style."

"But you love it wh—"

"It's doggy style." Her words cut through his protest, silencing him. "What's my favorite flower?"

"Roses."

"Wrong, it's peonies." Her voice grows stronger, the hurt and frustration evident in her tone. "We've been together for too long for you not to know the basics, Alex." Her voice takes on an edge he's never heard from her before.

"You want me to get you some peonies?"

"It's more than just the peonies!" She rockets to her feet, her anger finally unleashed. "It's about you not understanding what I need, and you don't even try! Newsflash, but I'm more than candy you can dangle on your arm and a warm hole to stick your dick in when you feel like it."

Her eyes are wild, and for a moment, I can almost see a hint of fae blood in her with the way her hair seems to glow in the moonlight. She's never raised her voice at him before, and it's long overdue.

"What's gotten into you?" He rests his back against the headboard. "We have sex almost every night."

"You're right; we do. You want to know what else? I fake it. Every time." Her voice is like venom.

"What?" He laughs, incredulous. "Are you about to start your period? You're acting crazy."

Oh, shit. I hop off the dresser, and the three of us ready ourselves to intercept should things get physically out of hand. She's not due to start her period until Thursday. Something he'd know if he cared to pay attention.

"Is your precious little ego too fragile to realize that you're what's wrong with this relationship?" She slides her giant ring off her finger and flings it at him.

He fumbles for it and watches in shock as it clatters to the ground, rolling to a stop at the edge of the rug. Scrambling out of bed and coming around to her, he reaches for her with a trembling hand. She doesn't shrug it off her shoulder, but instead meets his gaze, her eyes flooded with disappointment.

"Don't do this, sweetheart," he pleads, his voice thick with emotion. "Tell me what I have to do to make you happy. I'll change, I promise."

She just shakes her head and turns away. "A decade and a half, Alex. That's how long I've sat on your shelf, waiting for you to take me down and show me the world." A tear tracks down her cheek as she slowly backs away. "You're not a bad husband. Just a neglectful one," she whispers softly, her voice riding the edge of broken and angry. "Don't my dreams matter?"

"Of course they do, baby." He pulls her into his arms. "I'd die for you."

Then what are you waiting for? I glance at the others, and I know they're thinking it, too.

"But will you live for me?" The question hangs in the air, and I can almost feel the collective pause that follows.

"Tell me what I need to do," he begs, his eyes leaking tears onto her hair. They might actually be real ones.

He's weak. Promises her the world, and he'll give it to her, if he can throw money at a situation and put her away until he needs her again.

"You need to fix this, because I've given all I can, and it isn't enough," she murmurs.

CHAPTER TWO

REMY

idden from view, I watch Jocelyn as she sits across the table from Dacia at an outdoor café. Our charge doesn't have a lot of friends, not that she's not kind, she just keeps to herself. Jocelyn had wanted to go to vet school, and she'd even got into the best one in the country, but Alex had persuaded her to stay home instead. Told her she'd have all day to do her hobbies, and they never had to worry about money, so while it wasn't an easy sell on his part, ever the doting wife, she gave in. Without work colleagues or people to share her interests with, Dacia is one of the few people she ever spends time with.

The sun casts a warm, golden light over the scene, bringing out the vibrant colors of the surrounding plants and flowers. Fall is firmly upon us now, and I can't help but appreciate the beauty of the moment, even as the weight of our mission sits heavy on my heart.

Jocelyn laughs at something Dacia says, her eyes sparkling with amusement. She reaches for her mimosa, the condensation glistening on the glass as she takes a sip. I admire the way she enjoys life's simple pleasures, so blissfully unaware of the danger that lurks beneath the surface.

Her laughter is a reminder of what's at stake if we fail. Less than four years until go time. Thirty-nine months until everything changes.

"You should come by the studio sometime," Dacia offers. "You haven't been by in years."

Jocelyn sighs. "I guess I haven't been feeling very inspired. I can't remember the last time I did any pottery. Though I have been writing again."

"Oh?" Dacia leans in. "Poems?"

"Yeah." Jocelyn signals for the waiter to bring out some more bread. She's been carb obsessed for as long as we've been her guardians.

Dacia studies Jocelyn's face for a moment before asking, "How are things with Alex?"

Jocelyn's expression darkens. "Not great, to be honest. He's been distant and moody lately, and I just feel like we're not connecting anymore."

Her friend nods sympathetically. "I guess that happens." She bites her lip and looks around before speaking again. "Don't hate me for saying this. But when you two first got together, you were so happy and in love it was like you couldn't get enough of each other. I was a little jealous of what you had, to be honest. But lately—it seems like he's been holding you back."

Jocelyn looks down, her hands fidgeting with her napkin. "I don't know what to do. I don't want to leave him, but I can't keep living like this either."

"You deserve to be happy, Joss," Dacia says firmly. "And if that means leaving Alex, then so be it. Your parents would support you, and so would your friends."

Jocelyn looks up at Dacia, tears welling up in her eyes. "I just feel so trapped. Like I made the wrong choice by marrying him, and now it's too late to go back."

"It's never too late to make a change," Dacia reassures her. "And I'm always here for you, no matter what."

As they continue to talk, I realize that Jocelyn has been carrying a heavy burden for a long time. Her marriage to Alex is clearly not a happy one, and she's been struggling to keep up appearances for the sake of others. Even those who seem to have everything can be hiding a world of pain and unhappiness beneath the surface.

"You're not alone," Dacia reassures her. "I'm here for you, always. And like I said, your parents would be too, if you told them what was going on."

Jocelyn shakes her head, her eyes downcast. "I can't tell them. They love Alex. They'd never understand."

Dacia squeezes her hand. "Just remember you don't have to go through this alone, Joss. You have people who love you and want to support you."

Jocelyn looks away, her gaze downcast. I can see the pain in her eyes, and my heart aches for her. I wish I could take it all away, make everything right again, but I know that's not possible. All I can do is be here for her, protect her, and guide her towards her destiny.

"I'm sorry," Dacia says softly. "I didn't mean to bring up anything that might upset you."

"It's okay," Jocelyn replies, a tremor in her voice. "You ever feel like you have a vague idea of where you're supposed to be, what you're supposed to do, but aren't sure how to get there? I feel like I'm going crazy."

I let out a silent breath. She's feeling like this because she's gone thirty-six years without magic. It's way too long for a creature like her to cope with, even though she knows nothing about it, and it's starting to take its toll.

Dacia reaches across the table and takes Jocelyn's hand. "You don't have to figure it all out alone, you know. We're here for you. And maybe ... maybe it's time to start thinking about what you want, not just what Alex wants."

Jocelyn nods slowly, tears brimming in her eyes. "I know. I just feel so lost, like I don't even know who I am anymore."

"You're still the same Joss we've always known and loved," Dacia says. "The girl who used to make pottery in the garage and write poetry in the moonlight. The one who dreamed of going to vet school and saving every animal she could. You're still her, even if Alex can't see it anymore."

Jocelyn sniffles, wiping away her tears. "Thank you, Dacia. I needed to hear that."

"Of course," Dacia says, squeezing her hand. "And you know what? Maybe it's time for a girls' night. Just the two of us, like old times. We'll go to a musical or something, maybe even do some pottery if you're up for it. How does that sound?"

Jocelyn smiles weakly. "That sounds ... amazing, actually."

Dacia grins. "Good. It's settled then. And who knows, maybe we'll even meet some cute guys at the show."

Jocelyn laughs, the sound bright and genuine. For a moment, I forget about our mission, about the weight of responsibility that hangs over me. I'm just Remy, watching two friends reconnect and laugh together, and it's a beautiful thing.

They chat excitedly about their plans, and I can't help but feel a glimmer of hope. Maybe, just maybe, things will turn out okay in the end. Maybe Jocelyn will find her way back to the person she used to be. The person she's meant to be. And maybe, with our help, she'll fulfill her destiny and save the realms from certain destruction.

Only time will tell. But for now, in this moment, there's a sense of possibility in the air, a sense of hope. And that's enough for me.

As they continue to chat, Joss' eyes widen as Dacia recounts a recent trip she'd taken to a hidden waterfall, her voice filled with wonder and awe. I can't help but think of the breathtaking landscapes that exist within the fae realms, places where magic is so palpable that it takes your breath away. It's those places and the delicate balance they represent that we're fighting to protect.

If Joss is captivated by the beauty in this world, wait till she sees the sights of the one she's destined for.

When the time comes, I want Joss to be able to bask in the glory of the fae realms and revel in her magic—she's earned it after all these years. But there's unlikely to be time for that, at least to begin with.

The realms are in trouble.

I want to take her to Bedlam—arguably the most beautiful of the fae realms. But we also have *him* to worry about. The malevolent ruler of neighboring Romarie is cunning and ruthless, determined to maintain his hold on his realm.

Which wouldn't be a big deal if he wasn't also gunning for so much more, such as Bedlam, the underworld, and all those smaller, less inhabited realms with little protection from bullies like him.

Thankfully, we have the prophecy to pin our hopes on. And the focus of that foretelling is sitting inches away from me enjoying her mimosa. Only Jocelyn, as the rightful heir, has the power to stop him, and only if she claims her birthright *after* the age of forty. If she attempts to take her place too soon, she will fail, and the realms will be lost.

Blissfully unaware of the weight of all this, Jocelyn seems captivated by Dacia's tale, her eyes alight with curiosity and a hint of longing. In her gaze, I see a spark that I recognize from my own experiences in the fae realm—a hunger for adventure and a yearning for something beyond the ordinary. It's a quality that makes her so special, and it only strengthens my resolve to see her embrace her destiny at the right time, fulfilling the prophecy and restoring peace.

As the afternoon sun dips lower in the sky, casting elongated shadows on the cobblestone street, I can't help but worry about the challenges that lie ahead. Our task is daunting—to protect Jocelyn from the enemy's clutches and guide her safely to her destiny while still allowing her to live a normal human life for now. It feels like a tall order at times.

My mind races through the countless scenarios where things could go wrong. If we slip up, even once, we could jeopardize not only Jocelyn's life but the very existence of the realms we are sworn to protect. The stakes are immense, and the burden of responsibility feels like a physical weight upon my shoulders.

I glance back at Jocelyn and Dacia as they stand up from their table, their laughter and easy camaraderie filling the air. Jocelyn's face is flushed with a rare show of happiness, and it strikes me how precious these fleeting moments of normalcy are for her. I silently vow to do everything in my power to ensure she gets to experience as much of this life as possible before the time to embrace her destiny comes.

As they part ways, Jocelyn giving Dacia a warm hug and a promise to catch up again soon, I'm reminded once more of what we are fighting for. It's not just about the balance of the realms, the intricate dance of power and politics that fills our lives; it's about the moments of laughter, friendship, and love that make life worth living.

My brows furrow in determination as I continue to watch over Jocelyn: a guardian in the shadows, always vigilant, always ready.

For her, and for the countless lives that depend on us, we must succeed.

There is no other option.

CHAPTER THREE

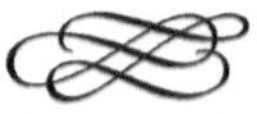

JOCELYN

I stare blankly at the ceiling, the dull ache in my chest growing with each passing second. The silence of the room amplifies my loneliness, and I can't help but wonder how I ended up here.

Just a little more than a decade ago, Alex and I were so in love, and our future seemed so bright. Now, as I lay in our king-sized bed that feels more like a chasm separating us, I can't shake the feeling that we're drifting further apart each day. He's always working, consumed by his career, while I'm left to navigate this empty house alone.

It's been a month since I told him he needs to fix this. Four weeks of late nights at work. Thirty days of empty promises, broken.

I hear the front door creak open, and I instinctively glance at the clock on the nightstand: 2:37 a.m. He's home, but he might as well be miles away. The bitter taste of disappointment lingers on my tongue as I close my eyes, hoping sleep will bring a temporary escape from this hollow life.

When I wake up the next morning, Alex is already gone, leaving nothing but the lingering scent of his cologne and a hastily scribbled note on the kitchen counter: "Working late again tonight. Love, A." It's just another reminder of the ever-widening gap between us.

I spend the day lost in thought, wondering if it's even possible to save our marriage or if we've already passed the point of no return. Desperation claws at me, urging me to do something, anything, to mend the broken pieces of our relationship.

As I drift back into the memories of that fateful night at the fraternity party, the vivid colors, sounds, and sensations envelop me.

The air is thick with the scent of cheap beer and sweat as I navigate the crowded room, feeling increasingly uncomfortable by my date's side. The laughter and shouts of partygoers blend into a cacophony of noise.

Chad, smirking and clearly tipsy, leans against the wall, a red solo cup in his hand. With a mischievous glint in his eyes, he loudly proclaims to his friends, "Look at my date, little Miss Jocelyn, attempting to mingle with the intellectual elite. Sure, she's easy on the eyes, but we all know she's not exactly the sharpest tool in the shed, right?"

My cheeks flare with indignation, the hurtful words a slap in the face. Just as I'm about to turn away, ready to flee the painful scene, Alex emerges from the boisterous crowd. His chiseled jaw is set, his eyes ablaze with conviction.

"Actually, Chad," Alex says, his voice smooth, confident, and tinged with a knowing smirk, "you're the one who's mistaken. Jocelyn is as brilliant as she is beautiful. We share a few classes, and she's clever. Really clever. You should hear how insightful her questions are. Even the professors know she's smarter than them. There's a reason she's number one in our graduating class. If you don't appreciate her, there's plenty more who will be lining up to take her off your hands."

The beginning of Alex and me is seared into my mind, a tale of love born from his unwavering belief in me and his willingness to confront the baseless judgments of others. That very night, Alex swept me away from Chad, and we embarked on our romance. For months, we basked in the light of our adoration for one another and soon got married. But, as time wore on, work cast its shadow over our love, plunging us into darkness. Now, I find myself sifting through the remnants of our marriage, desperately seeking a way to stitch the tattered pieces back together.

I can't do it on my own.

As I browse the internet, I come across their website: *The Love Architects; a team of passionate love experts who boast a track record of breathing new life into countless struggling relationships.*

Their offer seems almost too good to be true—they move in for six months, guaranteeing a complete marriage transformation, or you don't pay a single dime. Intriguingly, they also hint at providing hands-on demonstrations to enhance intimacy and sexual fulfillment, promising to rekindle the lost passion in any relationship. I chew my bottom lip. It's unconventional, and if people found out—but then I picture Alex's dismissive shrug when he told me to go on our planned vacation alone. Perhaps I am desperate enough. Anything's worth a try, right?

The thought of facing my parents, who have such a perfect marriage of their own, fills me with dread. They adore Alex, completely unaware of the cracks in our union. He's a master at keeping up appearances, presenting the image of the loving, attentive husband whenever they're around. I've grown weary of hiding the truth, and the weight of maintaining the façade is becoming unbearable.

Taking a deep breath, I bookmark the website to show Alex tomorrow. He doesn't normally work on Sundays, and it's the one day we ever enjoy breakfast together. Come hell or high water, this is our last shot at fixing things between us before I give up. I'm determined to save our marriage, even if it means enlisting the help of strangers to mend what we've allowed to fracture.

Niko

As soon as Joss and Alex turn in for the night, Vox and Remy return to Bedlam, the fae realm most fae guardians choose to live on. I find myself seated in the beige leather recliner near the window where she likes to read when the greenhouse is too hot during the day, a vantage point offering a view of the sprawling estate and the darkened sky.

I watch the moon hanging just above the horizon like a distant eye, its pale light casting long shadows across the grounds. My thoughts wander, and for a fleeting moment, I forget everything that's been weighing down on me. But as I sit here, alive but alone in this dark space, reality rushes back to me like a relentless wave.

The moon is always disorienting on Earth—only one visible to the naked eye, out of millions and billions of stars. It's astounding to think that such an insignificant little thing could wield so much power over this realm and its inhabitants. It makes them oscillate in sentiment, affecting their tides and emotional states; they're all prisoners to its pull.

The dark night air wraps around me like a comforting embrace, yet beneath the peace and quiet lies an underlying tension that urges me to dig deeper, search harder. I can almost hear the secrets of the night whispering to me, begging me to uncover the hidden beauty that lies within. Glancing over at Jocelyn's sleeping form, I can feel something stir inside me—the spark of hope that perhaps there is something left in this world worth fighting for.

Tonight, I'm thankful for the moon and its reminder that darkness is just a brief respite, and that maybe, somewhere in a different realm, she could've been ours.

A thought stirs in my mind. What would it be like if Joss left Alex? Could we convince her of her birthright, persuade her to leave for Bedlam?

Who am I kidding? The council hasn't come up with a solution for her greatest threat yet. So for now, Jocelyn has to stay with Alex, and it's our duty as her guardians to ensure she's kept happy. If she reaches a heightened state of heartbreak, there's a risk her magic will come unbound before the allotted time.

And then *he'll* be able to find her.

But is her marriage causing her more heartache than happiness? Would a divorce really be worse than this? Perhaps we've been going about this all wrong. Have we failed her?

The notion unsettles me.

I cross to the bed and pause at her side, observing her chest rise and fall. I snag Jocelyn's laptop, unlock it with her password, and bring it back to my chair.

Scouring her browser history, I find little of note—she only ventures into risqué territory in incognito mode—but I stumble across a website she's bookmarked. It's titled *The Love Architects: guaranteed to fix your relationship in six months or fewer, or you don't pay a dime.*

She's been searching for ways to be a better wife?

The thought disturbs me. She's not a failure, or a fixer upper. She's perfect just the way she is. But then I think of her with Alex, her life thrown into chaos by a man who seems to possess no heart or compassion. He's made her a prisoner in her own home. Her perfect marriage is a farce, and she's trying to find ways to make it work—to keep her life together.

And that infuriates me.

The clock on her laptop blinks at me; its hands barely moving. With a low groan, I rise to my feet, striding towards the bed while my mind tries to work out a different angle. My attention settles on Alex, his incessant snoring so intense, I have to put a silencing bubble around him every night just so Joss can sleep. He's everything that's wrong with this marriage.

I swear under my breath, closing out the tab and putting the laptop back where it belongs. I've spent so much of her life living in the background, waiting patiently for things to happen and watching from the sidelines. It's not who I am. I'm a Watcher; a God forged through devastating loss to lead, to protect, and to make a difference.

A half-formed thought takes shape as I study him. Can we convince him to change? Show him the error of his ways? I mean, who better to do it than the three males who've watched over her since she reached maturity.

A smile spreads across my face. With a little magic, I can hijack this website in no time. I've just got to convince the others this is a brilliant idea.

Jocelyn

As I wander through the local nursery, I'm surrounded by a sea of vibrant colors, each flower and plant competing for attention as I scour the place for some fruit trees to add to the greenhouse. Being here breathes life into me, and I've spent a small fortune just this year collecting plants.

There are worse things to be addicted to, I suppose. I could be a sex addict or a collector of those rare, exotic plants that require importing and take months to arrive. The ones that struggle to acclimate and eventually die as a result—now that would be a travesty.

The scent of damp soil fills the air, mingling with the faint, sweet fragrance of blossoming flowers. The atmosphere is calming, a welcome escape from the turmoil of my recent thoughts. I browse through the various plants, envisioning how they might bring a fresh sense of life to my home as I hunt for what I came for.

Lost in thought, I'm surprised when I suddenly find myself the focus of attention from a couple of guys. The first, a tall guy with sandy blond hair, leans casually against a display of potted azaleas. His hazel eyes twinkle with interest as he flashes a charming smile and says, "That's a nice selection of plants you've got there. Planning to start a garden?"

"A fall garden? This far north?" I reply skeptically, feeling a little flustered but also flattered at his lame attempt at striking a conversation. If they know what's good for them, they'll move on. No good has ever come from flirting with me. "No. Just picking up some citrus trees."

His friend, a shorter guy with dark, messy hair and a cheeky grin, chimes in. He's holding a small succulent as if he's contemplating whether to buy it or not. "Well, if you need any help, we'd be more than happy to lend a hand."

They need to take the hint. Anyone who lingers my way a little too long always seems to get hurt, as far back as I can remember.

I offer a polite smile, grateful for their offer but eager to continue shopping on my own. "Thanks, but I think I've got it under control."

As I turn to examine a display of dwarf lemon trees, I'm startled by a sudden, loud thud followed by a cry of pain. Whirling around, I see the tall guy doubled over, clutching his face as if he's been struck. The shorter guy looks equally shocked, his eyes wide with concern and confusion, the succulent he was holding now forgotten on the ground.

"Jesus, John, you okay?" the short one asks his friend. "What the hell happened?"

John just grunts, clutching his nose. Blood pools in his hands and drips into the sleeve of his jacket.

I rush over to help, but he waves me off, insisting that he's fine through gritted teeth. However, I can't shake the feeling that something strange has just happened, something that defies explanation. As I stand there, feeling a mix of confusion and worry, I can't help but wonder if there's more to this encounter than meets the eye.

Because this is what happens every time.

As I help the tall guy to his feet—I'm not just going to watch someone hurting and ignore him—my mind starts racing, replaying all the similar incidents from my past. The time when a flirtatious barista at the coffee shop accidentally spilled boiling water on himself while winking at me. The young man who tried to ask me out at the library, only to stumble backward into a bookshelf that toppled over and nearly crushed him. And then there was the guy at the gym who somehow managed to drop a weight on his foot right after complimenting my form.

Each time, I tell myself it's just a coincidence. But as the occurrences pile up, I can't help but start to believe that maybe, just maybe, I'm cursed. It seems as if any man who tries to get too close to me is met with disaster, and I don't understand why. It started shortly after I got married to Alex.

It's when our relationship changed, too.

With a sigh, I step back and let the two guys console each other, feeling a pang of guilt at the suffering I seem to bring to those who cross my path. I turn my attention back to the dwarf lemon trees, trying to push the unsettling thoughts from my mind. The truth is, though I'm married, Alex and I are more like roommates who have sex than a real partnership. Am I subconsciously pushing him away in fear that if I let him in, I'll inadvertently hurt him with my curse?

I shake off the memories and force myself to focus on what I came here for. Despite the odd encounter, I'm determined to enjoy my time at the nursery and find the perfect additions to my greenhouse. Maybe, in the midst of all the beautiful, thriving plants, I'll be able to forget my seemingly cursed existence, if only for a little while.

CHAPTER FOUR

JOCELYN

"Look at this." I turn my laptop towards Alex, tapping the screen with a red, manicured finger. "These guys move in and overhaul our entire marriage. Guaranteed to fix things between us, or we pay nothing." Tension runs through every muscle as I force myself to meet his eyes.

Not that the cost matters to him. Alex takes a bite of his toast, dropping crumbs onto my computer. His butter-greased fingers use my keypad to scroll to the FAQ section of the website. Sometimes when he's like this, it's hard to remember how much I loved this man, and how attractive I find him.

It's difficult to deny that Alex has an air of old money about him, the type that exudes that New England charm. His blond hair, cut in a style that speaks of his privileged background, often falls into his eyes, making him appear both boyish and sophisticated at the same time. His slight dad-bod still showcases toned muscles beneath his shirts, revealing a man who cares about his appearance but doesn't obsess over it. Those broad shoulders and the confident stride that comes with being a Vanderbilt can make my heart flutter, despite his infuriating habits.

Of course, he isn't actually a dad. His physique is the result of long nights at the office and a penchant for greasy late-night takeout, combined with a love for whiskey that adds a touch of ruggedness to his otherwise polished demeanor.

I glance over his shoulder at the FAQs on the screen.

Q: Do you really move in?

A: Yes, our couples find our presence helps keep both partners accountable. We're with one of you, 24/7.

Q: What are your methods?

A: Some say our skills are just like magic, while others think our methods are a little unorthodox. We couldn't guarantee results if we didn't take extreme measures to fix your marriage.

Q: Your Elite package mentions hands-on work. What do you mean by that?

A: Whether it's teaching the art of massage, the erotic art of cunnilingus, using toys in the bedroom, or anything in-between, we'll demonstrate and guide you step-by-step.

"These guys are going to see you naked? Fuck you? I'm not a cuck. No way." He shuts the laptop, dropping it onto the kitchen counter with a thud. "I don't like it."

"What? Who says anything about sleeping with them?"

"It's right between the lines, Jossy."

"It says they'll demonstrate, not that they'll actually do it, babe." My fingers drum on the tabletop. "We could at least call them for a consultation, ask questions, and see if it's a good fit for us."

"No."

The word lands like a sucker punch to my chest, leaving me breathless and reeling. My stomach churns, a mix of hurt and disappointment roiling inside me like a hurricane. I blink back the tears that threaten to spill over, refusing to give him the satisfaction of seeing me crumble.

My hands tremble in my lap, the weight of rejection settling heavily on my shoulders. My mind races, searching for any other solution, anything to mend the frayed edges of our marriage. But the stark reality dawns on me, cutting through the haze of desperation: there may be nothing left to save.

I take a shaky breath, attempting to steady my voice as I speak, but the words catch in my throat, choking me with their unspoken implications. The silence stretches between us, growing thicker and heavier with each passing second, until it's a palpable force, a suffocating barrier that seems impossible to breach.

My heart feels as if it's being ripped apart, the pain almost unbearable as I come to terms with the fact that the man I once loved so fiercely, the man who once fought for me, now refuses to even try. And in that moment, I know that our marriage is truly on the brink, teetering on the edge of a precipice from which there may be no return.

My chair screeches on the calacatta marble floors as I shove it back and stand up. "Alright," I manage to squeak out. I pick up my plate, leaving his on the table, and drop it into the sink. The glass shatters, but I ignore it, and storm down the hallway.

"Wh-where are you going?" Alex chases after me.

"It's been a month. Nothing changed, so I'm gone." I slip Rolls' leash off its hook near the door, and he bounds over to me so I can clip it onto his collar. The words I string together are broken shards of glass, all the pieces of my shattered dreams I can no longer choose to ignore.

"Seriously, Jossy?" He leans his shoulder against the door, preventing my exit. "Because of one little disagreement?"

"Fifteen years of holding my tongue about my real desires, Alex. Fifteen years of living vicariously through you, so I could keep the peace in our marriage. Fifteen fucking years!" I grind the heel of my hand between my eyes.

"What are you going to do?"

Rolling on the balls of my feet, I turn to pull on my white, down-filled jacket and zip it up. "What I should've done fourteen years ago."

I twist the doorknob and yank the door open, shocking Alex with my strength as he's moved out of my way. Rolls trots out with his head high.

"Wait!" Alex chases after me, barefooted, down the long, live oak-lined driveway.

The wind seems to propel me, whipping my thick blonde hair in my face.

"I'll call them!" he shouts, spinning me around with a hand on my shoulder. "Please."

I shutter my eyes and take a deep breath before I open them. "This is it, Alex. Let me put this in terms you'll understand. This? It's our Hail Mary. If you don't give it your all, you'll never see me again."

"Don't you love me?" Hurt crosses his face.

"I do, but I love me more." I tug the hood of my jacket tighter around me. "For years, I've allowed you to walk all over me. No more."

He pulls me into his arms. "No more."

Vox

THE BEDROOM IS DIMLY LIT, the soft burn from the bedside lamp casting shadows on the walls. We all gather here at the changing of shifts, the three of us convening in case of any major events or concerns. I stand near the window, brooding and lost in thought. My feelings for Jocelyn have grown deeper than I ever imagined, but I know the situation is far from simple.

In our current positions, it's considered treason for us guardians to be romantically involved with our charges or to reveal ourselves to them. None of us have dared to confess our growing obsession with her. Although we're gods, we aren't part of the council that governs us. If we were found guilty of treason, we'd be stripped of our godly status. We are three of the thirty fae guardians responsible for protecting and guiding immortals. In contrast, only ten gods sit on the council, overseeing the realms and making decisions that affect our worlds.

The hierarchy among the gods is based on a mix of age, wisdom, power, and influence. While some gods have the potential to ascend to the council, it's a rare occurrence, and demotions are even rarer.

The gods don't usually meddle with the day-to-day lives of

immortals, but fae like Jocelyn are special cases. Suppressing her magic until the council has handled her threat is important. Ever since she reached maturity, our goal has been to keep her happy. Strong negative emotions could unleash the bind on her powers, exposing her to the very threat we're trying to keep contained.

But the clock is ticking. Once she turns forty, the spell that binds it will end, whether or not the council is ready.

Niko strides into the room, his eyebrows drawn together in focused resolve and a spark of inspiration flickering in his eyes. He glances at Remy and me, his excitement palpable as he readies himself to divulge his thoughts. "I've got an idea. I found this website Jocelyn bookmarked, called 'The Love Architects.' It's a service that promises to fix marriages within six months or it's free. What if we hijacked their website and used it to convince Alex to change his ways? We could help Jocelyn without breaking any rules."

Remy raises an eyebrow, clearly skeptical. "You want us to become love doctors? Pretend we're part of some marriage counseling service? That's an interesting idea, but isn't it a bit ... desperate?"

I cross my arms, mulling over Niko's proposition. It's unorthodox and risky, but it could be an opportunity to help Jocelyn find happiness in her marriage without crossing any lines. The thought of her with Alex, unhappy and unfulfilled, gnaws at my heart. Perhaps this could be the turning point she needs.

A hidden longing flares within me—the desire to hold her and reveal myself to her, to let her see the man who would do anything to make her happy. Perhaps this plan could allow me to indulge in that secret yearning, to be the one who brings her the passion and love she deserves, even if it's done under the guise of fixing her marriage.

Niko, perceiving our reluctance, implores, his eyes filled with resolve, "It's worth a shot. We've been watching over her since she became an adult. Who better to help her find happiness than us? We can use this as an opportunity to help her marriage, and maybe ... just maybe, we'll be able to guide her toward a better life without jeopardizing our positions as her guardians. Though we'll probably have to spell Alex so he's a little more agreeable."

Remy paces the room, deep in thought, the floorboards creaking softly beneath his feet. "It's certainly an interesting plan," he admits, his voice laced with caution. "But are you sure this is the right way to go about it? What if she figures it out before we're ready? What if we develop feelings for her?"

The room goes silent at his words. It's a topic we've been avoiding, an unspoken truth that none of us have dared to confront—not out loud, anyway. The weight of the confession hangs heavy in the air, and we all exchange uncomfortable glances, knowing that our feelings for Jocelyn are a dangerous path to tread.

I'm already too far gone.

I look at Niko, who's also lost in thought, his brow furrowed in concentration. "We need to seek approval from the Fae Council. They're the ones we answer to, and if we're going to take such a bold step, we need to make sure they're on board with our plan. This has never been done before, and we need to be sure we're not overstepping our boundaries."

Niko nods, his determination unwavering. "You're right. I'll request an audience with the Council and explain our plan. It's risky, but if they see the merit in our idea, we might just have a chance."

Remy, still hesitant, sighs. "Fine. If the Council approves, I'll support the plan. But we must tread carefully. Our feelings for Jocelyn must not compromise our mission."

As Niko heads off to request the audience with the Fae Council, Remy and I are left in the softly lit room, the weight of our decision hanging heavy in the air. The shadows seem to dance around us, as if reflecting our uncertainty. We know it won't be easy, but we're willing to take the risk for the woman who means everything to us. All we can do now is hope that the Council sees the merit in our plan and grants us the permission we need to set it in motion.

Vox

"Why do they want to talk to all of us? We've been working together over two centuries before we were ever assigned to Jocelyn, don't they trust that we can make decisions aligned with each other?" I pace, glancing at Jocelyn's sleeping form across the room. "Who's going to watch after her?"

"They're sending in Socrates to take over from us while we convene." Niko winces.

"Socrates?! That asshole is going to take a shift with Jocelyn? We can't trust him." I seethe.

"I know, but he's the only one available right now. We don't have a choice," Niko grimaces.

"Because he's been fired from all his other charge jobs!" Remy growls, his frustration mounting.

Socrates used to be a great guardian—one of the best—until he wasn't. He'd been assigned to Jocelyn for a single shift during their honeymoon to Bali. After that, he changed, and I'm certain he purposely sabotaged his other jobs to secure a long-term assignment with Jocelyn. He's a powerful god—a fae guardian like us—and the mistakes he makes are calculated. They can only be explained as intentional.

"Alright," Niko interjects, "before we leave for the veil, let's place a protective spell on Jocelyn and her room. It should help to ensure her safety while we're gone."

We all bow our heads in unison and weave a powerful enchantment around Jocelyn and her bedroom. Niko etches protection runes into the walls and casts them around Jocelyn and Alex with a graceful swoop of his arms. The room is filled with blinding spectrums of electric blues, lush greens, and iridescent pinks that shroud their dwelling like colorful streamers. The hues sparkle and flicker like a thousand twinkling stars in the dead of night. The spell will be an impenetrable barrier against any harm that may come her way and will let us know if anything happens during our absence.

With the enchantment in place, we feel more at ease leaving Jocelyn in Socrates' care, albeit reluctantly. He arrives, wearing his typical lazy grin.

Socrates' voice is like velvet, smooth and alluring, but there's an underlying tension between us that makes it hard to appreciate. His laugh, despite our rivalry, has an infectious quality that could charm Jocelyn in even her most stubborn mood. He carries the subtle scent of sandalwood and spices, and as much as I loathe to admit it, I find the aroma pleasant. The man is infuriatingly attractive, with a chiseled jawline, smoldering eyes, and a disarming smile that could make Jocelyn's heart race. I feel a stab of jealousy as I think of her being near him, and I'm grateful for the cloaking spell that keeps her unaware of his presence.

He's dressed impeccably in a well-tailored suit and tie, as if he's prepared to impress. His dark hair falls perfectly around his face, framing his intense blue eyes that seem to hold a thousand secrets. As we brief him on everything he needs to know before we leave, he nods, seemingly attentive, but I can't shake the feeling that he's silently plotting his next move in our ongoing rivalry.

For years, he's tried to take over as Jocelyn's sole fae guardian.

Upon creating a portal and stepping through, we arrive just beyond the veil, greeted by the sight of the gods' council chambers. The structure is a harmonious blend of natural and magical elements, reflecting the domains of each god and goddess. Most fae only get to see this place once they've died—it's the equivalent of heaven for humans. As guardians, our ability to create portals allows us to travel to such extraordinary locations when needed.

Compared to Earth, this place is stunning. The colors here are more vibrant, the air feels charged with energy, and everything seems more alive. The fae realms are a place of wonder, where gods and fae walk among their creations, and the rules of the mortal world hold no sway.

The palace is an architectural marvel floating in the clouds above a gemstone field, crafted from iridescent crystal and adorned with intricate patterns that seem to shimmer and change as we pass by.

We're led through the palace's vast halls by a group of ethereal fae attendants until we reach the council chamber. The room is a grand

and awe-inspiring space, with the fae gods seated on thrones that seem to grow from the very floor itself.

Fae guardians may be gods, too, but we aren't as powerful as those on the council.

As we enter the grand chambers, we're immediately struck by the imposing presence of the assembled council of gods and goddesses. Luna, the moon goddess, presides at the head of the council, her radiant aura bathing the room in a warm, ethereal glow. As the provider of magic to all fae, her position among the pantheon is one of great importance.

However, it is Chaos, Luna's unpredictable counterpart, who holds the title of the most powerful god. Eons ago, he provided magic to the original Luna goddess, laying the foundation for the magical world we know today. His power is immense, but his erratic nature leaves him somewhat unmoored. The tension between order and chaos is palpable in the chamber.

The remaining gods and goddesses are arrayed on either side of Luna and Chaos, each exuding an aura of regal authority and divine power. Their eyes, ancient and wise, are fixed upon us, their expressions a mix of curiosity and concern as we stand before them, ready to plead our case. The air is thick with tension as we step forward, sensing the gravity of the situation.

Luna's piercing gaze meets ours, and she speaks, her voice a melodic blend of authority and wisdom.

"You have been summoned here to discuss your recent actions regarding your charge, Jocelyn. It has come to our attention that you intend to reveal yourselves to her and interfere with her marriage. This is a grave matter, as it goes against the fundamental principles of your role as guardians."

We exchange nervous glances before Niko steps forward, taking the lead as our spokesman. "We understand the severity of our actions, but we believe that Jocelyn's well-being is at stake. Her marriage has become a source of great pain, and we, as her guardians, feel it is our duty to protect her from further harm. I'd like to remind you that our role is to keep her magic from revealing itself before she's ready. If she's upset, we run the risk that her binds will come undone, and then she'll be captured."

The gods and goddesses exchange glances, weighing our words carefully. The air in the chamber is heavy with anticipation as we await their decision. Will they grant us the permission we seek, or will we be forced to watch Jocelyn suffer in silence?

With a deep breath, we prepare to plead our case, knowing that the fate of our beloved charge rests in the hands of the council.

~

Remy

THE SILENCE in the council chambers seems to stretch on for an eternity as the gods and goddesses contemplate our request. Finally, Luna speaks, her voice steady and clear.

"We understand your concerns and your desire to protect Jocelyn. However, we must also consider the consequences of granting such a request. The balance between the Fae realms and the mortal world is delicate, and any interference from us can have unintended repercussions."

A murmur of agreement ripples through the council, and we feel our hope dwindling. But before we can voice our objections, another goddess steps forward. It's Lilia, the goddess of love and passion.

Woven blonde braids hang to her waist, and it catches the sparkling light of the sun, a halo of spun gold. Like a choir of angels, her voice is more like a mother telling you all will be right in the world, rather than a bedroom voice speaking of illicit thoughts.

"With all due respect, Luna, we must also consider the well-being of those they are sworn to protect. If Jocelyn's marriage is causing her great suffering, and we have the power to help, should we not use that power responsibly?"

The council chambers erupt into a heated debate, as the gods and goddesses weigh the merits of our request against the potential risks.

We watch, our hearts pounding, as the fate of our charge hangs in the balance.

After what feels like hours, Luna calls for order, and the council members fall silent. She looks at each of us, her gaze assessing our resolve.

"We have reached a decision," she announces, her voice ringing with authority. "We will grant you permission to reveal yourselves to Jocelyn and aid her in her time of need. However, there are conditions to this agreement."

The three of us exchange anxious glances, awaiting the terms of our approval.

"First, you must ensure that your interference does not disrupt the delicate balance between the realms. Second, you must maintain the utmost discretion in your actions. The knowledge of our existence must remain a secret to the mortal world. And finally, you must accept the consequences of your actions, whatever they may be."

We bow our heads in silent reverence as we accept the heavy burden of duty laid upon us. Luna grants us her blessing, and with this we set off for Jocelyn, resolute to use all our strength to help her.

The gravity of what lies ahead thrums through our veins as we return to the mortal realm. We're prepared for any danger that awaits us and though we don't know what fate has in store, we're unwavering in our commitment to grant Jocelyn her due.

CHAPTER FIVE

VOX

As we step back into the mortal realm, a cold shiver runs down my spine, making my hair stand on end. Something is off, and I can't shake the unease clawing at the pit of my stomach. I glance at Niko and Remy, and it's clear from the furrowing of their brows and the tightness in their jaws that they share my disquiet.

"We were gone for too long," Niko murmurs, glancing around the hallway. "Where's Socrates?"

Before we have a chance to respond, the sudden noise of a commotion erupts from Jocelyn's bedroom. My pulse quickens, adrenaline flooding my veins, as we sprint towards the source of the disturbance, dreading what we might find.

Upon reaching the door, we discover Rolls, muzzled, and bound tightly. We swiftly unleash a burst of magic to free him, our eyes meeting in shared apprehension. Silently, we phase through the door, cautiously ensuring that we don't make a sound until we've cast a protective silencing bubble.

The sheets are tangled around Jocelyn's body, and the pillows are strewn across her bed. Her eyes dart back and forth beneath closed lids. A cold sweat covers her face, and she makes small noises as she tosses in her sleep.

Socrates is nowhere to be found.

"Damn him, where did he go?" Remy hisses, scanning the room for any trace of cursed guardian.

The air is acrid with the scent of sweat and anxiety, and the remnant of a nightmare lingers in the air.

Niko reaches out to gently touch Jocelyn's forehead. Her body shifts and twitches, as small noises escape her lips. "I think he might have left a nightmare spell on her before leaving. She's in distress."

The more I think about it, the more it seems like Socrates is intentionally trying to activate her magic. But what I don't understand is *why*? He's spent years trying to be her fae guardian. He's still bound by the same rules we are … so why is he trying to throw it all away? What does he stand to gain by this? Is he colluding with the enemy, or is it simply a situation where if he can't have her, no one can?

Fae guardians can't fall for their charges. The Edict of Separation forbids it, otherwise I probably would have said *fuck my job* and pursued what I really want.

Her.

I clench my fists in anger. "We need to find him and make sure he never gets close to her again."

"Forget him, we need to help Jocelyn," Remy reminds us. "We can't leave her like this. Nightmares can activate her magic!"

Niko nods and begins the soft incantation that has been passed down through generations of our people. The words are spoken with reverence, a calling of healing in the old language. Remy's eyes meet mine as Niko circles his fingers above Jocelyn's head, drawing in the air with his other hand. Still moving his fingers in circles above her, he reaches behind his back with his other hand and draws a dagger from its sheath. His voice rises in pitch until it vibrates throughout the room like a siren song. Slowly, Jocelyn's breathing evens out, and the tension in her face eases.

Once she's settled back into a peaceful sleep, we step back and discuss our next move.

"We need to report Socrates' actions to the council and make sure he's held accountable. I'm tired of that asshole trying to take her from us," Niko says, his jaw clenched in resolve. "For now, let's work on that website. Do either of you need to make arrangements at home for your extended absences?"

We live relatively solitary existences in the southern part of Rexuna, at the edge of Bedlam. Though we aren't roommates, we each have stilted houses next door to each other on an isthmus two and a half hours east of Serapi City. A maritime forest sits in our backyard, and a permanent portal lies in the middle of a clearing a three-hour hike straight east, through the towering pine trees. We could take a boat across the water to reach it twenty minutes faster. Once in the forest, though, only we can sift in or out. We're protective over our little slice of peace.

Remy shakes his head. "All I do is work. I could disappear forever, and no one would come looking for me." He glances my way, waiting for my response.

I didn't think the others were dating anyone, but a confirmation is nice. We don't ever get time off at the same time, as one of us is always watching over Jocelyn. Occasionally, the guys and I will camp in the forest, or go fishing. "I'm good too." I sink to the leather chair.

"Guess that settles it," Niko says.

We turn towards Jocelyn's sleeping form, illuminated by the glowing moonlight through her window, and we swear to ourselves that nobody will hurt her under our watch ever again.

Jocelyn

I STAND in the quiet kitchen, glancing at the lines I've scribbled on a piece of paper I spilled some tea on. Writing poetry is a habit I've taken up in the last few years to conquer some of my inner demons. The pressure to be perfect, and to have the perfect life, sometimes feels like too much to take.

Knowing that things used to be perfect between us is probably what kills me the most.

In perfect love's unyielding quest,
A heart that yearns but finds no rest.
A union built on laughter, grace,
The pressure mounts, I try to pace.

An image painted, vibrant, bright,
A dream I chase with all my might.
Beneath the weight, I feel I break,
Yet still maintain the perfect fake.

In the quiet kitchen, verses flow,
Reminders of the life I sow.
With every beat, I crumble more,
The pressure, love's unyielding war.

The doorbell rings, interrupting my musings. I check my hair in the mirror at the end of the hall, smoothing the flyaways from my ponytail. Today, I've got on a full face of makeup, and I'm wearing a fitted red dress that sits just below the knee. Through the patterned glass door, I can make out three enormous figures.

It's them.

Pasting on a smile, I tug it open, a greeting dying in my throat. I blink, taking in the men before me. Muscles on muscles, even the smaller of the three. Their presence alone is like a punch to the libido, a heady combination making me feel a little woozy. I can't help but imagine what it would be like to taste them, their skin, their hair, their lips.

The thought is more than a little foreign to me, as I have never once looked at another man after meeting Alex.

The one on the left is a beautiful mountain of a man, at least seven feet tall, with a buzz cut and hickory-colored eyes. The midnight pitch of his skin is in stark contrast to his pearly white smile, elongated canines and all—*a lot like mine.* He gives me a nod, taking in my outfit.

The one in the middle is shorter, but only by a few inches, with black hair just above his shoulders and a roman nose. He has the most striking blue eyes, so pale they're almost white, like chunks of an iceberg floating through azure water. Tattoos line the column of his throat, and dip into a black button-up dress shirt. He's less of a line-backer—like the first guy—and more like an elite swimmer.

On his right is a man with bright emerald eyes and blond hair that's longer on top than the sides. It sweeps across his forehead in a messy, but styled, way. His dimples punch his cheeks, and he tilts his head, taking me in. His high cheekbones contrast his square jaw.

None of them wear coats. The grin of the big one pulls me out of my lust-induced stupor, and I finally find my voice. "You must be The Love Architects!" I step aside. "Please, come on in."

Rolls doesn't bark, and instead waits patiently, wagging his tail as though greeting old friends and not strangers. Rolls is a quick judge of character, and he hates everyone. Except for these guys, apparently.

After pulling the duffel bags from their shoulders, they drop them at their feet to greet me. Instead of shaking my hand, they pull me into a hug, one at a time.

The big one holds me a little longer, his scent a mix of woods and spice, and something else I can't quite put my finger on. My insides dance and melt at the same time, so overwhelmed with the energy they give off. It's almost as though it pours off them and mingles with the oxygen in my lungs, urging me to take a deeper breath. Every molecule of my being floods with warmth, like I'm finally home. And their smell? It's like they've bathed in pheromones, turning my lower half into a panting, wanton hot wife. I swear I've smelled it before.

Weird.

"I'm Niko," the first one drawls, the deep tone of his voice vibrating through my body like a tuning fork in a glass of water. It's tantalizing and familiar, like I'm remembering a song I heard in a dream.

"And I'm Vox," the second one says with a nod, his voice low, like velvet-covered steel.

The last one looks me in the eye. "Remy." Voice gentle and smooth, like warm honey dripping off a spoon, he introduces himself.

"I'm Jocelyn. We're so happy to have you here." I watch as they slip their shoes off, arranging them neatly in the rack by the door. "Alex is running a little behind, but he should be here in a couple more hours. Let me show you to your rooms."

As I lead them up the stairs and down a hallway to the three guest rooms, my heart races, and my palms feel sweaty. It's strange to think that these men, strangers to me, will be living with us for the next six months. I can't help but feel both excited and nervous about what lies ahead.

I open each guest room to give them a tour. Each has an en suite bathroom, a large walk-in closet, and a Christmas tree in front of a floor-to-ceiling window. It's not even Thanksgiving yet, but I love decorating the trees for each holiday. They nod in silent approval, and with each room, my heart warms a little more, despite my lingering nerves.

"I'll let you all get settled in before my husband gets home. Make yourselves comfortable," I say. "If you need anything, just let me know."

The three men thank me, and I back away, feeling lighter and brighter than I had before. I can feel the energy they brought with them, and it's unlike anything I've ever experienced. I feel as though I can do anything—and I will.

I'm busy prepping supper in the kitchen when Niko enters, followed by Remy and Vox. My heart rate picks up under their attention, their presence even more electrifying in the space between the island and the stove.

"Thought we'd come down and help." Niko grins. "Put us to work. We earn our keep here."

I stand frozen with the long-handled wooden spoon in my hand, blinking at them while I process what they just said. "Help?"

"A marriage is a partnership, and we're going to teach you what is and isn't acceptable between husband and wife. Your first lesson? No more waiting on him hand and foot." Remy picks up a knife from where I'd stopped chopping an onion to stir the ground beef on the stove.

"Oh, alright." I bite my lip and glance around the kitchen, suddenly caught in overwhelm. I've always cooked for everyone. Never have I had to delegate, unless we've brought in a caterer or chef for a party. My eyes land on the ceramic bowl covered with a white flour sack. Gesturing with the spoon, I point to it, and ask for one of them to turn the dough onto the floured surface I'd already prepped on the island.

Niko and Remy get to work kneading and forming the dough into two loaves, and Vox puts together a fruit salad to accompany our meal.

As I cook, I can't help but be amazed at each one's contribution. They even help me prepare the table with real cloth napkins and silverware. If this were Alex, he would've pulled out paper plates or insisted on carryout if he were expected to help.

The four of us take our seats around the dinner table, adorned with red, scent-free tapered candles, while Alex's chair remains empty. Humiliation brews in my stomach as the minutes tick by and the food grows cold.

"Has he checked in?" Remy glances at the giant clock on the wall. It reads a quarter past nine.

Scooting back my chair, I grab my phone from where it's charging on the island.

"Going to be a little later, eat without me." I read Alex's text out loud. Tears well up in my eyes, and I turn away from the men so they can't see as all hope deflates in my chest. "I'll just save him a dish," I squeak out while I dig into a drawer for a matching Tupperware set.

As I search for the container, memories of my parents' loving relationship fill my mind. They've always been so happy together, and I've dreamt of having that same kind of love in my marriage. The pressure to maintain that image of perfection is overwhelming, and I can't help but feel like I'm failing.

I think back to how supportive my parents have always been, but I've always felt a little out of place, as though everything was a house of cards ready to crumble. It feels like that now as I think back to the first time I felt this way.

I step out of my parents' car and look up at the towering brick building that will be my home for the next four years. My heart races with excitement and trepidation as I clutch my backpack and follow my parents to the dorms. We make our way up the stairs, my dad lugging a heavy suitcase behind him. When we reach the third floor, I find my room and let out a sigh of relief. It's small, but cozy, with a twin bed, a desk, and a small window that lets in a sliver of light. My parents help me unpack, and we spend the next few hours organizing my things.

As the day wears on, my parents start to prepare to leave. A knot forms in my stomach at the thought of being alone in this unfamiliar place. My dad hugs me tightly and tells me to call if I need anything. My mom kisses me on the forehead and tells me how proud she is of me.

As they leave, I'm hit with a sudden pang of homesickness. But I push it aside and try to focus on the task at hand. I'm here for a reason—to get my undergrad degree in biology and later, become a veterinarian. I'll bury myself in my textbooks and assignments, determined to excel in my classes, and maybe even smuggle a few stray animals into my dorm for some much-needed companionship.

In the weeks that followed, I'd started to settle into my new routine. I made friends, joined clubs, and explored the campus. But as I immersed myself in my studies, I couldn't shake the feeling that something was missing. I longed for my family and the sense of security they provided. But most of all, I missed feeling like I knew who I was and where I belonged.

By the time I find a container, fat tears cascade down my cheeks where I'm crouched with an arm resting on the open drawer, hiding my sorrow from the strangers in my home.

"Hey." Vox's voice is full of concern as he kneels beside me, his eyes cloudy and troubled. He wraps an arm around my shoulders and whispers in my ear, "Let us help you."

He eases the lid out of my hand, setting it on the countertop while he helps me to my feet. Warm arms wrap around me, and I'm pulled against his firm chest.

The other men step closer, and soon, I'm surrounded in an

embrace of the warmest love I've ever felt. I burst into sobs and relax in their arms, a measure of safety I haven't felt in years.

Remy and Niko break away to reheat our stuffed peppers, and they usher me back to the table, not a word passing between us until our plates are clean.

The guys go for seconds, and I watch in amusement as they pile their plates high. I take pride in cooking. There's something meditative about it, but watching someone actually enjoy my cooking enough to go back for seconds? I might just find myself making excuses to feed these guys.

As we sit back down at the table—them with their second helpings and me with a glass of Moscato d'Asti—I find myself curious about these men who have come into my life and offered me comfort and support. I ask, "How did you three end up working together as Love Architects?"

Remy, who is sitting across from me, sets down his fork and exchanges a glance with Niko and Vox. He smiles warmly before explaining, "We used to work for the same company. Although we come from different backgrounds and experiences, we share a passion for helping others. There, our paths crossed many years ago, and we realized that together, we could make a real difference in people's lives. After working together for so long, we became good enough friends to become neighbors."

"I've tolerated them for a long time." Vox grins, adding, "We've found that by combining our expertise, we can provide a more comprehensive and effective approach to helping couples. I'm better at introspective counseling, whereas Niko keeps things fun."

I look at Niko, who has been quietly observing the conversation, and ask, "It can't be all fun and games though. What's the most challenging aspect of your work?"

He hesitates for a moment, as if carefully choosing his words. "Sometimes, it's difficult to see couples struggle and be in pain. You just want to reach in there, tell someone they're the ones screwing everything up, but you've got to have a little more tact. It's incredibly rewarding when we see them overcome their challenges and grow stronger together, even if it takes a little longer for them to get to the finish line."

Their words fill me with a sense of hope, something I haven't felt in a long time. These men, these Love Architects, have a genuine desire to help me and Alex. And though I'm still guarded, I can't help but feel a little more optimistic about the possibility of healing my marriage.

"Thank you," I say softly, looking at each of them in turn. "I know I don't know you well, but I appreciate your willingness to help. I just hope we can find a way to fix what's broken."

Vox squeezes my hand reassuringly, and the others nod in agreement. "We'll do everything we can to help you, Jocelyn. You're not alone in this."

As we continue our conversation, I find myself opening up to them, asking more about their personal experiences and how they've overcome challenges in their work as Love Architects. And for the first time in a long while, I feel a sense of camaraderie and hope.

A flicker of light in the darkness.

As we're gathering the dishes, the garage door rumbles open, and Alex walks in carrying a single, red rose. He pauses in the entry of our kitchen, eyes softening when they land on me.

"Sorry I'm so late," he apologizes, and sets the flower in the center of the table. He eyes the three giants in our kitchen, his face doing that thing where a mask slides in place and Mr. Hedge Fund Manager takes the reins.

He plasters a grin on his face, and one hand extends to welcome our guests. "Alexander Vanderbilt, great to meet you."

The men take turns introducing themselves, towering over my husband, who I just know is having a mental complex over it. I don't think either of us expected them to be so ... big. And handsome.

Although with the voices we heard on the phone, we were only fooling ourselves.

Remy gestures to the fridge. "We just put supper away. Why don't we have a chat now, and you can eat later? I wouldn't want to keep Jocelyn waiting any longer than she's already been made to wait."

Alex's eyes go comically wide, and I can't even be mad at Remy. Alex did make us wait, and he knew how important this was to me. To us.

In the years since we've gotten married, his hairline has receded a bit, but he's still got that handsome jawline dotted with salt-and-pepper stubble. The subtle tick-tick-tick of his Patek Philippe watch fills the quiet kitchen.

He swallows his surprise and nods, gesturing to the living room. "Yes, of course. Let's talk." His voice is rich, like Kentucky bourbon, and he's wearing the Creed Aventus cologne I got him for his birthday.

The men follow him, Niko and Remy engaging in conversation while Vox stares at the rose with an inscrutable expression on his face. I linger long enough for them to take their seats first.

As I settle on the couch next to Alex, I can feel the tension between us like a physical weight as I slip off my heels and tuck my feet under me, grabbing an ivory throw blanket to cover my legs. My heart aches with the distance between us, a reminder of how far we've drifted apart after years of marriage.

Vox takes the lead, his voice a compelling blend of midnight promises and unwavering confidence. "Let's address the elephant in the room. Not only were you late, but you disrespected our time. Where were you?"

Alex's skin pales as he struggles to keep his composure. "I-I apologize. I had a meeting with a business partner that ran late. It was irresponsible of me, and I understand that it was disrespectful to keep you waiting. I'm sorry."

Vox nods slowly. "Apology accepted, though your wife is the one who spent all day waiting at home for you, cooking your dinner, only for you to arrive late. She's the one you really need to apologize to." He crosses his tattoo-wrapped arms, giving Alex a stern look.

I can't help but feel a small sense of satisfaction at Vox's words. Finally, someone is holding Alex accountable for his actions.

But Alex looks to me, his eyes softening as he reaches out to take my hand. "Jossy, I'm sorry. I should've kept better track of time."

My usual self would've brushed it off, told him it was no big deal, and try to pacify his feelings. But having the guys here gives me an extra shot of confidence. "I expect you to make our marriage a priority going forward if you choose to remain in it."

Niko leans forward, his piercing amber-hued eyes locking onto Alex's. "And what will you do to make that happen? How will you show Jocelyn that you truly value your marriage?"

Alex's gaze flickers between Niko and me, and I can see the wheels turning in his head. "No meetings after five." He swallows, casting a nervous glance at me. "And no more weekend meetings."

I give him a shallow nod. "That's a good start."

Remy glances at his watch. "Here's how tonight is going to work. You'll draw Jocelyn a bath, which she will enjoy—alone—while you eat supper. After she's done, we'll start our first lesson of the night."

"And what's that?" I smooth the fibers of the blanket on my lap.

Remy glances at the screen and then looks up at us. "Tonight's lesson is about active listening and understanding each other's perspectives. We'll also be discussing how to express your emotions in a healthy way."

I raise an eyebrow, intrigued. Meanwhile, Alex nods, looking determined to prove himself.

"Alright," Alex says, his voice firm. "I'll draw the bath for you, Jossy."

As he heads to the bathroom to prepare the bath, I can't help but feel a mix of anticipation and anxiety. I know these lessons will be challenging, but I also know that they're necessary for us to grow as a couple. I'm tired of feeling like a wilted flower.

When the bath is ready, I give Alex a small smile before disappearing into the bathroom. The warm water and fragrant bubbles help to soothe my tense muscles and quiet my racing thoughts. Bubbles surround me, and I exhale, sinking deeper. A faint scent of rose and lavender from bath oils marinate the air around me.

I spend the time reflecting on our relationship and the changes I hope to see. Would I be able to navigate life after Alex if things don't change?

As I soak in the bath, my thoughts are interrupted by a low hum of music. It takes me a moment to realize it's coming from outside the bathroom door. Curiosity gets the best of me, so I quickly rinse off before slipping out of the tub and wrapping a fluffy robe around myself.

Opening the door, the music grows louder, and I recognize a familiar tune. It's a song Alex used to sing to me when we first started dating. Following the source of the music, I discover him, Remy, Niko, and Vox gathered around the fireplace in our living room.

They turn to face me, and Alex extends a hand. I take it as he wraps me in a hug. "How was your bath?"

"Good." I smile up at him. "What've you four been doing?"

"Talking about schedules for the rest of the month." Alex gestures to the couch, and we follow. I sit next to Alex, holding his hand as we wait for instruction.

I find myself shaking my head in shock. I really hadn't expected Alex to go along with all this so easily—not after his initial reaction to the idea. But he seems to soften in the presence of these guys. It's like they've cast a spell on him.

I suppress a grin at the thought of it.

Vox, Niko, and Remy pull chairs closer, so we're in a semi-circle.

Remy begins the lesson, explaining the importance of active listening and understanding each other's perspectives. "When one person is speaking, the other should be fully engaged, making eye contact, and not interrupting. Focus on truly hearing what your partner is saying, rather than formulating your response."

He asks us to share a recent issue we've faced in our relationship, and I hesitantly bring up Alex's frequent late nights at the office. Remy then guides us through a conversation where we each express our feelings and thoughts on the matter.

As I share my feelings of loneliness and neglect, I notice Alex's eyes widen slightly, as if he hadn't realized the depth of my emotions. He listens intently, nodding as I speak, and I can see that he's making a conscious effort to understand my perspective.

With a voice wobble, I manage to say, "It's just ... it's been so hard to feel so alone in this. We used to be so good. I just want to be there again."

Maybe things will change for the better.

When it's Alex's turn to share his thoughts, he explains how upset he is that I've been faking it in the bedroom this entire time. Heat rises in my cheeks as I wring my hands in my lap. "To be fair, I feel like the person I've spent over a decade with should know what makes me feel good, or should check in."

Niko clears his throat. "While true, I think the heart of the issue is letting Alex know what does feel good. Both now, and in the moment. Communication is key."

"Um." I falter for a moment. "I like massages."

Biting my lip nervously, I hesitate. While I do enjoy massages, Alex's technique leaves much to be desired. His touch is too rough, applying too much pressure in all the wrong places, and he never seems to find the knots that need attention.

"But massages don't give you an orgasm," Vox drawls. "Do they, Jocelyn?" The look he levels me with is enough to melt my bones. Or my underwear.

I clear my throat, feeling slightly embarrassed. "Well, no, not exactly."

Remy leans forward. "It's important to understand and communicate what you need in order to feel fulfilled in your relationship. This includes sexual needs."

I nod, feeling a sense of vulnerability wash over me.

Alex takes my hand in his and whispers, "What feels good, Jossy?" He turns to face me completely on the couch.

I squirm under everyone's attention, which is funny, considering a lot of the porn I watch is voyeuristic in nature.

Niko stands, and I glance at him as he asks where I keep paper and writing utensils. I gesture towards the desk across the room, and he rummages through it until he finds what he needs. He passes Alex and I each a sheet with a pen. "On your paper, make two columns. One titled 'what feels good,' and the other titled, 'fantasies.'"

I glance at the sheet of paper and chew on my bottom lip, considering what to write. This is a potential minefield, but I remind myself that it's all in the interest of improving our relationship.

Finally, I jot down a few things under the "what feels good" column:

kissing my neck
gentle touches along my skin
clitoral stimulation of any kind
doggy style
massages
cuddling

Under the 'fantasies' column, I write my list, hoping Alex will take it as something that can add to our marriage, not cause him to feel inadequate. Though the idea of sharing these out loud is kind of scary.

As I finish writing, I feel everyone's eyes on me. It's not often that I verbalize what turns me on, let alone write it down for everyone to see.

Niko speaks up, breaking the tense silence. "Now, take turns sharing with each other. It's important to be honest and open in this. Why don't you go first, Jocelyn?"

I take a deep inhale and glance down at my list. "Okay." I whisper my list, feeling nervous. And my last bit I squeak out fast, "doggy style."

"That all sounds good." Alex grins, smug as ever. "I can do more of all those things. What fantasies do you have?"

I can't help but wonder if Alex is playacting, trying to appear relaxed and agreeable in front of the others like he does when he's around clients and friends in the business world. Internally, I question his sincerity, but even if he's faking it until he makes it, hopefully this experience might make a genuine difference in our relationship.

"You never really talk dirty to me, but I think I'd love it." Nibbling on my lip again, I look at my husband. "You're so quiet every time, and I never really know if you're enjoying yourself."

"Oh baby, I am." He places his hand on my knee, giving it a squeeze. "What else?"

"I like the idea of being watched."

"Watched?"

Heat flames my cheeks, and my words are barely a squeak. "During sex or masturbating."

"You want people to watch us have sex?"

I nod, not looking up from my list.

He shifts uncomfortably. "And you want me to watch you get yourself off?"

I nod again, my words caught in my throat.

"Okay." I can hear the grin in his voice.

"And the rest of this kind of goes hand-in-hand. You're so docile in bed. Sometimes, I just want you to take control, chase me, dominate me, pin me down and fuck me. Leave your marks on my skin."

He chokes out, "Marks?"

"Bite me," I whisper, licking my lips. "Claw me."

"But I don't want to hurt you," he says softly.

"Sometimes," I look up at him through my lashes, "I want you to hurt me."

His throat bobs. "Okay, baby." He leans closer to me. "Then do you want to do that to me?"

"I want to bite and claw you."

"Where?"

Pulling in a deep breath through my nose, I look back down at the paper in my lap. "Anywhere. Everywhere."

Vox clears his throat, and our attention goes to him. "In any kind of BDSM relationship, there are parameters to consider. If you want any of that, you need to run it by me, Vox, and Remy as you explore this new dynamic. Just to ensure everyone's safety."

I'm practically panting with lust. I love that the three of them make me feel so unshackled. "What if I don't want him to have limits?"

Vox grins, and the sight of it has me squeezing my thighs together for friction. "You've got to leap before you can fly."

He's right. I need to start small with Alex. As far as I know, he doesn't watch porn—he's always working, and I'm always home. So he probably has no idea how rough I want him to be. I'll need to ease him into it.

"How about you read me your lists?" I turn to my husband.

Alex clears his throat and holds up his sheet to read his first column out loud. "I love when you're on top and the lights are on." He glances over the top of the paper and grins at me before returning to his list. "Because I like seeing you—it heightens my pleasure. Hearing your moans. When you do the little tongue swirl around the head of my cock, and the way you play with my balls."

He adjusts himself and continues. "And uh, for fantasies, well, costumes could be fun."

"What kind of costumes?" I sit up straighter, loving this idea.

"I'm not sure, but I'd like for us to role-play some with you sucking me off at a party or something. Or with you being my secretary and you have to blow me under my desk."

A pit of dread expands in my stomach as I choke on the bile that rises in my throat. My vision blurs as a tsunami of tears burst from my eyes, leaving me unable to see. With trembling hands, I drop the paper, jump to my feet, and stumble back until I'm out of the room, fleeing from his words.

"Woah, hey!" Alex shouts, but I don't hear the rest of what he says as I run up the stairs, Rolls on my heels and barking the entire way.

I lock myself in our en suite bathroom, sinking against the door and burying my head in my hands as sobs shake my shoulders. Rolls presses close to me, whimpering as he places a giant paw on me, his nails digging into my skin from the weight of him.

Pounding on the door ensues, and I suck in a breath, trying to hold in my cries.

"Jocelyn?" Alex calls through the door. "What the hell happened?"

He pounds some more, and I use the robe to wipe off my tears as I climb to my feet. I unlock the door, and step back so he can slip in.

"What the hell, Jossy?" He puts his hands on his hips, expression wild as I close the door behind him.

I place my hand on Rolls' head, allowing him to lend me strength for this conversation. "Are you cheating on me?"

"What? Are you crazy?" he shouts. "You've lost your fucking mind, Joss."

"Are. You. Cheating. On. Me?" I spit, gritting each word.

"That's what you gathered from my fantasy? For fucks sake." He throws up his hands, spinning around to face the center of the bathroom.

"Why won't you answer my fucking question?" I shriek. "Is that why you're always gone so long? Who is it? Tell me!"

"No one!" he roars so loud I jump, causing Rolls to bark and stand in front of me in a defensive move. He takes a deep breath as he lowers his voice, but it's still laced in anger as he turns towards me. "I work, then I come home to you. So no, I'm not fucking cheating on you, Jossy."

"But you'd love your secretary to come suck you off while you're on a work call, huh?"

"Are you on your period?" He stalks over to the trash bin, picking it up to inspect, seeing it empty before he tosses it down by the toilet. "Why are you acting so fucking crazy all of a sudden?"

"Call me crazy," I prowl towards him, stopping when my toes meet his, "one more time."

A loud knock sounds at the door, startling us both, and my face heats with shame that I'm acting so horribly irrational. "One second," I call out.

I adjust my robe and pad my way over to the door, turning the handle with a grimace. "Wow, guys." I wince as I swing it wide. "I'm so sorry."

The three love architects stand there with varying degrees of worry on their faces. "Are you alright?" Remy asks.

"Um, just going a little insane, probably." I squeeze my eyes shut, pressing my palms to my temples. "Maybe we should call it a night, try again tomorrow. I usually make a big brunch for us so Alex can sleep in on Sundays. Does that work for you?"

"Brunch sounds great, but I think we really need to talk this one out. Why don't you two join us in your bedroom?" Remy steps aside, gesturing to the bed.

"Okay," I murmur, my embarrassment flaming my cheeks.

I follow them into the bedroom, Alex and I taking spots against the headboard on our respective sides.

"Do you want to tell us what happened?" Niko asks as he picks up my leather chair as though it weighs nothing and brings it over to the bed. His muscles bulge, but he doesn't appear strained.

He sinks into it, and the other two climb onto the bed, facing us at the foot of it.

"I guess I was just triggered." I run a hand through my still-damp hair. "His fantasies made me feel inadequate."

"They seemed pretty run-of-the-mill fantasies," Vox mumbles, brow furrowed in confusion. "And there's not a snowball's chance in hell you're inadequate, Jocelyn."

"Hearing the bit about the secretary and the girl at a party really played to my insecurities about his constant absences, and I felt out of control. Like every fear was exposed." My fingers trace the edging of the silk pillow I've got clutched to my chest.

"Is there any merit to her insecurities, Alex? This is a safe space. And if you've got anything to confess, now is the time to do it." Remy's voice has warmth to it.

Alex takes a deep breath, and my stomach plummets as I close my eyes, dreading the confirmation. But it's not what he gives me.

"Never in our entire marriage, nor when we were dating, or before things were official between us, have I so much as looked at another woman. Or man." He slides his hand in mine. "Every fantasy I have, is you."

I open my mouth to speak, but he continues.

"And Gladys—" he looks to the guys—"my secretary—is a sixty-three-year-old woman who's been married for thirty years with nine grandchildren. I may not be the perfect husband, but a cheater is something I'm not."

My shoulders relax, and I bury my face in the pillow, letting the air out of my lungs slowly. When I inhale, I raise my head to look at Alex. "I'm sorry."

"It's okay, baby." He pulls me into his arms, and I sink into his touch.

"See? Aren't you two glad you talked it out?" Niko offers, and I nod.

"One more lesson, then we'll leave you two be for the night." Remy pulls out his phone and scrolls, introducing the topic of expressing emotions in a healthy way. "It's important to avoid blaming or accusing your partner when discussing your feelings. Instead, use 'I' statements to express how you feel and what you need."

We practice this technique, taking turns sharing our emotions and needs related to the issue we discussed earlier. It's not an easy exercise, but the love architects' guidance and support make it feel more manageable.

By the end of the lesson, I can see Alex and I starting to ease into a newfound connection.

"Okay, one more 'I' statement," I say with a playful smirk. "I enjoy it when you chase me around the house."

Alex grins and replies, "Well, I enjoy catching you and surprising you with tickles."

I giggle, feeling a small spark between us as we flirt. "Maybe we should make that a weekly thing."

Alex winks. "Deal."

Although it's just the first step on a long journey, I can already see the potential for positive change in our relationship. We're learning to communicate more effectively and to better understand each other's feelings and perspectives, which gives me hope for our future together.

CHAPTER SIX

REMY

*N*iko, Vox, and I sit together in the living room, carefully observing the dynamic between Jocelyn and Alex as they interact. The soft evening light filters through the windows, casting warm shadows on the floor, and a hint of tension fills the air. We all know the upcoming conversation won't be easy, but it's essential for the healing process.

Before we begin the conversation, we share a subtle glance, silently confirming that we're all in agreement. Our plan to make Alex more open to the intimacy lessons involves a discreet spell we discussed earlier. It's a delicate situation, and we believe this enchantment is necessary to help their marriage.

As Niko starts speaking, I subtly cast the spell, directing a soft wave of magical energy towards Alex. It's meant to make him more agreeable and open-minded for the upcoming intimacy lessons. Niko leans forward, maintaining eye contact with Alex as he says, "We need to discuss the next phase of our plan. The intimacy lessons are coming up, and we want to ensure you're fully on board and comfortable with the idea."

Alex's face tightens, betraying his unease. But as the magical energy reaches him, I notice his posture relax slightly, his expression becoming less strained. He takes a slow breath, trying to maintain his composure. "I understand," he says, his voice more even now. "It's part of the program, isn't it? If it's what we need to do to fix our relationship, then I'm willing."

I study his expression, searching for any hint of dishonesty or discomfort. "We want to make it clear that our goal is to help you and Jocelyn reconnect," I explain, trying to assuage his concerns. "Physical touch can be a powerful tool for strengthening emotional bonds, but we'll always be respectful of your boundaries and your relationship."

Vox nods in agreement, adding, "Open communication is crucial during this process. If you ever feel uncomfortable or want to stop, please speak up immediately. We're here to help, not to cause more distress."

As the conversation continues, we discuss the logistics of the intimacy lessons, ensuring that Alex understands the purpose of each activity and that Jocelyn is comfortable with the plan. It's clear that they're both apprehensive about the challenges ahead, but with the help of the spell, Alex seems more willing to face them.

With trust, communication, and a touch of magic, we hope to guide Jocelyn and Alex through the next phase of their journey, rebuild their connection and save their marriage.

CHAPTER SEVEN

JOCELYN

"Foreplay." Remy smirks.

My stomach flips as Alex's face blushes a deep crimson. I glance up, uncertain if I heard him correctly. For two weeks, the guys have had Alex observe me pleasuring myself, without giving him anything in return. The goal was for him to see what I enjoy without the pressure of me having to give back.

The pleasure was so intense, knowing Alex had been watching me. I didn't need to resort to watching porn since his presence already got me aroused—and I didn't want to give him a complex that he's not an oversized creature with the strength of ten men or a cock the width of my wrist.

Remy continues, "It's something that many couples take for granted, but it's an integral part of any relationship. We'll help you learn how to be more in tune with each other's needs and desires."

As soon as Remy finishes his sentence, Niko jumps in. "But first, we need to set some ground rules."

Alex nods, his face still flushed. "Of course. Whatever you think is best." He's got his ankle crossed over his knee, and he twitches his foot in a nervous gesture. The past couple of weeks have been a test of his patience, and true to his word, he's attended every lesson and hasn't worked late.

Niko takes a deep breath and looks at both Alex and me. "We need complete honesty from both of you. No holding back. No secrets. No fear of judgement. We want to help you build a strong foundation for your relationship, and that means being completely open with each other."

I take a moment to process his words before I manage to say something. "That sounds reasonable."

Alex nods in agreement, taking my hand in his and flashing me a warm smile. "Whatever we need to do to make this work."

"Anything?" Vox levels him with a dark look I can't place.

Alex pales slightly but stands firm. "Yes. Anything."

"Good," Vox says, his expression softening. "Then let's get started with the bath."

I watch as the four of them file out of the room, leaving me alone with my thoughts. This all feels so surreal. I have a feeling that things will be taken up a notch. Is this the part where they get hands-on? And is it really possible that these men—who no longer feel like strangers, but friends—could save our marriage? The rational side of me says no, but a part of me is curious and willing to try anything to fix what Alex and I once had.

Alex goes upstairs to start the bath while I make myself a mug of tea. Nerves make my hand unsteady, especially with the looming presence of the love architects in the room with me.

"Are you nervous?" Vox passes me the carton of oat milk.

"Thanks." I grab it, concentrating on fixing my tea. "And yup! I really am." I chuckle lightly.

While I've never been sick a day in my life, it still gives me some measure of comfort that Remy, Niko, and Vox provided proof of a clean bill of health.

"Is it about us touching you?" Vox's voice is low and gravelly.

I still my hand, dropping the spoon to face him. "Not exactly," I whisper.

Yes, it's about them touching me, but it's less about another man putting his hands on my body and more about *them* putting their hands on my body. And savoring their touch more than I would my husband's.

"What is it?" Niko approaches, and concern etches his face.

"It feels like cheating," I whisper. "Is that normal?"

"It's only cheating if Alex says no, and you do it anyway. But he said yes, didn't he?" Remy calls from where he's propped against the other counter.

I nibble on my bottom lip nervously. I can't get over the guilt for what goes through my mind sometimes. If Alex knew, I'm sure he would think it was a form of betrayal. "Well, yes—"

Remy grins. "If you're worried about being unfaithful, get that out of your mind now. You're doing this for your marriage. Alex is on board. We're on board. Are you?"

A smile teases my lips. "Yeah."

The lights are dim when I step into the bathroom, and the scent of lavender fills the air. The claw foot tub is filled with steaming water and the soft glow of candles illuminates the room.

"Come on in," Alex says, gesturing to the tub. He's got on a pair of low-slung pajama pants and a fitted t-shirt. "It's just how you like it."

I slip off my robe and slowly sink into the hot water, feeling the warmth and tension from the day melt away. Bubbles reach my chin, and I blow on them, sending a few into the air.

Alex presses a kiss to the top of my head. "I'll be up in a bit, but take your time." The soft keys of Helen Jane Long's *Expression* comes over the speakers, and I let myself melt into the moment.

For the first time in a long time, I can breathe. As the music surrounds me, I feel my body relax and the stress and worries of the last few years drift away. I drag a deep breath into my lungs and allow myself to be enveloped by the peaceful atmosphere. I can almost feel the potential of my relationship with Alex healing itself.

As my fingers and toes begin to prune, nerves swim in my stomach over what's to come. How hands on will the men get? How far will I let them go to help us? And will Alex tolerate it?

A soft knock on the door jolts me from my thoughts. "Jossy," Alex's voice calls out. "May we come in?"

I grab the bubbles that cling to my skin and sink lower in the water, covering all the good bits. "Okay," I squeak, heat pooling low in my belly.

My eyes have already adjusted to the candlelight, but the light behind the men is bright as they file in, so they probably can't see much of me anyway.

Alex enters first. Then Niko, Remy, and Vox each step further into the bathroom, making the space suddenly feel much smaller. But there's something comforting about their presence, like a security blanket wrapping around me.

The guys prop themselves against the wall while Alex approaches the tub. He leans down, eyes trained on mine, and my breath catches in my throat. "Are you ready for this, Joss?" he asks, his hand reaching out to caress my cheek.

I nod, my heart thudding a dangerous beat in my chest. "I think so."

Alex's fingers trail along the arm I have propped on the rim of the tub, sending a shiver through my body. "Remember, this is for us." He looks deep into my eyes. "We're in this together."

He kneads my shoulder and my head lolls back in a groan of pleasure. As I close my eyes, I feel the four men move around the room, their presence palpable. I try to keep my breathing steady, but it's difficult with so many eyes on me, especially when I know they're not just any eyes. These are the eyes attached to the hottest men I've seen in my entire life. Like they've walked out of every dirty fantasy I've ever had.

A small gasp escapes my lips as I feel a warm breath on the nape of my neck. I open my eyes to see Alex move closer, his hand dragging leisurely down my arm and sending delicious sensations through my body. His mouth presses against my shoulder and I sigh, feeling my body melt into the water.

"Drain the tub," one of them whispers to Alex, and he sinks his fingers into the water, pulling the drain open. As the water starts to swirl and disappear, I brace myself for what's to come.

Niko hands him a giant, fluffy towel, and Alex holds it open for me to step into.

Heat flushes my cheeks as I cover all my lady parts and rise out of the water. Alex wraps the towel around me, cocooning me in warmth. His hands brush my skin, sparking a tingling sensation in all the right places.

"Come," he says, his voice gentle. I take his hand and he ushers me into the bedroom, where more candles light up the space, twice as bright as the bathroom.

Alex leads me to the bed and asks me to lay on my stomach for a massage. I'm not fond of his massages—they're not very good—but the gesture is sweet.

I crawl onto the bed, positioning myself in the middle while Alex strips down to his boxers and climbs onto the mattress to sit next to me. He slides my towel, so it rests over just my ass, exposing my back to him.

As he starts on my back with massage oil, I try to relax, but the movements are stiff and more painful than anything. The guys must be able to tell by the look on my face because they stop him.

"I'll demonstrate first." Vox clears his throat, and I peer back at him just in time to catch him shucking his own shirt and pants.

Holy shit.

This is happening.

And if I thought these men looked good with their clothes on, it is *nothing* compared to seeing one of them in their boxers. If I don't spontaneously combust, I'm going to have a heart attack.

This is how I'm gonna die.

Vox carefully climbs onto the bed and positions himself on top of me, his strong body resting delicately on my hips, the heat of his presence seeping through. He tenderly guides my arms to the sides, and places his hands atop mine, exerting a gentle, steady pressure. His hands then begin to move in slow, rhythmic circles, kneading my muscles with the perfect blend of firmness and tenderness.

In a low, velvety voice, he explains to Alex the techniques he uses with each precise motion, imparting valuable advice on how to provide the best possible massage. Vox's skilled hands work wonders on my tense back, expertly coaxing my knots to unravel and melt away.

As Vox continues to work his magic, I can't help but let out a few moans of pleasure as I melt like putty in his hands. It's not just the relief from the tension in my muscles, but the rush of sensations surging through me.

Pinned beneath him, my mind runs wild with all the dirty things he could do to me. When he shifts his weight, my breath quickens as I feel his arousal jutting against my ass. But with its massive size, I dismiss it as my imagination.

Wishful thinking.

His fingers linger on me as he moves out of the way for Alex to return to his position, only he's on top of me now, just like Vox had been.

Unlike before, his movements are smooth and calming, coming in long, deep strokes, thanks to Vox's coaching.

"When you feel comfortable," Niko whispers to Alex. "You can start being more brazen with your hands. Dip a little lower, linger a little longer."

I can feel my whole face flush with embarrassment and anticipation as the words sink in. These guys are really here to help me fix my marriage. And part of that means showing me all the ways I can make my husband happy in bed.

But then Alex scoots onto my thighs, taking the towel with him, and all thoughts of embarrassment fly from my mind and shoot straight into mortification as I watch Remy head straight for my nightstand.

He sinks to his knees and pulls open the one drawer not even Alex goes in. I let out a tiny squeak of alarm and he chuckles, looking over his shoulder to wink at me.

Wink at me!

He holds up my biggest vibrator, a pink tentacle monstrosity, and gives it a playful shake.

My hands fly to my face, and I groan. "How did you even know where to look?"

"Where else would you keep your toys? The pantry downstairs? In the greenhouse? Rolls' kennel?"

My jaw drops in shock, and then I laugh as I shake my head in disbelief. What have I gotten myself into?

Niko stands up, a mischievous glint in his eyes. "We're not here to judge your bedroom activities, Jocelyn. We're here to make sure you're getting what you need—and that Alex can deliver."

Alex is the one to break the tension, resting his forehead against my shoulder blades as he whispers, "If you want this to stop, it'll stop."

I shake my head. "No, it's okay." I flush. "Just a little embarrassed."

"Everything that happens stays in this house." Vox reclines against the headboard, crossing his ankles. "By the time we're through with you two in six months, he'll be drawing orgasm after orgasm out from you right in front of us. This is only the beginning, but only if you want it to continue."

An involuntary whimper escapes my throat at the prospect, and a lazy grin settles upon his face.

"Guess that settles it then." He smirks.

Alex's hands continue their ministrations on my back, running up and down my spine. It's much better than it used to be, but he still needs a lot of practice.

"Can you flip over to your back?" Alex asks me.

"Okay," I answer breathlessly, though my movements are hesitant. Do I just bare myself to the room or what? I look around, blushing fiercely. What if this isn't something they're expecting?

Remy takes a deep breath and flashes a reassuring smile in my direction. "It's okay, Jocelyn," he says softly. "Just do what feels natural to you. We won't judge you."

I pull a deep breath into my lungs and flop onto my back, exposing my breasts to the four of them. Immediately, Alex's hands move to them, kneading them as he holds out a hand for the vibrator.

Niko passes him the tool, and I suddenly realize why they want me to lay here. They're going to coach Alex through how to use it on me.

I feel myself blush anew, but I can't deny the heat that is already pooling between my legs. Already, I'm more aroused than I've ever been in my entire life. Who knew I had a little hussy in me all this time?

Vox slides off the bed, his eyes smoldering with a burning intensity that speaks of untold, hidden desires. He kneels down beside me and takes one of my hands in his.

"Show him where it feels good," he demands in a low, husky voice as he guides my hand down the flat plane of my stomach to the juncture between my legs. "This is a chance to bring your voyeuristic fantasies to life."

My breath catches in my throat and a shiver of pleasure shoots through me as my fingertips brush against my center. I can feel everyone's eyes on me, and heat spreads through my cheeks.

Alex hands me the vibrator and I take it hesitantly, feeling awkwardly exposed.

Vox takes my other hand, now both of them guiding me.

"Show him where it feels best," he encourages, his hot breath tickling my ear.

Alex looks at me expectantly, his eyes half-lidded and seductive. *He really is going to let this happen.*

I tentatively place the vibrator against my clit, and a deep flush of pleasure washes over me. Alex gasps and Remy's eyes widen as I experiment with the toy, my breaths coming rapidly.

"Just like that, Jocelyn," Vox murmurs, his grip on my hands tightening.

Niko kneels beside me, his hand trailing down my shoulder.

Alex looks transfixed, the others mesmerized by my pleasure, and I realize I'm not embarrassed anymore. I'm glowing, reveling in a new level of intimacy and pleasure that I'm sure I could never have reached on my own.

I close my eyes, and I can feel the vibrations traveling through me as I move the vibrator in circles around my clitoris. The pleasure builds until I'm panting and gasping, my skin on fire.

The vibrator quiets, and I reluctantly open my eyes. All four of them are staring at me, and I can see the heat and anticipation in their eyes. I feel like I'm alive for the first time in decades, and it's in this moment I know that I'm in for the ride of my life.

"It's my turn, right?" Alex ruins the moment by breaking the silence and flashing me a lascivious grin.

He slides the vibrator out of me and tosses it to the other side of the bed. It bounces, bumping into Remy's foot. Picking it up, Remy tosses it end-over-end, catching it without looking as he stares me down.

"Okay." I bite my lip, feeling exposed now that my post-orgasm bliss has faded.

"Actually," Niko props his head in his hands where he's got his elbows resting on the bed and levels Alex with a look I can't quite place, "tonight was all about Jocelyn's pleasure. She spends her days and nights serving you, and after more than a decade together you still don't know what makes her feel good, other than what she's told you. Until you can prove you can, this is what we're working on."

Alex's mouth drops open, and I tuck my lip between my teeth to hold in the grin. "But we've been working on this for weeks now! When is it my turn?"

Surprisingly, the guys say nothing, other than leveling him with a look.

Alex sighs and leans over me to press a chaste, but meaningful kiss to my forehead. "I'll do better," he says, sincerity swimming in his eyes.

He slides off the bed, offering me a hand to help me up, and I accept. When I stand, I grab the towel pooled on the floor and pull it around me, securing it at my chest.

"Now what?" I turn to face the men, heat flushing my cheeks as I avoid their gazes.

"You'll get ready for bed while Alex preps his lunch for tomorrow."

Alex sighs but nods his agreement. He turns to me, a softness in his eyes I haven't seen in years. "I'll be up when I'm done." He presses his lips to my forehead and leaves the room, a strange sense of peace settling over me.

I think I'm going to love having these men here.

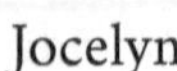

Jocelyn

THE SUN'S rays begin to pierce through the thin curtains, illuminating the room in a dappled golden light. I wake up with a pounding headache and an almost physical weight on my chest. Last night's events play on repeat in my mind, a dizzying whirlwind of memories that make it impossible to think straight.

Dragging myself out of bed, I feel the icy chill of the hardwood floor beneath my feet. My body aches as if it's been through a battle, but the warmth of my memories—the sensation of being held by Vox, Niko, and Remy—make it hard to shake off. My heart races as I remember the intensity of the intimacy lesson, our bodies working together and the overwhelming sense of connection we shared.

With trembling hands, I trudge over to my little coffee bar and pour myself a cup, needing something to ground me back to reality. As I cradle the steaming mug, the aromatic scent of java fills my nostrils, and I can't help but reflect on what happened.

I've never felt so alive, so desired, as I do with Vox, Niko, and Remy. The intimacy lesson had been a whirlwind of sensations, a revelation of connection that I've never experienced before. It leaves my head spinning and my soul yearning for more.

I take a seat by the window, the sun warming my face as the new day unfolds around me. The world outside seems so distant, as though it exists in a parallel universe. I can't help but feel like I'm on the precipice of something life-changing, yet terrifyingly uncertain.

As the morning wears on, a new thought begins to worm its way into my mind. It's more than just a fleeting fancy, and it sinks its teeth deep into my very core. What I feel for them—Vox, Niko, and Remy— is more than just physical attraction. It's a connection that goes beyond the surface, something that I have never felt with my husband.

This realization sends me spiraling into a vortex of doubt and confusion. What in the fuck am I actually doing? I felt something with them. I can't put my finger on it, but the connection was so intense, it's like it was more than just a contract. Do they genuinely care for me, or am I just a job to them?

My thoughts race, my heart aches, and the weight of my decision feels like an anchor around my neck. I start to practice what I'm going to say to them, telling them that I can't do this anymore; that I need to end our arrangement. How can I possibly allow these men, who are supposed to save my marriage, to tempt me like this?

I can envision the words, clear as day in my mind. Yet, every time I try to speak them aloud, the words get caught in my throat, and I can't bring myself to voice them.

As the day wears on, my resolve weakens. The thought of losing them is unbearable, but the thought of continuing down this path fills me with even more dread.

In the end, I decide to say nothing. I can't bring myself to ask them to leave. For now, I'll continue down this dangerous path, hoping that it doesn't lead to something I'll regret. As the sun sets, casting long shadows across the room, I steel myself for the uncertainty that lies ahead, my heart heavy with the weight of the choices I must make.

CHAPTER EIGHT

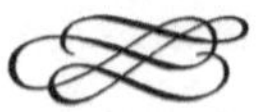

VOX

It's been a week since I helped Jocelyn get off, and it almost broke me. If a fraction of that had taken place without Alex there, I would've been worshipping her with my tongue, fuck whatever the guys think. Or the council.

We've all retired to our rooms for the night, and I'm in the one next to hers. It's Niko's turn to watch over her this evening. We've kept our same rotation, but the longer this goes on, the more I know I'm in too deep.

Do the others feel this? The pull to claim her, make her ours, consequences be damned? While Alex is making an effort, it isn't near good enough because he's not good enough for someone like Jocelyn.

Hell, I'm not good enough, and I'm twice the man he is. If it wouldn't totally devastate Jocelyn, I'd slip something into Alex's drink, and be done with the asshole. Maybe shove him off a cliff, out of an airplane, or drive a knife into his skull.

He reminds me so much of Lourdes, the bastard who killed the last of my blood. I told my sister he wasn't a good man. Even hundreds of years later, the pain of not ending him when I had the chance is like an open, festering wound.

Alex has never laid a hand on Jocelyn, but I know he's capable. I see it in the subtle shifts of his demeanor—the tension in his jaw, the narrowing of his eyes, and the slight edge in his tone when she does something he doesn't like, and as a guardian, it's easier for me to spot than it would be for anyone else in her life.

It's partly down to instinct and partly due to our training. As fae guardians, we offer a constant, protective presence, ensuring that she never faces a tragic fate like the ones that changed the lives of all three of us. Our deepest grief gave roots to ancient power, only unlocked during unimaginable loss, and we turned it into something bigger than any one of us. It's how each of us came to be fae guardians.

I toss and turn, unable to find a comfortable position. My mind is restless, consumed by thoughts of Jocelyn and the complicated situation we find ourselves in. The others have to be grappling with similar feelings. We've all been drawn to her, captivated by her strength, her vulnerability, and her inherent goodness. It's a magnetic pull that's becoming harder to resist with each passing day.

I wonder if Remy is also lying awake, contemplating the choices we've made and the sacrifices we've agreed to for Jocelyn's sake. Of the three of us, he's the one who puts duty above all else—always.

As I lie in bed, my mind wanders—as it always does in times of stress—to the life I left behind when I chose to become a guardian. The wild beauty of the fae lands, the lush forests teeming with enchanting creatures and mystical flora, the ethereal cities made of crystal and light. The sense of belonging that comes from being surrounded by my own kind, the camaraderie of fae warriors and the warmth of the fae families I used to know.

I remember the vibrant celebrations and the shared joy of our people, dancing and laughing beneath the moonlight. The thrill of racing through the air, feeling the wind beneath my wings as I soared through the sky, unhindered and free.

And even though I still get to enjoy the life of the fae realm outside my eight-hour shifts on Earth, the time spent among humans with their countless rules and expectations can feel overwhelming, especially when I know just how good things could be for Jocelyn if only there weren't threats keeping her from the beauty of the fae realms. The mundane reality of Earth weighs on me during those hours, as if gravity itself has become more oppressive. The laughter and playfulness of my true home feels like a distant memory, pushed to the back of my mind as I focus on our sacred duty to protect Jocelyn.

This world can be cold and unforgiving, governed by rigid social norms that seem to constrain the spirit rather than uplift it. The vibrant colors of the fae realm are replaced by gray concrete and unending routine. I long for the warmth of the magical world I return to each day, the familiarity of my old life, and the comforting presence of unhindered nature.

And yet, even with these feelings of homesickness and longing, my desire to protect Jocelyn never falters. She is a beacon of light in this dreary human world, a reminder of the beauty and magic that still exist beyond the veil. And in her eyes, I see a glimmer of the fae spirit that lies dormant within her, waiting to be awakened.

The sacrifices we've made are worth it. For Jocelyn, for her future, and for the hope that one day, she will claim her birthright and embrace her true self.

The three of us will help her navigate the treacherous waters of both worlds. We'll teach her to control her powers, reveal the secrets of her ancestry, and help her forge new alliances in the fae realm.

But until that day arrives, we must continue to walk the fine line between love and duty, between what our hearts desire and what our obligations demand. It's a delicate balance, one that grows more precarious with each passing day.

The loneliness and longing for home are real, but they're tempered by the growing love and admiration I feel for Jocelyn.

I think about the future and the inevitable moment when Jocelyn will learn the truth about her royal blood and the magical world that has been hidden from her. It's a daunting prospect, one that will undoubtedly cause her pain and confusion. But it's also a chance for her to finally claim her birthright, to embrace the extraordinary power that lies dormant within her.

This will all be over soon. All the pretenses. We'll get to unleash her magic, show her the beauty of her real fae appearance, and bring her to the fae realms. Probably Bedlam, as it's safest.

We'll keep her away from the monster who created her, although if she wants the Romarie crown, it's hers.

As I stare into the darkness, I can't help but worry about the consequences of being in her orbit now. Will our growing attachment to Jocelyn ultimately lead to our downfall? Will our devotion to her cause irreparable damage to the mission we've been entrusted with? Or will it be the very thing that saves us all, forging a bond that transcends time and space—one that will unite us in the face of the challenges to come?

These questions haunt me, filling my mind with doubt and uncertainty. But one thing remains clear: no matter what the future holds, we are inextricably bound to Jocelyn. Our fates are intertwined, our hearts forever linked by the invisible threads that have drawn us together.

With a heavy sigh, I finally close my eyes, seeking solace in the promise of tomorrow. As sleep slowly overtakes me, I hold onto the hope that, in the end, love will be our salvation, a beacon of light guiding us through the darkest of storms.

Remy

AT OUR ONE-MONTH CHECK-IN, the gods send Ballad, a fae guardian with fiery red hair and near-translucent skin that seems to shimmer in the dim light. He's always been a quiet presence, and while we trust no one after what Socrates pulled, he's one of the better options to look after Jocelyn while we meet beyond the veil tonight.

Socrates was placed on administrative leave after he tried to sabotage the bind on Jocelyn's magic. Because it didn't actually cause her magic to be released, he got to keep his job. He'd called it an accident, but how do you explain Rolls getting tied up and muzzled?

I give one last glance at Jocelyn's sleeping form, her chest rising and falling softly, before tipping my hat at Ballad and sifting to the hallway downstairs. As I wait for Niko and Vox to join me, the subtle scent of peonies fills the air, providing a small sense of calm in the tense situation. The guys and I picked them out for Jocelyn when we made a grocery run for her so she and Alex and could have a date night last night.

When Niko and Vox arrive, we huddle together, speaking in hushed tones despite having placed the silencing bubble around us. "Alright, we need to be careful with what we say at this meeting." I cup the back of my neck, feeling constricted. "Let's focus on our progress and avoid mentioning any emotional complications you may or may not be experiencing."

I won't admit it out loud, because I can barely admit it to myself. *I'm in trouble.*

Niko nods, grinning mischievously. "Agreed. We'll stick to the positives and play it cool. It's not like we haven't done this before, right?"

We've had plenty of charges over our couple hundred years being fae guardians. None like her, though. None that felt like less of a burden and more of a privilege.

Vox sighs, running a hand through his hair. "Yeah, but it feels different this time. We've never been this close to our charge before. I just hope we can keep it together."

Jocelyn's house is still, as if holding its breath for the verdict, reflecting the uncertainty we feel—the dimly lit hallway, with its rich, earthy colors, and the soft whisper of the fan in the background heighten our sense of urgency. The three of us talk to cut through the tension that sits in the air like stubborn fog. Niko keeps making stupid jokes as he always does when he's nervous and wants to cheer everyone up. I just keep going over the facts, trying to keep us focus on our duty, and Vox continues to wax lyrical about how hard this all is and how much he loves Jocelyn. He's always been the rawest and most emotional of all of us.

I glance at the clock on the wall and clear my throat. Almost time.

"So, do you think we've stuck to the conditions set by the gods?" Niko asks, his voice losing its usual playfulness.

"We have to believe that we have," I reply with a steely resolve. "If we waver in our duty, everything we've worked for could be lost."

Vox's eyes fill with concern. "But what if we can't keep our feelings in check? I'm not sure how much longer I can keep up this façade."

We exchange understanding looks, acknowledging the shared struggle we've been facing, though I'm too chicken shit to put it into words. It's becoming increasingly difficult to maintain a professional distance from Jocelyn, but we must do so for her sake.

With a nod, I say, "We'll get through this together. We just have to stay focused and remember our purpose."

After a moment of shared determination, Vox sets up a portal to the gods' council beyond the veil. We step through the shimmering doorway, the air tingling with magic, and find ourselves in the grand chamber where the gods and goddesses have assembled.

Seated in the council are Luna, Erida, Zephyr, Solara, Noctis, Nympha, Terron, and Aetheria. Each deity exudes an aura of power, their presence commanding attention and respect. The grand chamber they occupy is a breathtaking display of celestial beauty, with walls adorned with intricate, golden patterns that mimic the constellations in the night sky. A high, domed ceiling seems to extend into infinity, giving the room a sense of boundless space.

The air is thick with the fragrance of exotic flowers, mingling with the scent of aged parchment, a testament to the vast knowledge contained within this space. Soft, ethereal music plays in the background, carried on a gentle breeze that brushes against our skin like the touch of a lover. The temperature in the chamber is warm but not overwhelming, as though it were the perfect summer evening.

The floor beneath our feet is made of polished marble, reflecting the light from the numerous floating orbs that illuminate the room with a soft, golden glow. In the center of the chamber, a large, round table made of the same marble stands, surrounded by elegant, high-backed chairs where the gods and goddesses sit.

Their gazes turn toward us as we enter, their expressions a mix of curiosity and authority. The atmosphere in the room is both awe-inspiring and intimidating, reminding us of the power these beings hold and the gravity of the situation we are facing.

Luna isn't present yet, but Chaos has an irritated scowl on his face where he's seated near the window. He strides over to us, leaving his scowl in place when he hands a parchment to me.

I unroll the scroll, and my eyes quickly scan each line of the missive, skimming through the contents until it hits me with full force.

I furrow my brow as I read the contents of the scroll, the implications settling heavy in my chest. Chaos's irritation now makes sense. I glance at Niko and Vox, who have been reading the scroll over my shoulder, and their expressions mirror my own concern.

"What is the meaning of this?" I demand, looking back at Chaos. "Our plan was solid, and now you're telling us there's a new threat we didn't anticipate?"

Chaos sighs, his eyes filled with frustration. "It seems that Socrates has been meddling again, forming alliances while on leave. He's become more dangerous than we initially thought, and it appears that he's attempting to sabotage our efforts to protect Jocelyn even further."

Niko clenches his fists, anger radiating off him. "We need to do something about him. We can't allow him to fuck this up."

Just then, Luna enters the chamber, her radiant aura casting a warm glow over the room, so at odds with the anxiety coursing through my veins. According to the scroll, she's aware of the situation, so she addresses us immediately. "We understand your concern. Rest assured, we will deal with Socrates and ensure that he no longer poses a threat to Jocelyn or your mission."

"But what about this new alliance he's formed?" Vox interjects, his tone edged with worry. "How can we protect Jocelyn from this faction? Do we know who else is involved yet?

Luna's gaze is steady and reassuring. "We will keep a close watch on Socrates and his associates. You must remain vigilant and continue your efforts to guide Jocelyn through this darkness. We have faith in your abilities, and together, we will overcome this minor challenge."

"Minor?" Vox paces, visibly agitated. "All this time we've been her guardians. Keeping her magic contained. Protecting her. Making sure she remains happy despite the shit life threw at her?"

Chaos bursts into mocking laughter. "Is that how she ended up with Coriander?"

"Alexander, you mean?" I offer.

"Same thing." He grins, throwing a dagger back and forth between his hands with unerring accuracy.

"Free will is important. We can't make all her decisions, especially when it comes to love," I argue. "If it were up to me, she'd be happily single for the rest of her time on Earth." Though I can't say I regret that it's led to us getting to meet her face-to-face less than four years early.

Vox scoffs. "Love? Is that what you call it when she cries herself to sleep every night? When he belittles her and tells her she's crazy every time she shows the littlest bit of emotion?"

Niko places a hand on Vox's shoulder, calming him slightly. "We may not be able to make all her decisions, but we—"

"Wait, back up there. Emotions?" Nympha stops swirling the ball of water in her hand and it lands in her lap, though it doesn't soak her. She presides over the waters of the Fae realms, from the smallest streams to the vast oceans. She also governs the emotions of the Fae, ensuring balance and emotional stability.

Something I can't quite place coils in my stomach. Unease, maybe.

"What are you suggesting, Nympha?" Luna leans in, the glow of her skin pulsing even brighter.

"If she's more emotional—more than usual—it could be that her magic needs to be expelled. We're not meant to go more than a few days without using our magic, and she's never used hers." Nympha pauses for a moment, studying each of us in turn. "I think we need to consider the ramifications of making her wait any longer to come to the fae realms."

Wild panic soars through my chest. "But—"

Terron, God of earth and stability, interrupts me. "If her husband is so terrible, I'm not so sure you're doing your job, guardians. You mean to tell me that you've allowed Jocelyn's husband to berate her and emotionally abuse her for years, and have done nothing about it until now?"

Niko steps forward, his eyes burning with a fierce intensity, so unlike his usual happy-go-lucky demeanor. "We've done what we can without revealing ourselves. We've watched over her from the shadows, intervening when necessary, without alerting either of them to our presence. What would you have us do? Kill the bastard?"

"If you must." Chaos waves his hand dismissively.

Luna shoots to her feet. "Now, now," she hums.

"What have you done to ensure her happiness?" Noctis croons, her shadows coiling around her and spilling onto the marble floors.

"We've provided her with opportunities to grow and find joy in her life," I explain, trying to keep my voice steady despite the growing pressure in my chest. "We've guided her toward fulfilling hobbies and encouraged supportive friendships. We've done our best to keep her safe and help her find happiness within the limits of our mission."

"But you've failed," Erida interjects softly, her eyes filled with sorrow. "You've allowed her to remain in a toxic relationship, and now her magic is at risk of spiraling out of control. This situation is untenable."

Luna steps forward, her glow casting an air of authority over the room. "Enough. It's clear that the situation has become more complex than we initially anticipated. We must adapt our plans accordingly." She turns to us, her eyes filled with resolve. "Guardians, we must accelerate our timeline. It's time for Jocelyn to learn the truth about her heritage and reclaim her powers. We will deal with Socrates and his new allies, and we trust you to guide her through this next phase of her life."

"But what about Alex?" Vox asks, his voice laced with uncertainty. "How will she handle the truth about the life she's going to be living and that he probably won't be in her future?"

"We will help her through it," Niko says resolutely. "We've always been there for her, and we will continue to be by her side. We'll support her and help her find the strength to face the challenges ahead. It will be hard for Alex, but he isn't our priority—Jocelyn is."

Zephyr speaks up, his voice calm and soothing like a gentle breeze. "Jocelyn is stronger than you give her credit for. With your guidance and the support of the council, she will rise above the obstacles in her path and embrace her destiny."

The council members nod in agreement, their expressions filled with ancient wisdom.

As Luna's gaze meets each of ours in turn, a sense of gravity settles over us. "I want to remind you all of the importance of your mission. Jocelyn's future and the balance of both the mortal and fae realms depend on your success. Do not take your responsibility lightly."

I nod, the weight of her words settling heavily on my shoulders. "We understand, Luna. We'll do everything in our power to protect Jocelyn and ensure her transition goes smoothly when the time comes."

Niko steps forward, his expression resolute. "Before we go, what can you tell us about this new alliance Socrates has formed? We need information in order to counter their moves effectively."

Luna regards him thoughtfully, then looks towards a god seated at the far end of the chamber. I hadn't even noticed him there. He rises and approaches us, his eyes filled with a deep, ancient wisdom. He is Thoth, the god of knowledge, and he holds a scroll of his own.

"I have been monitoring the situation closely," Thoth begins, his voice measured and calm. "Socrates has indeed formed a new alliance, one that aims to disrupt the balance of power in the fae realm. They believe that by controlling Jocelyn's fate, they can manipulate the outcome of events to come."

I exchange a glance with Vox and Niko, worry gnawing at the edges of my thoughts. If Socrates and his allies succeed, Jocelyn's life could be in grave danger, not to mention the potential consequences for the realms themselves.

Thoth continues, "I have gathered some intelligence on the

members of this alliance, but their identities remain shrouded in secrecy. I will continue to investigate and report my findings to you as the situation evolves."

Vox's jaw tightens, his frustration evident. "Thank you, Thoth. We appreciate any information that could help us keep Jocelyn safe."

Luna speaks up again, her voice filled with authority. "We will handle Socrates and his alliance, but we need you to focus on the task at hand."

As the meeting comes to a close, we make our way back to the portal, our determination solidified. Jocelyn is more at risk than ever with danger on two fronts now. We thought we had shy of four more years to deal with the power-hungry monster in Romarie, and it seems as though Socrates is now forcing our hand. Are they working together? I rub my temples and glance at the determined faces of my fellow guardians. We won't rest until Jocelyn's future is secure and the realms are safe from harm.

❧

Niko

I STAND in the hallway outside of Jocelyn's room the following morning, my heart heavy with the weight of our mission. Remy and Vox stand beside me, their expressions equally grave. Ballad keeps watch over Jocelyn, his flaming red hair a beacon in the dark room.

The hallway is narrow and adorned with tasteful paintings and there's a soft, plush carpet under our feet. The warm, earthy tones of the walls create a sense of coziness, but the dim lighting makes it feel more somber, reflecting the weight of the moment. A small table with a potted plant sits near the end of the corridor, adding a touch of life to the space.

Remy clears his throat, drawing our attention. "We need to discuss what to do about Jocelyn and how to break the truth to her. We must be careful about it." He leans against the wall, arms crossed, his stance conveying authority.

80

Vox nods, his face a mixture of concern and … relief? "I'm ready to tell her the truth. But I think we need to get her away from her daily monotony before we tell her we've been lying to her this entire time. I don't want her to hate us." He stands with one hand on his hip and the other on the back of his neck, the tension visible in his posture.

I run a hand over my cropped hair, mulling over our options. "What if we plan something that'll create some tension between Jocelyn and Alex? Something that might make her more amenable to leaving him, at least temporarily?" I lean against the opposite wall, my eyes scanning the floor as I think.

Now that we're going to unbind Jocelyn's magic, we don't need to keep up the pretense of saving her marriage.

Remy raises an eyebrow. "Like what?"

I can't help but smirk. "How about a camping trip? We all know Alex hates camping. It could cause enough friction to make Jocelyn see that there might be more to life than her current situation."

Vox chuckles, albeit somewhat nervously. "It's perfect. We just need to make sure we're there to support her and show her what she's been missing all these years."

Remy nods in agreement. "We'll be there for her. We'll help her rediscover her love for the outdoors and maybe even encourage her to use some of her magic. It could be a good way to start preparing her for the truth."

"So it's settled then," I say, feeling a sense of resolve settle over us. "We'll set up a camping trip and use it as an opportunity to start breaking the truth to her gently. We'll need to figure out the details and how to get her on board, but I think it's our best shot."

As we finalize our plan, I can't help but feel a renewed sense of trepidation. "We need to be careful not to push her too hard, though. She's been through enough, and we don't want to alienate her."

Remy nods in agreement. "We'll have to be subtle about it. Maybe we can suggest the camping trip as a way for her to relax and unwind from the stress of daily life. She's always loved nature, and it could be a good reminder of happier times. It's why they got that property up north."

Vox chimes in, "Let's put it together as a surprise, though we should probably give Alex some opportunity to actually show up. It'll seem disingenuous otherwise. I think we can all agree he'll fumble at the one-yard line, though."

"No one is arguing that." I sigh. "We should also think about how to introduce her to her magic during the trip," I suggest, trying to cover all our bases. "Perhaps we can create situations where she'll need to rely on her instincts and innate abilities."

Remy strokes his chin thoughtfully. "That's a good idea. We can set up some challenges, maybe even have some fun with it. Get her to connect with her magical side in a more lighthearted way before we dive into the heavier stuff."

Vox grins. "I like that. It could be a bonding experience for all of us. We'll be there to guide her and teach her without overwhelming her."

As we continue discussing our plan, I can't help but worry about Jocelyn's reaction to the truth. The fact that she's married to a mortal complicates matters even further. We need to be sensitive and considerate of her feelings, but we also need to be honest and prepare her for the challenges ahead. And the possibility of her father finding her once her magic is unlocked looms over us, adding another layer of danger to our mission. For almost forty years, keeping her magic locked away so she's safe from him has been our *only* mission.

Remy claps his hands together. "Alright, let's get to work on planning this camping trip. We'll arrange the flight with their pilot, get all the necessary supplies, and come up with a way to convince Jocelyn to go without raising suspicions."

Vox nods, determination etched on his face. "We'll need to move quickly. With Socrates and his alliance working against us, we can't afford to waste any time."

I take a deep breath, steeling myself for the task at hand. "We can do this. We've always been there for Jocelyn, and we'll continue to be by her side. Together, we'll guide her through this next phase of her life and help her embrace what comes next."

With our plan in place and our resolve stronger than ever, we set out to make the camping trip a reality. In the meantime, I'm going to do whatever I can to drive a wedge between Jocelyn and Alex now that we don't need this asshole.

As we prepare for the trip, my thoughts linger on how excited I am to finally show Jocelyn what true magic is. She's always been a bit of a dreamer, so to get to witness the power she possesses, even as I worry about the consequences of unleashing it, is something to look forward to. This is no longer a mission about keeping magic contained, but about helping Jocelyn reach her fullest potential—she's going to need the help to contend with the fae courts. It's as if every moment of our lives has been leading up to this next phase. *Are we up to it?*

I glance at Remy and Vox, recognizing that despite the shared pain of losing our families in terrible, unimaginable ways, we have grown as individuals, each with our own strengths and passions that contribute to our mission.

Remy's strategic mind, honed by his study of ancient fae texts, has been invaluable in our plans to protect Jocelyn. Vox's empathetic heart, which he uses to heal and comfort others, has helped us connect with her on a deeper level.

For me, I've found purpose in advocating for those who have been wronged and seeking justice within the fae courts. It is this pursuit of fairness that drives me to ensure that Jocelyn is given a chance to choose her own destiny. I give as all an internal nod. We've got this.

It isn't as if we haven't faced peril before. My mind drifts to that fateful day when my peaceful community of lion shifters was raided by a faction of berserkers. They swept through our village, destroying everything in their path, fueled by an ancient, bitter feud. We were caught unprepared, and I could do nothing but watch in horror as my family, friends, and neighbors were slaughtered before my eyes. I was still a child, hidden in the tall grass behind our house when they came.

In the wake of the devastation, the unbearable pain of losing everyone I loved pushed me onto the path of becoming a fae guardian. As soon as the grief unlocked the ancient power within me I vowed to use it to fight for those who had been wronged and seek justice within the fae courts.

The events of the past are a stark reminder of how crucial it is that we protect Jocelyn from power-hungry monsters like her father.

CHAPTER NINE

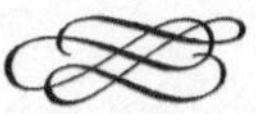

JOCELYN

"*D*o you know what the guys have planned for today?" Alex asks, casually buttoning up his dress shirt before handing me his tie. "Could you help me with this, please?"

I accept the tie from him, draping it around his neck. "No idea."

It's fascinating to me that Alex, who has so many skills and talents, still struggles with tying his own tie. I mentally make a note to ask the guys to teach him someday.

As I carefully loop the fabric and tighten the knot, Alex remains silent. His eyes follow my hands, observing the intricate process. The air between us is filled with a comfortable, familiar warmth.

Once I finish, I step back to assess my work, satisfied. Alex reaches up to adjust the tie, his fingers brushing against the fabric as though he needs to make it perfect, but it already is. His cheeks flush a delicate pink, betraying his emotions. He looks into my eyes, a mixture of gratitude and vulnerability filling his gaze.

"Thank you, Jocelyn," he murmurs softly, his hand still on the tie. The simple moment feels both tender and intimate, a reminder of the deep bond we once shared. "They pulled me aside last night to discuss it."

"What is it?" I pause in the doorway to the walk-in closet and turn to face him.

He clears his throat. "Dirty talk."

"What?" I ask, not sure if I'm hearing him correctly. I knew this was coming but knowing it and experiencing it are different things.

"The first lesson will be them demonstrating it, and I'm to take detailed notes." He cups the back of his neck. "And apparently, it ties nicely into foreplay, so that, too."

"Oh," I squeak, feeling my cheeks heat.

He chuckles, pulling me into his arms. "Yeah. I can't believe we're doing it."

I rest my head against his. "You don't know how much I appreciate you doing this." Sighing, I tighten my hold around his waist. "I feel closer to you than I have in years."

Alex pulls back slightly, looking into my eyes. "I want that too, Jocelyn. I want to feel like we're a team again." He leans in and kisses me softly, his fingers tangling in my hair. "And if learning some new tricks is what it takes, then I'm all in."

My tongue stumbles over the words as I mouth them. "Am I getting intimate with them?" A million thoughts race through my mind, accompanied by a swarm of butterflies and a stomach-churning dread. These men consume most of my thoughts. The fear should be paralyzing, but instead I feel a strange curiosity within me—to see what it would be like for them to consume me completely.

"They're teaching me how to perform oral tonight," he grumbles. "Sex positions are in a few weeks, I think."

"And you're still okay with this?" I tug on my bottom lip with my teeth. At this point, I fear him saying no more than I fear him saying yes.

"I trust you." He presses a kiss to my temple. "I know it's me you'll be thinking of."

But that's the thing, isn't it? I'm not so certain that's true any longer.

~

THE WHISTLE of steam above the pressure cooker tells me our chuck roast is done. Remy turns the handle, and steam wafts into the air, bringing with it the delicious smell of spices: peppers, cinnamon, garlic, onion, cumin, and oregano.

"Have you ever had birria tacos?" Niko presses a fresh corn tortilla between two sheets of parchment paper, flattening it with a heavy skillet. I shake my head, watching as he carefully peels the tortilla from the paper and places it on a hot skillet.

"No, but I love any kind of tacos." I take a sip of my wine, the deep red liquid warming me from within. "I could eat them every day, for every meal. If I hadn't married Alex, I probably would've married a taco."

The guys chuckle, and Vox leans in. "Just wait 'til you try these."

Vox wears his usual black jeans and fitted t-shirt, his ink on full display. Remy is the more reserved of the three, wearing dress slacks and a button-up, though it's rolled at the sleeves, showcasing forearms that any nurse or phlebotomist would swoon over. Niko is somewhere in between, with a leather jacket over a plain white t-shirt and dark jeans.

I help shred the meat while Niko finishes making the tortillas, and we set up an assembly line once all the ingredients are prepped. Remy dips the tortillas into the sauce, I fill them, Niko drops some butter in the pan, and Vox crisps them up.

We made fifty of them, which sounds like a lot, but the guys have the appetites of a small army. It brings me a lot of pleasure to feed such hearty men who burn it off just as quick in our home gym in the basement.

I don't even need to ask someone to set the table, because while I'm busy opening another bottle of wine, the guys take care of it.

We sit down at the table, and I glance at my phone, checking the time. It's almost eight, and Alex should've been here by now.

He promised he'd stop working after five. I really hope he's not slipping back into old habits because he'd been doing so good.

The sound of the garage door opening interrupts my thoughts, and I smile at the thought of Alex finally being home. But as he walks in, the smile quickly fades away. He looks harried and agitated, his tie askew and his hair disheveled.

"Hey," he greets us, dropping his briefcase on the floor.

He gives me a quick kiss on the cheek before plopping down in his seat beside me. The guys exchange glances, and Vox clears his throat.

"Was there an accident?"

Alex looks up, meeting Vox's eyes across from him. "Sorry, no. I got stuck on a call with an overseas potential fund investor."

"A text would've been the right call here, Alexander." Vox's words aren't unkind, but the tone borders on it.

"You're right." Alex turns to me and takes my hand in his. "I should've texted I was going to be late."

I can feel the tension thickening in the air like the heavy aroma of buttered sauce. Niko and Remy exchange a knowing look that makes me uneasy.

I eat my tacos in silence, but don't offer any platitudes, all while trying to ignore the mounting pressure in my chest. It's not the first time Alex has come home late, but it is something he promised he'd avoid. At the least, he could've let me know.

Are we really back at square one?

Devouring four enormous tacos, I lean back in my chair, stuffed.

"Told you." Vox grins at me, gesturing to the platter of tacos in the middle of the table. "They're fire, aren't they?"

"The best thing I've ever put in my mouth," I breathe.

I realize a moment too late how my words could be interpreted, and I blush at the thought. Remy chuckles, and Niko shakes his head with a smirk.

"I'm glad you have a healthy appetite," Alex says, drawing me out of my thoughts.

The guys clear their throat, exchanging another look that makes me feel like they're just as eager as I am to get the evening started.

I push back from my seat, taking my plate and empty wine glass. "Thanks for your help, guys, this was delicious."

As I walk into the kitchen, I can hear Niko whisper something to Alex. "Hey, man, it's time."

~

I'VE BEEN INSTRUCTED to go about my business for the evening, and then meet everyone in our bedroom at ten, sharp. I feel an excited nervousness creeping up inside me and can't help but wonder what the guys have planned.

Rolls and I go for a walk near our woods, enjoying the cool night air. The crisp scent of autumn surrounds us, a heady mix of earthy leaves, smoky wood-burning stoves, and sweet apple cider. Above us, the leaves are beginning to change, creating a mosaic of vibrant oranges, fiery reds, and deep yellows that dance against the black sky. It's peaceful out here. The only sounds are the crunching of leaves beneath our feet and the occasional hooting of an owl.

Long ago, I gave up trying to get Rolls to play fetch. He's giant, lazy, and prefers leisurely strolls—his tail swaying back and forth like a metronome as he sniffs out every new scent in his path. Despite his size, he moves gracefully with a predator's gait—each step landing silently on the forest floor like a CIA agent moving in stealth mode. A breeze rustles through the treetops and sends a shower of leaves raining down around us, an explosion of colors catching in Rolls' fur as he waddles by my side.

After our walk, I seek refuge in the Victorian greenhouse, surrounded by lush greenery and the soothing sound of water trickling in the little pond that houses a tiny turtle and some fish. I nestle into my favorite reading nook, hoping to get lost in a fantasy world for a while. The fragrant scent of tropical plants and the warm air on my skin are a welcome respite from the chaos inside me.

This is my favorite place on the whole property, and a big reason why I stay despite the shit I put up with. If I leave, he'll probably get the house. Alex's parents bought us the house as a wedding gift, and I'd had the greenhouse built just like the one in Practical Magic shortly after. It's been my sanctuary, a place to escape and be alone with my thoughts. I've got every manner of plant in here, some so tall, it reaches the twenty-foot ceiling.

Being in here feels like I'm in a real-life fairytale. Growing up, I always had my nose buried in a book. The countless hours spent reading allowed me to experience adventures and visit worlds beyond my own, fueling my love for storytelling.

As a child, I'd often hide under the covers with a flashlight, reading until the early hours of the morning. I remember feeling so inspired and amazed by the worlds these authors created, transporting me to places filled with magic, romance, and danger. Those cherished memories have stayed with me, and now, nestled in the greenhouse's quiet serenity, I can't help but feel that familiar sense of wonder as I immerse myself in another story.

As I glance out the window, I catch sight of the guys moving back and forth through the front yard, lugging furniture wrapped in dusty tarps. I'm curious about what they're up to, so I peer through the glass panes, careful not to disturb the fragile ecosystem of the greenhouse.

From my vantage point, I can see my husband and the guys working up a sweat as they maneuver the unwieldy pieces of furniture through the giant front door. Alex curses and grunts, his face contorted in exertion. Despite the noise and commotion outside, I can't help but feel a sense of amusement at their antics. The vibrant colors of the flowers and the gentle trickle of the pond offer a welcome reprieve from the chaos beyond the glass walls.

As I watch them work, the beauty and tranquility of the greenhouse envelop me, and I forget, if only for a moment, about how in less than an hour, three of the hottest guys I've ever seen in my entire life will have their hands all over me.

It's quiet when I trudge up the stairs at nine thirty. Rolls sleeps just outside my bedroom door in his little nook, snoring lightly, but I pass right by the door and head towards another spare bedroom to shower quick. I spend extra time scrubbing, and making sure I'm well-groomed, anticipating the sensual experience that awaits me. Once I'm done, I slip into my favorite navy-blue lace negligee that Alex loves so much, and pad back down the hallway to my bedroom.

I knock on the door, hugging my midsection while I sway from side to side. My heart pounds in my chest as I wait for one of them to let me in. When the door finally opens, my eyes widen at the sight before me.

Remy, Niko, and Vox stand before me, each dressed in sharp suits that outline their chiseled physiques. Their hungry gazes roam over my body, taking in every inch of skin that's exposed by my sheer lingerie. Heat spreads across my cheeks at their scrutiny, and I try desperate to keep myself composed as anxiety threatens to swallow me whole.

"I wasn't sure if you guys wanted me to wear something sexy, or ..." I fidget, suddenly feeling way underdressed. "Sorry, I can put on some—"

"On the bed, Jocelyn," Vox orders with an intensity that sends sparks shooting through me. My knees go weak at his authoritative tone, but I manage to make it to the bed.

I scramble onto the surface and kneel. The three men move closer, surrounding me like predators about to pounce on their prey.

"Good girl," Vox says soothingly, his large hand resting on my cheek.

Behind them, I can just make out a giant mirrored wall spanning the entire length of the far side of our bedroom. This must've been what they were busy doing all night.

"Is Alex behind there?" I squeak.

"Yes, and he's been instructed not to intervene. He's taking notes, and he can hear everything we're saying. If you wish to stop at any time, for any reason, call out your safe word. Do you remember what it is?"

My safeword? I scramble my brain for what they're talking about but remember putting one down on our intake questionnaire. "Viking."

He grins. "You say it, and we stop. Got it?"

I nod.

At that cue, the men in front of me reach for their ties, loosening them until they fall to the floor.

My stomach swoops as they work on each of their buttons, eyes trained on me. They're slow and methodical, removing their clothes until they remain in just their underwear. Seeing the three of them with all those rippling muscles, bare chested and in just their boxers, reveals a side of them that I've never seen before. They are dominating and fierce, ready to take control and guide me towards pleasure in a way that I've never experienced. I'm intrigued and overwhelmed by the intensity of my own desire.

"Did you wear this just for us?" Niko purrs, fingering the strap of my lingerie.

I nod, until he commands me to speak out loud.

"Yes," I whimper.

"Yes, what?"

"Yes, sir." My whole body trembles.

"Good girl." Niko grips my chin, tilting it so I can look him directly in the eyes as he takes a step closer.

His touch lights a fire inside me, and my chest heaves from the sheer anticipation of what's to come. I can already feel my body responding to their commands, each touch and word sending a ripple of pleasure across my skin. I realize then that I've never wanted anything as much as I want them to take control of me.

"Listen up, Alex," Remy's voice rumbles throughout the space. "Tonight, we'll teach you the distinction between a compliant homemaker and a good girl, and why her pussy craves to be the latter."

Desires engulfs me, but at the same time, I feel slightly ashamed of how much I want this. I've been so timid and submissive for so long, never daring to voice my desires, let alone act on them. But now, with these three men in front of me, I feel like I can finally let go and embrace my sexuality fully. And as I shutter my eyes, I picture Alex watching me through the two-way mirror. I want to impress him, to make him proud of me and my ability to follow their commands, though a part of me is nervous he'll be upset after all. A larger part of me is hopeful that just maybe, he'll take good enough notes he can replicate this with me, too.

When I open my eyes again, Vox is the one directly in front of me, and he cups the back of my neck before dropping his forehead to mine and whispering,

"You're going to give your new-and-improved husband the most amazing gift he's ever received."

"What's that?" I'm practically panting, my mouth dry and heart racing.

"A very wet, very pink pussy." Niko chuckles in my ear, and my eyes dart to his.

But before they can connect, Vox's mouth comes crashing down on mine in a rough, claiming kiss, his groan echoing in my mouth as he tastes me. His firm, demanding hands grip the edges of my lingerie, and he tugs, ripping it clean in half and spilling my breasts in someone's hands—not Vox's. I'm vaguely aware of this, but there's something about the way their hands caress my body that has other parts of me heated.

My heart threatens to pound right out of my chest as Vox's tongue slides between my lips, his hands grabbing ahold of me firmly but gently at the same time.

Somehow, I end up on my back, hands pinned above my head. Vox tugs on my lip with his teeth before breaking away, panting heavily.

"Take her hands," he calls gruffly to Remy, who pins them to the mattress.

Vox trails a finger down the column of my throat, then draws one of my breasts into his mouth, the suction making me rock my hips against him. My whimper is swallowed by Niko's mouth on mine. He licks at my lips with incredible precision, his teeth nibbling at my bottom lip and his tongue takes over, dancing with mine while his hand wraps around my still-damp hair.

Remy is on my other side, one hand holding my wrists, while his other hand snakes down the flat plane of my stomach to the junction between my thighs. His fingers tease me over my underwear, slow, tortuous circles around my clit.

My hips chase the movement, trying to create more friction. He chuckles. "Such a greedy little pussy. Be a good girl and next time, I'll feed you my cock."

I whimper, and someone chuckles. "Oh, she likes the sound of that, doesn't she?"

Arousal pools in my belly as Remy tugs my damp panties to the side, exposing me to hungry eyes, hungry hands. His thumb flicks at my clit over and over until I'm grinding desperately against his hand as someone sucks on my neck. I don't know who, it could be both Niko and Vox, but I'm so far gone I can't tell which way is up.

Just before I reach my orgasm, all hands stop, and the men back away, leaving me a writhing, whimpering mess. But just before I can make a protest, I can feel the heat of lips and tongue against my knee when Vox pulls my leg up, wrapping an arm around my thigh. His mouth sucks at the inside of my knee and then lower, below the kneecap. By the time his tongue is circling my inner thigh, I'm desperate for release.

When I buck my hips, Vox uses that opportunity to flip me onto my stomach, and the air whooshes from my lungs just as he drags my hips back, bringing me onto my knees and exposing myself to the room.

A loud rip of fabric meets my ears and fingers slide down the valley between my ass, stroking the tender cheeks. Fingers hook into the top of each cheek and a heavy body presses against me.

I groan as Vox's tongue runs along my seam, the rough texture sending goosebumps racing over my flesh. Fingers are still pulling at my cheeks as he angles me so he can reach my clit with his tongue.

The sound of my groan fills the room as he inserts his thick fingers into my pussy. I'm so drenched, they glide right in.

"Such a pretty pussy, baby. So fucking tight, and wet." He groans between licks, the vibration against my clit sending pleasure shooting up my body. "And so sweet. I can't wait to feel these lips around my cock."

He alternates between toying with my clit and working his fingers deeper into my pussy, stretching me out as he curls them against the front wall of my cunt. My fingers curl and I grasp at the bedding beneath me, trying to hold onto something as he works me close to orgasm.

His forbidden words wash over me and my hips roll back as I fall apart, I'm coming so hard, I cry out his name against the bedding as he inserts a third finger into my pussy. His tongue keeps a steady rhythm on my clit, helping me ride out the orgasm as long as I can.

I collapse onto the bed when he slips his fingers out of me, and he pulls me into his arms, holding me against his bare chest.

"I love the way you sing for me," Vox croons in my ear.

Whatever he says next, I don't hear, because I'm falling asleep in his arms. For the first time in more than a decade, I'm fucking sated.

~

Vox

MY HEART THUNDERS in my chest as Jocelyn's weight rests against me. I'm done for, hooked deep by her presence, unable to imagine life before this moment and dreading the possibility of life after.

The sharp sound of Alex coming out of the narrow, mirrored wall we installed jolts me back to reality. Before we got started, we did another spell on him to keep him amenable to what we were doing. Good thing, too. Because when she called my name instead of his?

Fuck.

My goal was to give Jocelyn a taste of what she's missing by being with him, and get her to think that just maybe she could be fulfilled without Alex.

Mission: accomplished.

The others usher Alex downstairs to go over his notes and answer questions he might have.

I reach for my phone. My finger shakes as I press the shutter button, capturing Jocelyn in all her beauty—hair fanning out across the bed, peacefully resting against my chest. Taking a few more shots, I carefully store them away into an encrypted folder on my phone, safe from prying eyes. The love of my eternal life, and yet I'm forbidden to be with her like this—it's enough to rip me apart seeing her remain so unfulfilled in this mortal world. If I can't have her, at least I'll have these images that will keep her close forever.

But I've got her here now. Naked, the taste of her release on my lips like a drug, and her body intertwined with mine.

I'd risk it all. Throw my entire life away if it meant I could do this forever. I can't be the only one feeling this pull, this desire to claim her, to make her ours. Just below the surface, I can feel her magic, pawing at me, desperate to break free and create a beautiful dance with mine.

I skim my fingers on her bare hip, tracing the ridges of her bone. With a long, slow breath, I look down at her, admiring the way the soft blue glow of the backyard spotlight filters through the window curtains, casting an otherworldly hue over her sleeping form. The effect is striking, as if her fae order is on full display.

I drink in the sight, savoring the way her body seems to glow from within. It's a mesmerizing display, one that speaks to the raw power of her magic, even as it remains suppressed.

I know I could make her happy.

Because I'd die trying.

CHAPTER TEN

JOCELYN

My eyes flutter open to the warmth of the morning sun on my face. The rays dance on the ceiling, making intricately woven patterns with their trajectory. It takes me a moment to remember where I am, but then the events of the previous night come flooding back. A smile spreads across my face as I turn to face Alex, who is watching me with a mixture of concern and apprehension.

"Hey," I murmur, reaching out to touch his arm. "I'm sorry we didn't get a chance to talk last night. I fell asleep before I could even say goodnight."

Alex's expression softens as he takes my hand. "It's okay," he says, his voice gentle. "But I think we need to talk about what happened last night."

I nod, feeling a knot form in my stomach. I can't help but feel guilty for what happened. The guys' lesson had been intimate, and while Alex could only observe, I had been an active participant. If it'd been me in his shoes, I would've lost my damn mind.

And here I am ... starting to feel a pull towards the other men in the house that I can't explain, and it scares me.

"I just ... I want you to know that I'm okay with what happened," Alex says, his voice hesitant.

"You weren't jealous?"

"I mean, I know that it was all for the sake of the lesson, but I couldn't help feeling a little jealous." His eyes take on a dreamy quality as if he's not quite present. "But it was kinda hot, too."

"I understand why you would feel a little jealous. I'm actually really surprised you're taking it so well," I say softly. "But please know that it was just a lesson. It didn't mean anything beyond that." *Lies. All lies.*

A chill snakes its way through my veins, and I take a deep breath, trying to steady myself. I know that I can't tell Alex the truth, not yet. Not until I understand what's happening to me, and what it means for our future together.

"I love you, Alex," I say, squeezing his hand. "That will never change."

Alex smiles, and for a moment, I feel a sense of relief. But the nagging feeling in my gut tells me that this is just the beginning of a much bigger problem.

WHEN ALEX LEAVES for the office, I finally work up the courage to leave my room. Rolls scrambles to his feet as soon as I open the door, and even though I know he's a giant goof, his lopsided grin makes my heart melt. "Hey, big guy," I coo, ruffling his ears. "You hungry?"

He bounds after me as I trudge down the stairs, and I feel a sense of apprehension as I enter the kitchen, and I almost turn around so I can run upstairs and hide. The guys are making breakfast, their easy camaraderie filling the room. It's like nothing has changed, but everything has.

I'm a grown-ass woman, but right now, I'm feeling a little like I just fooled around with my crush and now I have to act like nothing happened because if I really examine my feelings on the issue, people will get hurt. And I'm not just talking about Alex.

"Good morning." Vox saunters towards me, warm mug of coffee in his outstretched hand.

"This for me?" I take it, sipping on it gingerly, pumping as much bravado into my voice as I can. "Thanks."

Remy chuckles, then reaches into the refrigerator, pulling out a carton of eggs. "Did you sleep okay?" His eyes flicker to mine, and I can see the same unspoken tension there that I'm feeling.

"I slept fine," I reply, my voice barely above a whisper. I try to keep my gaze steady, but I can feel myself getting lost in the intensity of their stares.

"Need any help with breakfast?" I offer, feeling like I need to assert my place in this new dynamic. I may not know what's going on between us, but I do know how to make a damn good omelet.

Vox's lips curve into a smile, and I feel my knees go weak. "I could use a sous chef," he says, his voice low and intimate.

I can feel the heat rising to my cheeks as I step closer to him, our bodies almost touching. The air is thick with tension, and I can feel myself getting lost in his gaze. "What can I do?" I whisper.

He leans in close to me, his breath hot against my ear. "You can start by cracking these eggs," he murmurs, his fingers brushing against mine.

My pulse quickens as I follow his instructions, my mind racing with all the things I want to say to him. I know that things between us are changing, but I don't know what it means. All I know is that I can't resist the pull towards him—towards all of them.

As we cook breakfast together, I can feel the tension between us growing stronger. The guys are watching me with a mixture of concern and desire, and I know that things will never be the same between us after last night. But in this moment, as we stand together in the kitchen, all I can think about is the heat between us, the way Vox's eyes are on me, and the way my heart is pounding in my chest.

But as much as I'm drawn to him, I can't help but feel guilty about Alex. We've been married for years, and even though things have been strained between us lately, I can't just throw it all away for a fling with the guys. I booked them to *save* my marriage, not destroy it.

I steal a glance at Vox, and he catches my eye. "What's on your mind?" he asks softly, his fingers brushing against mine as we finish cooking.

I take a deep breath, feeling the weight of the confession on my shoulders. "Nothing," I say, forcing a smile. "I'm just a little tired."

Vox's expression darkens for a moment, and I can see the concern in his eyes. But before he can say anything, Niko interrupts us with a boisterous laugh.

"Come on, Jocelyn," he says with a playful grin. "We didn't keep you up that late."

"You did fall asleep pretty quickly after I made you come," Vox adds with a smirk.

"Funny that." I raise a brow, pumping as much false bravado into my voice as I can muster. "I thought it was because you guys bored me to sleep."

Vox chuckles, his deep voice rumbling through the room. "Ouch. You wound me." He glances at the others. "Good thing we're about to go over what worked and what didn't after breakfast."

"Huh?" I straighten.

"We went over Alex's homework last night while you slept. Never did get a chance to go over what you liked and didn't like about it." Remy hands me a plate, and I take it over to the table.

I lower to my seat. My mind races with a mix of excitement and fear. The idea of rehashing last night excites me, but the fear of being vulnerable in front of them puts a knot in my stomach. Nevertheless, I take a deep breath and steel myself for the conversation.

As we eat, the men discuss their plans for the day. I try to listen, but my mind keeps wandering back to the previous night's events. Niko catches me staring at him, and winks at me.

"Don't think about it too hard," he says with a grin. "You'll get plenty more practice soon."

I choke on my spit, coughing violently. The other men start laughing, and I can feel my face turning red with embarrassment.

"Smooth, Niko," Remy says, shaking his head.

"What? I'm just trying to keep her motivated." Niko chuckles.

Vox leans in closer to me. "He's right, though."

Memories of their mouths and tongues all over me replay in my mind, sending my lust-riddled brain into a frenzy.

After breakfast, we all gather in the living room. The men sit on the couch, passing around a notebook while I sit nervously in a chair across from them, with Rolls panting by my feet. The notebook is filled with drawings and diagrams that I can't quite make sense of.

"So, let's start with what worked." Remy flips through the notebook before setting it on his lap to look up at me. "Jocelyn?"

"Everything," I breathe, gripping the arms of the chair and shifting in my seat.

The men exchange satisfied smirks.

"Be more specific," Niko says.

I swallow hard before speaking. "The way you touched me, the way you kissed me ... it was all amazing."

Vox leans in, his voice more of a purr than anything. "What about the dirty talk?"

"It was ... really hot. Just the right amount." My face flushes as I recall their explicit words. "It made everything more intense."

"Good," Remy says, nodding. "That's what we want to hear."

Niko pulls out his phone and starts scrolling through it. "And what about things you didn't like?"

Parsing through my memory of last night, I pick at the hem of my shirt and avoid their eyes until I can articulate what I want to say. "I can't even be mad about my lingerie because it was the hottest thing that's ever happened to me."

Last night was far better than any of my wildest dreams. Better than any porn. It was taken straight from every dirty fantasy I've ever had, and my body aches for more.

"I'll buy you new ones." Vox flashes me a grin that lights up his entire face, and if I were standing, the sight alone would make me crash to my knees.

I clear my throat. *Be cool, Jocelyn. Be cool.* "You don't have to do that—"

"And if I want to?"

"I think I'd be okay with that," I whisper, tucking my chin to my chest as I examine my hands splayed across my lap.

Remy's eyes meet mine, and I swear there's a flicker of something there. Something that makes my stomach drop and my heart skip a beat. But then it's gone, replaced by a smirk.

"What else do you want Alex to work on?" Niko reclines, crossing his legs at the knee.

"Um, well," I hesitate. "Isn't there anything I need to work on?"

"No," the three of them say at the same time.

"I'm far from a perfect wife, I—"

"Jocelyn." Vox rises from his seat on the couch and comes to crouch in front of me. He's on his knees, his hands on either side of mine, as he gazes up at me. "We've been here for over a month, witnessing almost every interaction you have with Alex. Trust when we say you've been the perfect wife. He's lucky you've put up with his shit this long."

I swallow, my mouth suddenly dry. "Thank you," I manage to get out.

Though, it's not as comforting as it sounds. If I'm not the problem, and it's my husband, then why have I been his doormat for so long? Why did we have to resort to such extreme measures to fix things between us?

Tears well in my eyes, and Remy and Niko approach me now, crowding around to console me.

When I finally find the words to speak what's in my heart, they come out choked. "What happens if I don't even last six months? I've been a shell of who I am for over a decade, and I can't even remember who I used to be. What are my dreams? Aspirations? Hopes for the future? Does none of it matter? Do I matter?"

Remy's hand brushes against my cheek, wiping away a stray tear. "Of course, you matter, Jocelyn," he murmurs softly. "You matter more than anything else in this world." His voice is so gentle, but so full of conviction that it causes my eyes to meet his.

What I see there makes me catch my breath. Remy's eyes are filled with a fiery intensity, and I suddenly realize that there's more to him than meets the eye. There's a raw, primal power in him that I never noticed before. For a moment, I'm captivated by his gaze, and all thoughts of my troubled marriage seem to float away.

"Thank you," I whisper.

Rolls interrupts our moment by whining to be let out, reminding me of reality. I turn to Niko, feeling suddenly self-conscious under Remy's gaze. "So, what now?" I ask him, biting my lip nervously while Vox climbs to his feet and opens the door for Rolls.

Niko exchanges a look with Remy before turning back to me, a serious expression on his face. "Now, we tackle the real problem."

Remy wraps an arm around me, comforting me. "That's right," he says quietly. "We have something of a surprise in store for you—a pleasant one, I promise."

"A surprise?" My voice sounds faint as I push to my feet.

I've come to hate surprises. Alex is terrible at gift giving, and any time he 'plans' a surprise, I must handle all the logistics, which takes all the fun out of it.

"Come on." Niko offers his hand. "We're not going to give away the surprise just yet, Jocelyn. You're going to have to trust us."

I pause, my breath caught, before placing my hand in Niko's. As our fingers intertwine, a surge of electricity races up my arm, igniting my senses. An ephemeral vision blossoms within my mind, fleeting and elusive.

It hovers at the edge of perception, a fragmented memory or a wisp of déjà vu. Yet, the emotions it conjures are as vivid as the vision is transient. A swell of joy washes over me, followed by an undertow of sorrow. The happiness of grasping such a moment, and the anguish of watching it slip through my fingers like sand.

It's over before I can savor it, fading into nothingness. I blink, stumbling back, but Niko's grip on my hand keeps me.

"What is it?" he asks, eyebrows furrowed in concern.

I shake my head. "Uh, nothing. Just déjà vu I guess."

The three men cast glances at each other but say nothing more. As I'm led through the living room, up the stairs, and to the end of the hallway to a storage room full of odds and ends.

Niko opens the door to reveal the surprise. In the center of the room, there's a beautiful pottery wheel, a kiln set up in the corner, and a table laden with various types of clay, tools, and glazes.

My breath catches in my throat, and I can't help but gasp in awe. "This is ... incredible."

Remy grins, his eyes shining with pride. "We did some digging and found out that you used to love pottery when you were younger. We thought it might help you reconnect with a part of yourself that you may have lost along the way."

Niko squeezes my hand gently. "It's a way for you to rediscover your dreams, aspirations, and hopes for the future, Jocelyn. A way to remind you that you matter."

Tears well up in my eyes once more, but this time they are tears of gratitude. I look from Niko to Remy, and then to Vox, who stands near the door, a warm smile on his face. "Thank you," I whisper, my voice thick with emotion.

But as I sit down at the pottery wheel, a nagging thought pulls at the edge of my mind. Is this all just an act? Are they doing this to ensure their success, so they get paid at the end? I try to push the thought aside, but it lingers, and I can't help but remind myself that this is their job. They're supposed to make me happy, to ensure the relationship works out. And yet, there's a part of me that can't shake the feeling that they genuinely care about me; that their concern runs deeper than a simple transaction.

I hesitate, feeling both excited and anxious to rediscover a piece of myself. As I turn towards the pottery wheel, the others watch me closely, offering silent support.

Slowly, I begin to work the clay, feeling the familiar sensation of the material between my fingers. It's a strange mixture of nostalgia and newness, and I find myself growing more and more engrossed in the process.

As I shape the clay, the world around me seems to fade away. For the first time in years, I feel a sense of focus and purpose that has been sorely missing from my life. Whether or not their caring is genuine, the love architects have given me a chance to rediscover something that truly makes me happy. I'm not sure where this journey will lead me, nor who will be with me at the end, but at least for now, I have a sense of direction and the support of those who, it seems, genuinely care for me.

And that is enough.

CHAPTER ELEVEN

NIKO

ocelyn has spent almost all day in the craft room we've been creating for her in a spare room. Her first several pieces were a little wonky, but after a while, she seemed to get the hang of it.

I watch her from the doorway as she carefully molds a lump of clay into a beautiful vase. She's so focused that she doesn't even notice me standing there. It kind of reminds me of the years we'd kept watch over her when she'd been completely unaware of our presence.

I can't help but feel a sense of pride, watching her rediscover this passion that had wilted under the duties of this giant home.

She's got her hair tied on top of her head, and pieces fall into her face. Wearing nothing but pajama shorts and a tank top, she's bare footed, and covered in splatters of clay.

Even now, without a trace of makeup on and her hair a mess, she's magnificent. Getting to taste the sweetness of her lips and her breasts has only heightened my growing obsession.

When she makes to blow a strand of hair out of her eyes, she startles when she notices me leaning against the door frame.

"Niko! When did you get here?" She flushes, pink tingeing her cheeks. Resting her hands palms-up on her knees, she turns towards me.

Her breasts nearly spill out of her skin-tight tank top, and I stalk towards her as she turns back towards her work.

"Just a few minutes." I grin. "What are you working on?" I peak over her shoulder.

On the wheel, a vase made of clay is taking shape in Jocelyn's hands. It's not perfect, but it's beautiful in its imperfections.

"I'm just trying to get the hang of things again," Jocelyn admits, wiping her brow with the back of her hand.

I watch as her fingers move in graceful arcs, coaxing the clay into a smooth, delicate curve.

I can't help but admire the way she handles the clay, with such precision and care. I've always known her to have a keen eye for detail, and it's fascinating to see it in action.

"Looks great," I say, bending down slightly to get a closer look. "What inspired you?"

I'm in her orbit, barely able to resist the urge to touch her. To shape her, mold her like she does the clay, just as we did several nights ago. I want to feel her smooth skin against mine, to explore every inch of her body and make her mine.

Wait. *Make her mine?*

Where in the gods did that come from?

"I was trying to make a dog bowl big enough for Rolls, but it's kind of turning into a vase instead." She chuckles.

"Well, you know what they say about art. It has a mind of its own." I can't help but smile at the thought of Rolls using a beautiful vase as his water bowl.

Jocelyn is the kind of person who goes to great lengths to make her furry friend happy. I'm not sure what we'll do with him when she has to come to the fae realms. Bedlam is probably more accommodating to creatures from Earth than Romarie or any of the other realms, on account of their high queen being from Minnesota.

As Jocelyn continues to work on the vase, I lean against the table and watch her with intense interest.

Music croons from the speakers, a slow jazz number that has Jocelyn really leaning into her work. But when the song switches to something else on her playlist—some Black Veil Brides—her hands slip, causing her vase/dog bowl to crumple.

"Aw, shit!" She slumps, resting her wrists on her table.

I walk over to her phone and navigate to another playlist. This one she's titled ...

"Disrespectfully, Break My Back?" I chuckle, scanning the songs on the list. "Is this what I think it is?"

I arch a brow at her, appreciating the way the light caresses her flushed face. Her mouth parts, as if to speak, but no words emerge. Instead, her entire face and chest deepen into a captivating shade of scarlet.

Each of the songs on the playlist were added in the last forty-eight hours. *This girl.*

Hitting play, I listen as Russ' NASTY plays over the Bluetooth speakers on the wall.

"Jocelyn." I set her phone down, propping myself on the ledge of her table. "Do you want us to play these during lessons on sex positions? Is that why you made this?"

I watch as her chest heaves, her nipples poking through the thin fabric of her tank top drawing my attention.

"We could," she whispers.

"I'll save them for then." I pick her phone back up and select something a little more mellow, more sensual.

As Hozier's "Take Me to Church" begins to play, Jocelyn looks up at me with a mix of emotions on her face. Her eyes are wide and curious while her lips are slightly parted, as if she's trying to say something but can't find the words.

I step closer to her, my hand hovering just above her shoulder. She can feel my touch without me even making contact. It's electrifying and we both know it.

"Can I help you?" I reach over her, brushing against her skin as I grab a fistful of clay.

She's caught between me and the table, eyes wide as she nods. I slide in behind her so she's practically in my lap, and our bodies are aligned. My arms encircle her, guiding her hands as we begin to shape the clay together. The soft material yields under our combined pressure, mirroring the growing connection between us.

The sensual rhythm of the spinning pottery wheel sets the tone as Jocelyn leans back against me, the warmth of her body radiating through my chest. Our hands become one, working together, intimately connected through the clay. I can feel her heartbeat quicken; her breaths becoming shallow.

Hozier's haunting voice fills the room, the lyrics echoing the raw desire building between us. Every touch, every movement, is a dance of longing and restraint. The wheel spins, and so does the world around us, leaving only the two of us in this moment.

Jocelyn's skin is flushed, and beads of sweat dot her forehead, her hair clinging to her neck. As our creation takes shape, the air between us grows heavy with unspoken desires. Our fingers intertwine, slick with wet clay, as we mold the masterpiece that's a testament to our connection.

The music swells, and I can't help but brush my lips against her ear, my breath a warm whisper against her skin. "You're doing great, Jocelyn," I murmur, my voice thick with the emotion coursing through my veins.

She shivers at my words, her body responding to my touch; to the intimacy we're sharing. And for a moment, it feels as though nothing else exists but this—the art, the music, and the undeniable bond between us.

The soft, steady rhythm of the pottery wheel echoes in the room, amplifying the intensity of our shared experience. Jocelyn's breathing grows heavier, in sync with the rise and fall of my own chest. Our hands move in unison, fingers pressing and caressing the clay, shaping it with a passion that mirrors our growing connection.

As Hozier's voice washes over us, his lyrics entwining with the tender intimacy of our actions, I can feel the delicate tremble that runs through Jocelyn's body. The electricity between us is palpable, and I can't help but tighten my hold on her, pressing her closer to me.

Our creation, a physical manifestation of the bond we share, continues to take form under our skillful, tender ministrations. The clay responds to our every touch, a testament to the powerful connection that guides our movements. The curve of the vase begins to emerge, a graceful, natural contour that echoes the enchantment of the moment.

Jocelyn's breath hitches as I lean in, my lips brushing her neck, planting a feather-light kiss on her sweat damp skin. The scent of her fills my senses, and I can't help but breathe her in, drowning in the desire that courses through me.

Her desire is there, too. It perfumes the air, beckoning me closer, begging me to sate her. To run my fingers over her soft skin, to watch it part beneath my touch, and to coax her body until it sings under my ministrations.

Her hands, so sure and steady before, falter ever so slightly at the contact. She bites her lip, struggling to maintain control, but the intensity of our shared experience is too much for either of us to ignore.

The song reaches its climax, and so do we, our fingers pressing harder into the clay, as if trying to leave an indelible mark on the world, a testament to the passion that binds us together. As the last note fades, our creation stands half complete.

In the silence that follows, Jocelyn turns her head to meet my gaze, her eyes searching mine for answers. Our breaths mingle, and it's as if time has stopped, leaving us suspended in this moment of vulnerability and desire.

Here, in this room, our hearts have found their rhythm, beating in time with one another, bound by the power of creation, and the undeniable connection that has brought us together.

The sudden sound of heavy footsteps echoing in the hallway jolts me, and I leap off the stool, creating distance between us.

As I regain my composure, I can't help but feel a mixture of guilt and concern. The intensity of our connection had taken us both by surprise, and I worry about the potential consequences of allowing it to go further. Jocelyn, too, appears shaken; her cheeks flushed and her breath coming in short, uneven gasps.

The door to the room swings open, revealing Remy, who stands in the doorway with a knowing expression. He glances between Jocelyn and me, clearly aware of the charged atmosphere that still lingers.

"Am I interrupting something?" he asks, a hint of amusement in his voice.

Jocelyn stammers, trying to find the words to explain the situation. "We, uh, were just ... working on the pottery." She gestures to the half-finished vase on the wheel.

Remy raises an eyebrow but doesn't press the issue. "Well, I just wanted to let you know that dinner is ready. We should probably head to the dining room."

Jocelyn and I exchange glances, silently acknowledging the unspoken understanding that had blossomed between us during our time at the pottery wheel. As we carefully extricate ourselves from the room, we can't help but steal furtive glances at each other, acutely aware of the shift in our dynamic.

At dinner, the tension between us is palpable, though we both try to maintain a semblance of normalcy. Our fingers brush against each other as we pass dishes around the table, each touch sending a shiver of electricity down my spine. We laugh and talk with the others, but our eyes keep finding one another, drawn together like magnets.

As the evening progresses, I can't shake the nagging thought that gnaws at the edges of my mind. Falling for my charge is a dangerous path, one that could lead to heartbreak and ruin. I'm teetering on the precipice, and I can't help but wonder if I'm already too far gone to turn back.

Jocelyn

THE SOUND of rain pelting the window stirs me from my sleep, and I groggily flop over, noticing Alex is gone from bed. I sit up, squinting at the clock on the wall as my eyes adjust to the hazy morning light.

Eleven?

That can't be right. I fumble for my phone on the nightstand and realize he's been gone for hours, and somehow, my alarms never went off.

Frowning, I pull on some clothes and make my way downstairs, where I find Niko and Remy sitting at the kitchen island making lunch and trading stories.

"Good morning," I mumble, pausing in the doorway. The two look up and immediately give me a smile.

"Good morning," Remy says, gesturing to the plate of avocado toast and scrambled eggs he's just set in front of me. "Fuel up. We have a busy day ahead of us."

"What do you mean?" I ask, cautiously taking a seat at the countertop and tugging the plate a little closer. My favorite.

"You're going to see in just a few," Niko explains, pushing his plate aside and resting his elbows on the table.

"Okay." I smile, glancing towards the living room. "Where's Vox?"

"Right here." The man in question strides through the garage door, carrying a giant box of supplies. "Just doing a little reconnaissance."

He sets it down, revealing a number of flashlights, cameras, and other gadgets, as well as a few manila folders. At my curious look, he grins. "That is your mission briefing, my lady," he says grandly, pulling out a folder labeled 'Case #766: Jocelyn'.

There's something about his easy smile that is both comforting and terrifying. As if he's seen a thousand tragedies and won't rest until he's fixed one more.

"But flashlights and—" I use the footrest to propel me out of my seat to get a better look in the box he sets on the counter. "Wait. Camping supplies? Alex hates camping."

"And you love it, so we'll fly there, and then we'll spend the day getting it all set up."

"How the hell did you convince Alex?"

Vanderbilts don't camp. Though I'm not sure which is rarer—camping or days off.

Niko and Remy share a look. "He mentioned the other day that he hasn't used any of his vacation time this year ... or any of the previous years," Remy explains.

Niko grins, patting his belly, which is less of a belly and more of a steel door. "Just promise unlimited S'mores."

I shake my head, laughing. They are crazy. Crazy, but maybe genius. "He's going to hate it. But he can't just leave on a whim, so we'll have to push this out a few weeks. Is that okay?"

The guys glance at each other, but Vox is the first to speak. "Yeah, that'll give us some time to convince him, right?"

A week later, I still haven't found the gall to propose our camping trip to Alex. But tonight, it's our anniversary, and I've just finished preparing a romantic dinner for the two of us. I can't think of a better anniversary gift than for Alex to agree to go, considering I had to cancel our Maldives trip. Especially if it'll be my birthday.

It's just an ordinary one—thirty-seven—but we don't tend to do much for my birthdays, anyway.

The guys have the night off, off running errands somewhere. The candles are lit, the table is set, and I'm wearing the dress Alex once said was his favorite on me. It's a night to remember, or at least, it's supposed to be.

As I wait for Alex to arrive home from work, I can't help but feel a sense of unease. It's been a long time since we've had a night like this. I'm hoping tonight will be the turning point in our strained relationship, but I'm also terrified that it might only highlight the widening gap between us.

The clock ticks on, and Alex is nowhere to be seen. As the minutes turn into hours, my unease transforms into frustration, and then into anger. I've put so much effort into making tonight special, and yet he hasn't even bothered to call or text to let me know he's running late.

Every single anniversary we've had after our first one, he's ruined. I try to be the perfect, doting wife. Killing myself in the gym until I couldn't take the constant flirting from other guys and their subsequent mysterious injuries, so I built one at home, but at least now I maintain the arm candy-status so many people in Alex's industry seems to appreciate. I make him his favorite foods, ask him about work, pour everything I am, everything I have, into this man.

And this is the thanks I get.

Am I unworthy of love? Or is it my curse?

By the time Alex finally walks through the front door, the candles have burned down to stubs, and the food has gone cold. My anger has turned into a simmering resentment, and I struggle to hold back tears as I face him.

"Alex." My voice trembles with emotion. "It's our anniversary. I planned this entire evening for us. I wanted it to be special, a chance for us to reconnect. And you didn't even bother to let me know you were going to be late."

He looks at me, seemingly surprised by my outburst. "I'm sorry, Jocelyn. I lost track of time at work. I didn't realize it had gotten so late."

His apology only serves to fuel my anger. "You lost track of time? On our anniversary? Do you even care about us anymore, Alex? Do you care about me at all?" The tears I've been holding back finally spill over, streaming down my cheeks.

Alex hesitates, searching for the right words. "Of course, I care about you, Jocelyn. I just ... I've been so caught up in work lately, trying to provide for us. I didn't mean to neglect you or our relationship."

Provide for us? He was born with a silver spoon in his mouth, a trust fund kid who wouldn't need to work for the next thousand years and he'd still be richer than a god. As I listen to his excuses, I realize that I've reached my breaking point. I can't continue to live like this, feeling ignored and unloved. It's time to make a stand.

"Alex," I say, my voice firm despite the tears. "I can't do this anymore. I need you to be present in our lives, in our marriage. I need to know that you're committed to making this work, that you're willing to fight for us. If you can't do that, then I don't know if there's a future for us together."

He stares at me, his face pale and his eyes wide. It's clear that he wasn't expecting an ultimatum, but it's the only way I can think of to force him to confront the reality of our situation.

After a long, tense moment, Alex finally speaks. "I ... I'll do whatever it takes, Jocelyn. I love you, and I want to make this work. I promise I'll be better; I'll be more present."

Nodding, I feel a mixture of relief and trepidation. "Alright. Then we're going on a camping trip together. We need to reconnect and spend some time away from everything that's pulling us apart. You'll need to get approval from your work partners for the time off, but I need you to commit to this. Can you do that?"

He swallows hard, but then nods. "Can I have a minute to think on this?"

"Sure."

His words evoke mixed feelings within me, a blend of longing for the connection we once had, and a pang of guilt for the growing attachment I have to the love architects. However, I know that Alex and I need to find our way back to each other if there's any hope for our relationship.

Only time will tell if Alex can truly keep his promise, but for now, I cling to the hope that our camping trip will be the first step toward healing our broken relationship.

As I sit across from Alex in our dimly lit living room, the weight of the conversation we're about to have settles heavily on my chest. I take a deep breath, trying to steady my nerves. He looks up from his phone, sensing the still-simmering tension in the air.

"This is it, isn't it?" he asks, his voice laced with concern.

I clasp my hands together, gathering my courage. "The fact that you brought the love architects into our home says a lot about what you're willing to try. But I'm not sure if it's enough." I pause, searching his face for any reaction. His expression remains impassive, but he sets his phone down and gives me his full attention.

"I feel like we've been drifting apart, and I don't know how to fix it on my own. I miss the connection we used to have, the love that we shared." My voice trembles again as I try to hold back the fresh bout of tears threatening to spill over.

Alex shifts in his seat, his eyes downcast. "Jocelyn, I know I've been distant. I've just been so caught up with work, and I'm sorry."

My heart aches as I press on. "The guys have planned a camping trip for us, and they'll be there too. I think it could help us reconnect and remember why we fell in love in the first place. I know you don't like camping, but it's important to me, and I believe it could make a difference for our relationship."

Alex sighs, rubbing the back of his neck. "I don't know, Jocelyn. Camping really isn't my thing and taking time off from work is always a hassle."

I take a deep breath, steeling myself for what I have to say next. "Alex, this is an ultimatum. Either we go on this camping trip together, try our best to reconnect, and make a genuine effort to save our marriage, or I don't see a future for us. I can't keep going like this."

His eyes widen and his face pales. "Jocelyn, I ... I didn't know you felt this way. I'm sorry."

I shake my head, fighting back tears. "It's not just about apologies, Alex. We both need to make an effort. If we don't try to fix this now, I don't think we ever will. This camping trip is a chance for us to start over, to rediscover what made us fall in love in the first place. If you won't do it for that, do it because you've managed to ruin every single birthday I've had for the last decade."

He hesitates for a long moment, clearly torn. Finally, he nods. "Alright. I'll talk to my partners and see if I can get some time off. I can't promise anything, but I'll do my best."

I exhale, relief washing over me. "Thank you, Alex. I really think this trip could be a turning point for us."

As the conversation comes to a close, I can't help but feel a mixture of hope and trepidation. I'm putting everything on the line for this trip, praying that it can mend our broken connection and bring us back together. I know it's not going to be easy, but I'm willing to fight for our love.

Over the next few weeks, we both work on preparing for the camping trip. Alex manages to secure time off from work, and I can see he's trying to be more present and attentive. The guys are supportive and excited for the trip, eager to help us reconnect.

As the day of the trip approaches, I feel a mix of anxiety and anticipation. This could be our last chance to save our marriage, and I desperately want it to work. I know we'll have some challenges, but I hope that by facing them together, we can find our way back to each other. To how we used to be.

Our entire first year of marriage was near-perfect. We had a great anniversary trip, and once we got home, everything changed. It was like he was an entirely different person. One who no longer cared about my hopes or dreams, and I became this ghost of a woman, only there to serve and not be heard. I start mentally preparing my suitcase, blissfully unaware that the camping trip will not only test our love but also change the trajectory of my life forever.

CHAPTER TWELVE

JOCELYN

The morning of our big camping trip finally arrives. Rolls is with his favorite sitter, we're at cruising altitude, and I've packed extra-warm gear in case the weather gets colder. The anticipation of reaching the land that Alex and I own together fills me with a sense of excitement. It's my sanctuary, my happy place where I can escape the pressures of the world, and I long to share it with someone who genuinely loves it as much as I do.

I close my eyes and picture Alex's face, feeling a swell of hope inside my chest. He said he'd do whatever it takes to make our marriage work and that show of willingness means the world to me. Just as I'm envisioning how things might pan out for us in the sex department out in the wilds of nature, my phone dings.

Slipping it out of my pocket, my heart sinks as I read the message from him. He's supposed to catch a commercial flight tonight and then have a driver take him to the trailhead.

Relaying the message out loud for the others, my voice shakes. "Alex says he's going to have a chopper bring him in. He can't get out of his work meeting in the morning."

I scrub a hand over my face, sinking to the giant bench seat. Feet meet my periphery, and I glance up, finding Remy crouching in front of me.

"How many times has he missed family vacations?"

I pocket my phone. "Every time."

Remy edges in a little closer. A heavy silence hangs in the air, ripping me apart as I remember all the no-shows of the past few years. The tingling heat of humiliation radiates across my face, and I can't bring myself to look up at him.

"You're probably wondering why I'm still with him," I whisper.

He brushes my chin gently and firmly forces me to meet his gaze. "Good people sometimes do terrible things. I have no doubt he loves you, but he prioritizes the wrong thing. When he gets here, we'll have a heart-to-heart."

My body shakes with silent sobs, and I bury my head in my hands.

"You do still want to be with him, right?" he asks softly.

I nod and wipe away my tears. "Of course, I do." My voice cracks as I speak. "I just don't always know if he wants to be with me ... and ... I'm not so sure I can keep going on like this."

"He'd be crazy not to."

"You think so?"

"I know so."

Our pilot comes in the intercom. "We're ready to begin our final descent. Please fasten your seat belts. We'll begin our approach in ten minutes."

"Thank you," I say with tear-filled eyes.

As the plane begins its descent, I can't help but feel a pang of longing as I imagine the vast expanse of our property, the towering trees and the vibrant green foliage that serves as a reminder of nature's beauty. My heart aches at the thought of finally sharing this experience with Alex, and I hope that this trip will bring us closer together.

"We'll get camp set up, and we'll spend the rest of the week working on marriage-building exercises, alright?" Remy extends his hand and helps me over to a bucket seat and I strap in. He finds one next to me, and the others are in the aisle across from us.

"We'll get this straightened out," he whispers and breaks into a grin. He pulls his camera out of the bag in front of him and holds it up to eye level. "Ready?"

I shrug. "Ready as I'll ever be." He snaps a few photos of us and calls it good.

As we begin our descent, I continue the exhausting process of trying to remain positive about Alex. I've lost track of how quickly my feelings have changed for the man I married more than a decade ago: from love, to frustration, to hurt, to something more like pity and, with each disappointment, a little loss of hope. I know now that I'm going into this trip with a new mindset.

Maybe we won't make it through this rough patch, but I refuse to let our marriage end without giving it my all.

My eyes fall on Niko who keeps checking on me every few minutes, his face etched with worry. Vox sits next to him with his nose in a book.

Pressure causes my ears to pop, and the plane jolts minutes later as we touch down. It's small enough we don't have a flight crew aside from two stewards and the pilot. I'd made a fuss about Alex getting the plane on account of global warming, but he travels so much for work he'd insisted on it. Said he'd be home more.

If anything, he uses it as an excuse to work more.

After taxiing, we hop out of the plane onto the dirt runway. The fresh smell of nature hits me, and I can't help but take a deep breath in. This is exactly what I need right now, time away from the city and all its distractions.

Two Land Rovers take us to our trail, and Niko gets my door. He's got on dark technical pants and a fitted t-shirt that does little to hide his massive biceps. The same ones that helped me mold and shape that vase in the craft room not too long ago.

He doesn't know it, but I fired it in the kiln just like that. I want to remember that moment. Him. Long after they've packed up and moved onto their next couple.

The air is crisp and cool, and I breathe deep, taking in the scent of pine. This far north, it's almost winter, but growing up, I loved camping in the cold. There's just something about getting bundled up and roasting S'mores in front of a roaring fire before crawling into your tent at night and having to share body heat to keep warm.

Remy hands me my backpack, helping me cinch it around my waist while he fixes the hydration bladder tubing and mouthpiece.

"Have you done much camping?" I study the way his lips tighten in concentration as he untangles my pack straps.

They split into a grin, and my eyes dart to his before he catches me staring. Too late. He notices but doesn't say anything about it. He's so close, I can smell the mint on his breath. "The guys and I camp all the time." He smirks. "We once spent a night on a hidden plateau that overlooked a valley filled with fireflies. It was like watching a live symphony of lights."

I laugh, recalling my own camping experiences. "As an only child, I used to go camping with my parents a lot. Once, we went hiking on a trail covered in these leaves so colorful, that they blew my mind. Then we stumbled upon a family of deer, grazing peacefully. It was such a magical moment, like something out of a fairy tale."

Alex and I own a little under six hundred acres of pristine wilderness, a compromise to the massive amount of carbon footprint he generates with his constant traveling. I've been here a good thirty or forty times to camp, but Alex has never stayed the night. The property is a mix of dense forests, rolling hills, and clearings that provide breathtaking views of the starry sky at night.

Camping alone isn't so bad when you pretend there aren't wolves stalking these woods.

"Another time," Niko adds, his eyes sparkling with amusement, "Vox, Remy, and I went camping near a beautiful waterfall. We spent the day exploring the area and found a hidden cave behind the cascading water. It felt like our own secret hideout. We stayed up late telling stories and seeing who could pee furthest off the waterfall."

"Omigod," I laugh. "You guys are terrible." I gain a little pep in my step at the excitement of showing off my favorite place in the world. "Half a day hike that way," I gesture to the east, "lies a waterfall. I bet it's even better than the one you guys found. Should we see if there's a cave behind it once Alex gets here?"

"We'll have a vote. If your waterfall is better, I'll jump off it. Naked as the day I was born." Niko grins.

"What?!" I stumble. "It's too cold, you'll get hypothermia."

"Too chicken we'll make you do it if ours is better?" Vox throws his arm around my shoulder, keeping pace with me so I don't trip. "Didn't take you for the timid type, Joss."

Crossing my arms over my chest, I hook my thumbs in my backpack straps and park myself on the path. "You're on. But if I win, all of y'all have to jump."

"Deal." Remy grins. "But if we decide ours is better … you're getting wet."

Heat flushes my cheeks, despite the cold air. "And if they're both good?"

"Guess we'll all have to test the water to see." Remy grins smugly.

Pointing the way, I let Niko lead the way down the trail. Tall and broad-shouldered, he walks with fluid athleticism, scanning the forest as he goes. I get the sense that he's always on guard, but at the same time, he exudes a calm confidence that's reassuring. He's the outgoing one of the three, but his eyes are always on alert.

Vox brings up the rear, lost in his book. How he can read and hike at the same time is beyond me. He's the most enigmatic of the group. He rarely speaks but when he does, it's with a precision that leaves no room for misunderstanding. He's the quiet observer, always watching and analyzing. There's an intensity in his gaze that can be unnerving at times, but it's also what draws you in.

As we hike deeper into the woods, I feel a sense of freedom wash over me. The trees tower above us, their branches reaching towards the sky like outstretched fingers. The sunlight filters through the leaves, casting a warm glow on everything around us. It's as if the world has slowed down just for us.

The trail is rugged, and it's slow going as we navigate around boulders and overgrowth. It's challenging, but I'm grateful for the workout. It gives me something to focus on besides the state of my marriage and my growing attraction to the guys I hired to save it.

Niko leads us to a clearing where we set up camp for the night.

Remy steps up beside me, breaking me out of my reverie. "You know, Jocelyn, there's something to be said for getting away from it all. You can clear your mind and just be in the moment."

I nod, appreciating his words. "I know what you mean."

Remy's eyes meet mine, and I feel a jolt of electricity pass between us. It's as if he's reading my thoughts, understanding the pain that I'm carrying inside.

"You hired us to fix your marriage, but know that you're our client, Jocelyn. If you decide at any point you want out, you let us know." His voice is gentle but firm, and I can tell he means what he says.

I turn to face him, taking a deep breath before responding. "I know, and I appreciate everything you're doing for me. It's just ... I don't know if it's even possible to fix things between Alex and me. I'm not so sure I want to anymore." Admitting that out loud is scary.

Remy's hand lands on my shoulder, giving it a reassuring squeeze. "It will work out exactly how it's meant to."

I turn to face him, noticing the way his fingers linger on my skin. There's a warmth in his touch that makes me feel safe and protected.

As soon as we're settled in, I help Niko build a fire while Vox starts cooking dinner on our portable stove. Remy sets up our tent and spreads out our sleeping bags.

I sit back and watch as they work together like a well-oiled machine. There's a sense of unity between them that's palpable, even as they go about their individual tasks. It's clear they're a family, and no matter the situation, they have each other's backs.

For a moment, I envy their bond.

Is this what it would've been like if Alex worked just a regular job, and rather than spending the limited time we get together in some Sims-like fantasy world, we spent our lives just living on love? No high-rise work parties, private jets, or a house so big we've got an intercom system to communicate in it.

As the sun sets and darkness envelops us, I can feel the weight of my thoughts bearing down on me. Remy's words replay in my mind, and I wonder if it's really possible to fix things between Alex and me. Is it even worth trying?

Lost in thought, I almost don't notice Remy settling in beside me, until he speaks.

"Can I share something with you, Jocelyn?" His voice is soft, barely above a whisper.

I nod, turning to face him as I spear a marshmallow on the end of a stick. His eyes are intense as they lock onto mine.

"Do not measure your worth by Alex's inability to see yours. You are an incredible woman, Jocelyn, and you deserve to be loved just as fiercely as you love." His words hit me like a ton of bricks, and I can feel the tears pricking at the corners of my eyes.

I'm not sure how much time passes before he speaks again. "I know it's easier said than done," he continues, "but you are worthy of love and respect, no matter what happens between you and Alex."

I let out a shaky breath, my cheeks damp now. No one has ever spoken to me this way before. It's as if Remy can see into the depths of my soul and knows exactly what I need to hear.

"Thank you," I whisper, my voice barely audible above the sounds of the crackling fire.

I shove my marshmallow into the flames dancing over the logs, watching as they catch on the ball of sugar, consuming it. Pulling it out of the flame, I blow the fire out and slide it onto my already-prepared bed of graham cracker and chocolate balancing on my lap.

The guys watch in rapt attention as I bite into my S'more, savoring the way the marshmallow melts on my tongue. In a few more bites, it's gone, and Vox settles on the log next to me.

"You've got a little chocolate here." He drags his thumb across my lips and captures the chocolate that rests on the edge. His mouth hovers near mine as he delicately brings his thumb to his mouth and wraps his lips around it.

My insides combust with a sudden heat, and I can feel my body responding to the intimate gesture. Vox's eyes lock onto mine, and I can see the raw desire burning in his gaze, charged with something we both want but can't have.

I jump to my feet, desperate to put some space between us before I do something I'll regret. "I've got to go to the bathroom," I squeak as I pivot for the trees behind us.

As I walk away from the campsite, my mind reels with conflicting emotions. Part of me is confused and scared by the intensity of the attraction I feel for the guys, but another is excited by the possibility of exploring the potential of something more with them.

But I can't do that to Alex. I made a vow to him on our wedding day, and even though things aren't perfect between us right now, cheating on him is not the answer. And while I've done intimate things with the guys, it was in full view of Alex, and we had his permission. Doing it here, while he's stuck at home?

No. I can't.

Wind whips through the woods, ruffling my hair as I use the dappled moonlight to find my way to a far enough spot to do my business.

I'm just squirting hand sanitizer into my hand when snow starts to spit. I knew it was cold—I can see my breath—but hadn't checked the forecast.

Adrenaline still courses through my veins from my encounter with Vox as I make my way back.

But even as I rue the situation, my body has other ideas. The image of Vox's strong arms wrapped around me, his lips hot and insistent on mine, flashes through my mind.

I clamp down on the thoughts, willing them away as fast as they come. But it's like trying to contain a wildfire with spit. Futile.

And then I hear it.

A twig snaps in the underbrush, and my heart jumps into my throat. I spin around, trying to peer through the darkness. But there's nothing there. Just the rustling of leaves and the hoot of an owl somewhere in the distance.

I take a step forward, then another, my heart still racing. My hand goes instinctively to my pocketknife, ready for anything that might come at me.

That's when I see him: a tall figure emerging from the shadows.

"Remy?" I say, breathless with relief.

He nods in response, coming closer until we're face to face. I can feel his body heat radiating off him as he speaks. "Probably best to go in pairs around these parts on account of the wolves. Just wanted to make sure you were alright."

I nod, feeling sheepish for overreacting. But as Remy turns to lead me back to the campsite, I can't help but notice the strong line of his jaw and the way his muscles move beneath his shirt. My thoughts, already a tangled mess from Vox's and Niko's attention, become even more jumbled.

But when we arrive back at the fire, something has changed. The tension in the air is thicker now, a perceptible energy that seems to hum along my skin.

"Is everything okay?" I ask, my eyes searching their faces for any hint of what's happening.

Niko and Vox exchange a look, and then Vox speaks up, his voice low and husky. "We need to talk."

My heart skips a beat as all three of them turn to face me, their eyes filled with a burning intensity that sends shivers down my spine. I can feel the heat of their gaze on my skin, and it's like there's an invisible force drawing me towards them.

"What is it?" I ask, my voice barely above a whisper.

Vox moves closer to me, his hand reaching out to cradle my cheek. "I didn't mean to make you feel uncomfortable."

"Oh," I squeak. I guess we're going there. "You didn't make me uncomfortable. I'm just trying to wrestle with my conflicting emotions."

"Conflicting emotions?" He drops his hand, using it to fiddle with his scarf.

A war rages within me as I consider whether I should divulge my deepest, most conflicting feelings. I hesitate, biting my lip, and then, as if a dam has burst, the words come pouring out. "I'm trying to reconcile how I could feel something for men who aren't my husband." Stuffing my hands in my coat, I continue, "I know it's wrong, and I don't want to hurt Alex. But being around you three ..." I trail off, unable to put into words the powerful pull they have on me.

A sinister thought creeps its way in: I know exactly how I could find myself in this position. I'm a long-neglected housewife who's been begging for love and attention from her husband.

Snow clings to my lashes, and I blink them away as Niko steps forward, handing me a mug of tea he'd been brewing over the fire.

"Should be cool enough now." He inclines his head, and I bring it to my lips. "And what you feel? It's natural to question your marriage. Anyone would if they'd had to endure what you have."

Notes of chamomile blooms on my tongue, and I close my eyes, letting the warmth of the drink soothe the heartache in me.

When I open them, Remy is digging through his backpack, setting toiletries on the ground. Vox joins me on the fallen log we've drug near the fire.

"It's normal for you to feel this way towards men who fill a gap in your marriage." He leans in, voice pitched low. "It doesn't mean you're going to act on it. But if you did? None of us would blame you."

But that's the real quandary, isn't it? Alex would absolutely blame me. I feel like I'm at the edge of a cliff, and all it'll take is a heated glance or a lingering touch to send me tumbling over. I swallow hard, trying to push that thought away.

"I know," I reply, sipping my tea again. "But I can't help feeling like I'm betraying Alex in some way."

Remy drops a bottle of shampoo next to the other items, his voice gruff as he speaks, "You're not betraying anyone by acknowledging your feelings. It's natural to crave affection and attention."

Niko nods in agreement, his eyes gentle as they meet mine. "You're our client, Jocelyn. Not Alexander. If you decide right now you want to call it quits, you can do that. If you go through the rest of this process and still decide at the end that you and him are through, you can do that, too. We'll help you through it, whether you're together or not."

Snow begins to accumulate on my coat as they speak, and I can feel the cold seeping into my bones. But their words warm me more than any fire ever could. Even if I don't fully understand my emotions, these three men are here for me. And that means the world.

"Thank you," I whisper, feeling tears pricking at the corners of my eyes. "I don't know what I'd do without you guys."

Vox shoots me a crooked grin, his eyes crinkling at the edges. "You'd have far less orgas—"

The howl of a wolf pierces the cold evening air, cutting off Vox's words. We all freeze, listening to the eerie sound. There's something haunting about it, something that makes the skin on my arms pebble. The hairs on the back of my neck stand at attention as we listen to the wolf's howl fade into the distance as it joins others.

"Maybe we should call it a night," Niko suggests, his eyes scanning the darkening woods warily.

I nod in agreement, feeling a sudden urge to be tucked away in the tent in my fabricated semblance of safety. Jumping to my feet, I help the guys seal our food into a rucksack so we can string it in a tree.

As we crawl into the tent, I can't help but feel a shiver run up my spine. The howling of the wolf still echoes in my mind, and I can't shake off the feeling that we're being watched. Despite the warm sleeping bag, I find myself curling up, arms tight around my chest, as if trying to protect myself from the wolves lurking in the forest.

Remy turns his flashlight off, plunging us into complete darkness. The only sound is our breathing and the occasional rustle of fabric as one of us adjusts in our sleeping bags.

Sleep finds me quickly, safe in their company.

Sometime in the middle of the night, a breathy whisper breaks the silence. "Are you cold?"

Just my face is out of the sleeping bag, so it doesn't build condensation and make me colder. I turn towards the voice, heart beating fast as I see Vox's silhouette near mine now that my eyes have adjusted to the dark. He's so close I can feel the heat radiating from him.

"Yeah," I manage to reply, my own voice barely above a whisper. "As long as it doesn't get any colder, I should be okay, though."

Vox doesn't move away. Instead, his hand brushes against my cheek, and I feel a sudden surge of heat spreading through me. His fingers trail down my neck, sending shivers of pleasure through me.

"Are you sure?" he murmurs, his breath hot against my skin. "Because you're shivering."

I can't speak, can't even think as every nerve ending lights on fire at his touch.

"Jocelyn, you don't get a medal for being a hero," Niko's gruff voice calls from the other side of me. "Here." He sits up, unzipping his sleeping bag. "We can zip everyone's together. Share body heat."

Light illuminates the small space between us, and I squint as Remy checks his phone. "Fuck, zero bars."

"How cold do you think it is?" My trembling hands work to unzip my sleeping bag.

Remy grunts. "Was supposed to stay in the teens." He moves closer, helping the others join our blankets together. "But it's definitely hovering around zero degrees right now."

We get our blankets situated, and as soon as Niko and Vox settle back onto their pillows next to me, delicious heat leeches into my skin. But as much as I try to focus on the warmth around me, my mind keeps drifting back to Vox's touch. The way his fingers felt against my skin, the heat of his breath on my neck.

I turn to face him, my eyes locking onto his in the darkness. His gaze is intense, almost like he's searching for something in the depths of my own eyes.

"Thank you," I whisper, suddenly overcome with emotion. "For being here for me, for helping me."

Vox's hand reaches out again, and this time there's no hesitation as his fingers tangle in my hair. He pulls me close, bringing my head to rest on his chest. His scent fills my nostrils, and I can feel his heart beating against my ear.

"Always." He grabs my hands and puts them under his shirt, warming them. "We'll always be here for you."

I close my eyes, reveling in the sensation of being wrapped up in warmth and safety. But even as I lay there, cocooned in his embrace, my mind wanders to a dark and dirty place. A place where Vox's hands aren't just on my hair, but they're exploring every inch of my body.

I try to shake the thoughts from my mind, blaming them on the cold and the sudden surge of emotions I felt moments before. But it's no use; they persist, growing stronger with each passing moment.

Niko drifts closer, enveloping my back in his heat. The two press against me, sandwiching me between them, and I feel their bodies growing more and more familiar against mine.

Vox continues to hold me close, his fingers tracing patterns on my skin, and I can't help but imagine what it would be like to have the three of them all over me again. Without the watchful eye of my husband.

I bite my lip, trying to suppress the thoughts, but they only intensify. It's wrong, I tell myself, so very wrong. But the temptation is too great, and I find myself responding to their touches, yearning for more.

They seem to come to the same conclusion—about it being wrong —and their ministrations stop.

We lay there in the darkness, our breaths mingling in the frigid air. My heart is wild, and heat radiates from their bodies, even as they keep their distance.

"I'm sorry," Vox whispers into my hair, his voice cracking slightly. "That was inappropriate."

"It's okay," I manage to reply, even though my mind is racing with conflicting emotions. "I understand."

Niko clears his throat, his arm tightening around my waist. "We'll keep you warm," he says gruffly. "But we need to keep it platonic."

If I'm so conflicted in my feelings, why does their touch feel so *right*? As though their hands were made to explore my body, and their lips to caress my skin. But I know it's wrong, despite what my body might try to conjure up, and I can't give in to these illicit desires.

I nod, but in the darkness, they can't see the tears that are forming in my eyes. This whole situation is too much for me to handle. It's like a cauldron of emotions and desires that I've never felt before, and I don't know how to deal with them.

But even as I try to control my feelings, their warmth seeps into me. We lay there in silence for a while longer, the only sounds coming from our breathing and the occasional rustling of our blankets. Eventually, exhaustion takes over and we all fall into a deep sleep.

But even as I'm drifting off, I can't shake the images from my mind of how different things could be if I just gave in.

CHAPTER THIRTEEN

VOX

Jocelyn's body presses tight against me, seeking every bit of warmth I can offer her as she sleeps. In this moment, I would willingly give her every last ounce of my heat. The freezing air surrounds us, but within the confines of our zipped-together sleeping bags, our combined warmth creates a sanctuary from the cold.

Remy, Niko, and I huddle close to Jocelyn, our bodies a protective shield against the frigid air that has invaded our tent. The unexpected snowfall from the night before has left us in a winter wonderland, but Jocelyn's presence brings a warmth to my heart that the cold cannot touch.

As I lie here, I can't help but remember the first time I realized my attraction to Jocelyn was more than just physical. It was the end of her senior year in college, and she'd just experienced a painful breakup. I felt an overwhelming urge to reveal myself to her, to comfort her, and to show her the depth of my feelings.

To love her.

I wanted so desperately to prove to her that my affection went beyond mere attraction. I longed to demonstrate how much I valued her—not just for her beauty, but for her intelligence, her vibrant personality, and the depth of her soul.

But as one of her guardian fae gods, I knew that revealing myself to her would be a violation of the Edict of Separation, a betrayal of my duty. So I remained in the shadows, watching her pick up the pieces of her broken heart, and wishing that I could be the one to mend it. Instead I've had to watch her navigate relationships with men who couldn't see her true worth. Men who saw her as nothing more than an object to satisfy their desires.

Now, as our bodies press together in the confined space of the tent, I feel that same longing surge through me once more. I wish I could take away the pain she's endured in her marriage to Alex and replace it with the love and devotion she truly deserves.

But for now, all I can do is hold her close, share my warmth, and hope that somehow, one day, we will be able to overcome the obstacles that separate us and forge a love that transcends the boundaries of our worlds.

With her nestled in my arms, my thoughts drift to the way she responded to our touch, the way she bit her lip as if suppressing desires that echoed our own. The way she tastes, and how I can coax her to cry out under the weight of my tongue. The intensity of these memories is almost too much to bear.

I shift slightly, attempting to alleviate the pressure building in my pants caused by these forbidden thoughts.

Niko stirs beside me, his hand entwined in Jocelyn's hair as he sleeps. I cast him a longing glance, wondering if he, too, is tormented by similar desires. Remy left the tent a short while ago, likely to answer nature's call.

We can't act on these feelings. While our purpose has changed—we're no longer attempting to mend her marriage—soon enough, we'll get to tell her about her heritage.

Teach her all about how to wield magic. How to fuel her powers.

She doesn't know that she'll maintain her youthful appearance for eternity—we're still grappling with how to approach that topic when the time comes.

"You up?" Remy's voice pulls me from my thoughts as he crawls back into the tent.

"Yeah," I whisper in response.

"We need to talk, right now."

Whatever the issue, it doesn't sound good. I use my magic to warm a pillow, placing it in Jocelyn's arms as I carefully slip out of the tent to face whatever awaits.

We create a silencing bubble around us so that if Jocelyn wakes up, she won't be able to hear our conversation.

At least a foot of snow blankets the ground, and although the temperature has risen slightly, the wind whips through the trees, sending large snow drifts crashing against the tent. I shiver despite the magic warming my body.

"What's the matter?" I ask as Remy paces back and forth, his eyes filled with concern.

"I sifted to Alex's workplace, and he won't be coming," Remy says, his voice heavy with frustration. As fae, we can teleport anywhere, provided we know what the place looks like. And as gods, we can use a portal to go anywhere, anytime.

"What do you mean he's not coming?" Niko's voice takes on a dangerous edge.

"Are you kidding me?" I shout, grateful for the sound barrier we've put up. "He knows this is his last chance!" While I'm thrilled he's doing exactly what we want—sabotaging his own marriage—I'm livid for Jocelyn. She's going to be crushed. "How are we going to cause tension between them now if he won't even be here?"

Remy's face is grim. "His partner is having him meet with a client for lunch in New York City ... but that doesn't mean we can't work this to our advantage."

"What did Alex tell his partner? And what do you mean, work this to our advantage?"

"Well, this will be the final straw," Remy growls. "This will confirm to Jocelyn what we all already know, that Alex cares more about his job than his marriage."

In a fit of anger, I grab a snow-covered log and hurl it into the trees with such force that we don't even hear it land.

"She's going to be so heartbroken." Niko squats down, tucking his head in his hands.

"That fucking bastard," I growl. "We should just kill him."

"You can't just kill him, Vox." Remy rests a hand on my shoulder and I shrug it off. "The first person they'll suspect is Jocelyn."

"How are we going to tell her?" I glance towards the tent where Jocelyn is still sound asleep.

"Orgasms. If we give her orgasms, it'll soften the blow," I offer. "We could mate her."

Remy sucks in a breath. "Watch your mouth, you never know who could overhear!" he hisses.

"Sound barrier, asshole." I throw my hands up. "The three of us know her better than *anyone*. Who better to love her than us?" I begin to pace. "Who better to give her everything she ever desired? Do you really want her with some upper crust fae asshole as her mate? You and I both know that's exactly what they'll try to orchestrate once she goes to the fae realms."

"What you're saying is treason," Remy breathes.

"You can't honestly tell me you don't feel something for her," I growl.

Niko rises to his feet and runs a hand over his face. "We could just tell her now. Get it over with and bring her to the fae realms. Probably Bedlam, since Rolls will have to come with ... but, why not?"

"Really, Niko?" Remy's voice is near shouting. He gets defensive when he feels backed into a corner. "Just how do you see that panning out?!"

"She's the fucking heir, Remy. She has to come back some day. Why not now?"

"If we bring her back there now, we'll never see her again!" He shoves me, but I don't budge. Nor do I retaliate. He's on the verge of a breakdown, and he's afraid. Afraid of losing her. "They'll see how close we are. Closer than guardians should be with their charge."

"You love her, too, don't you?" I unclench my jaw. "I'm not afraid to admit it, so why are you?"

"Because the minute I do, they'll take her from us!" Tears spring from his red-rimmed eyes.

I pull him into my arms, holding him as I tilt my head to the skies.

Guardians aren't supposed to fall for their charges. In doing so, we've broken the Edict of Separation.

Punishable by death, which means we're stripped of our god status and sent to Aggonid's realm—the fae underworld. But if we frame it as helping mend her broken heart—

The sound of the zipper unzipping startles us back, and we drop the sound barrier.

"Wow, that's a lot of snow." Jocelyn pokes her head out. "How long have you guys been awake?"

"Not long." I grin at her bed head. It's messy from Niko running his fingers through it while she slept. Pretty sure he's got a hair fetish or something.

"Hungry?" Remy asks her, walking towards the tree where we've got the rucksack of food strung up.

"I could eat." She grins. "After we eat, I'd like to hike to the top of the hill; see if I can't get a signal to see what time Alex will be here."

Remy drops the rope securing the rucksack, sending the bundle of our food crashing to the ground. "Shit." He scrambles to pick up everything that's spilled out of the bag.

We all help, picking up granola bars, trail mix, and packets of freeze-dried foods.

"Sorry." Remy scowls, stuffing a granola bar into his mouth.

If Jocelyn weren't watching, we could've used magic to stop the food from hitting the ground, but she still has no idea magic is real.

No idea the three men who are supposed to fix her marriage are really fae.

Or that she is, too.

Jocelyn has on a fuzzy beanie cap with a fluffy, white ball on the top that flops around when she moves.

As we finish gathering the scattered food, Jocelyn tilts her head, a confused expression on her face. "Do you guys feel that?"

Remy clears his throat, glancing at us nervously. "Feel what?"

Jocelyn's gaze lingers on him for a moment but shakes her head. "Huh. Never mind. Let's just get breakfast ready and plan our hike."

We settle down around the campfire, preparing a simple breakfast with the salvaged food. The warmth of the flames and the smell of hot coffee fill the air, creating a cozy atmosphere despite the cold. Jocelyn hums softly as she sips her coffee, her eyes bright with excitement for the day ahead.

"I freaking love camping," she whispers.

We chuckle. Little does she know, it's the fae blood in her calling to be one with nature. Helps her feel a little closer to source this way.

As we eat and chat, I can't help but feel a sense of unease. We haven't yet found the right moment to tell Jocelyn about the change in plans regarding Alex's arrival. I glance at Niko and Remy, silently communicating our shared concern.

Remy catches my eye and gives a subtle nod, acknowledging the agreement that we'll find a way to break the news to her soon. But for now, we focus on enjoying the beauty of our surroundings and the camaraderie we share. All too soon, the truth will be revealed, and we can only hope that Jocelyn will be able to handle the unexpected twist in her journey.

Jocelyn

As we finish our breakfast, I feel a renewed sense of excitement for the hike we have planned. The snow has coated the world around us in a blanket of glittery white, and I'm eager to explore the serene beauty of the landscape.

The four of us set out, bundled up in our warmest clothes, following a narrow trail that leads up to the hilltop. The climb is a bit challenging, but invigorating, and I find myself relishing the physical exertion. Niko, Remy, and Vox are attentive, offering support and encouragement whenever I need it.

After a considerable amount of hiking, we finally reach the top of the hill. The view is breathtaking, the vast expanse of snow-dusted trees stretching out before us. I can't resist snapping a few pictures on my phone, knowing I'll want to remember this moment.

"I can't believe how beautiful it is up here," I say, awestruck.

Remy grins at me. "It's even more stunning with you in it, Jocelyn."

I can't help but blush at his words, touched by the compliment. But my thoughts soon drift back to Alex, and I remember the purpose of this hike. I pull out my phone, noticing that I have a couple of bars of signal. I quickly dial Alex's number, hoping to find out when he'll be joining us.

The phone rings a few times before he finally answers. "Jocelyn, hey! How's the camping trip going?"

"It's amazing, Alex. You should see the view from the spot we picked out," I reply, my voice filled with enthusiasm. "When are you planning to come up here? We can't wait for you to join us."

There's a brief pause on the other end, and I can sense the hesitation in his voice when he finally responds. "Jocelyn, I ... I have some bad news. A client in New York needs to meet with me tomorrow morning, and I can't reschedule. I'm really sorry, but I won't be able to make it to the camping trip."

My heart sinks, and I can feel the disappointment and frustration rising in my chest. "Alex, we planned this trip for weeks. Can't you have someone else handle it, just this once?"

"I wish I could," he says, his voice filled with regret. "But this is a high-profile client, and they specifically requested me. I can't risk losing their business. I'm sorry, Jocelyn. I promise I'll make it up to you."

I grip the phone tightly, trying to keep my anger under control as the frustration turns to rage. "Alex, I've been more than patient with you. I've given you so many chances to make things right between us, and this camping trip was supposed to be our last shot at fixing our marriage. I told you that this was important, that this was your last chance. And now you're telling me you can't make it?"

I can hear the guilt and anxiety in his voice as he replies, "Jocelyn, I know how important this is to you, and I swear I wouldn't miss it if I had any other choice. But this client is crucial for our business, and I can't afford to lose them. I promise I'll make it up to you as soon as I can."

I shake my head, my anger boiling over. "No, Alex. You don't get it. There won't be any more chances after this. This was it. You had one job: to be here, with me, for our marriage. And you failed. If you can't prioritize us, then maybe it's time for me to reevaluate where I stand in your life."

The silence on the other end of the phone is deafening. Finally, he whispers, "Jocelyn, please don't say that. I love you. I'll do whatever it takes to make this right."

I let out a bitter laugh. "You should have thought about that before you chose your client over your wife. We're done, Alex." With that, I end the call, my chest heaving with a mix of anger and sadness.

As I turn to face Niko, Remy, and Vox, they can see the pain in my eyes. "Alex isn't coming," I say bitterly. "He chose work over our marriage. Again."

Remy wraps an arm around my shoulders, offering comfort. "I'm so sorry, Jocelyn."

"Yeah," I reply, my voice heavy with disappointment. "So am I."

Determined not to let Alex ruin our time together, we continue our hike, taking in the stunning snowy landscape and enjoying each other's company. But as we trudge through the snow, the weight of my crumbling marriage weighs heavily on my heart.

THAT EVENING, as the sky above us turns into a mesmerizing canvas of vivid hues, the weight of the call with Alex lingers heavily in the air. I find myself staring into the campfire, the orange and yellow flames dancing hypnotically, their warmth a soothing balm for my aching heart. I'm seated on a rough-hewn log, wrapped in a cozy blanket, with Niko, Remy, and Vox gathered around me. The campsite is surrounded by tall, snow-laden trees, and the sounds of the forest form a gentle melody in the background.

The concern etched on their faces is evident, and it's clear that they're trying to think of a way to help me feel better. I can't help but compare this moment to my crumbling relationship with Alex. Despite the brief time we've spent together, the love architects have shown more genuine care, empathy, and understanding than my husband has in years. The connection we've formed feels more profound and more fulfilling than anything I'd ever experienced with Alex. The thought of losing them, of having them leave once our camping trip is over, is even more devastating than the end of my marriage.

Tears begin to slide down my cheeks as I come to this realization. The firelight reflects in the droplets that fall to my ungloved hands, turning them into liquid amber. Vox notices my tears and reaches out to wipe them away, his touch gentle and soothing. "Hey. What's wrong?"

I choke back a sob, unable to hold back my emotions any longer. "I don't want you guys to leave. You've become so important to me, and I can't stand the thought of losing you. I've given up so much for a man who didn't care enough to try and save our marriage. Now, I feel like I'm losing the only people who truly understand and care for me."

The guys exchange concerned glances before Remy speaks up. "Jocelyn, you're not losing us. We care about you, and we're not going anywhere unless you want us to."

They crowd around me, knees sinking into soft snow. As I look into their eyes, I see the truth in their words. The thought of having them by my side, supporting me as I face the daunting task of rebuilding my life, brings a measure of solace to my aching heart.

Maybe I'm not so alone, after all.

Crawling into our tent, midnight has fallen, casting its inky cloak over the forest. The world beyond our tent exists in shadows and whispers, but inside our temporary haven, a soft golden glow emanates from the lanterns we've hung. The chill outside attempts to invade our space, but the warmth from the three men surrounding me is a far stronger force, keeping the cold at bay.

"We're sorry about Alex," Niko murmurs, his voice low and gentle, rich with empathy. His fingers tenderly brush a stray strand of hair from my face, tucking it behind my ear. "We know this trip meant a lot to you."

"It did," I admit, my words a mere whisper, laden with the weight of my disappointment. "But I'm not sure it matters anymore."

Remy's hand finds mine beneath the layers of blankets, his fingers intertwining with mine, strong and reassuring. "We'll always be here for you, Jocelyn. No matter what."

The tent fills with the sound of our steady breathing, each of us lost in our thoughts. My heart aches with the overwhelming emotions that bubble to the surface, the hurt and frustration refusing to be suppressed.

Vox shifts closer, his body pressing against my back, his warmth seeping into my very bones. "You deserve so much better, Jocelyn," he whispers into my ear, his breath warm and comforting.

I bite my lip, feeling the tension in the air. It's undeniable that there's an attraction between us, and the intimacy we've shared with Alex's knowledge now feels different; it's no longer an experiment or a lesson, but something far more profound and complicated.

My breath catches as Niko's hand grazes the curve of my hip, the simple touch sending a shiver down my spine. I glance at him, his eyes dark and unreadable in the dim light of the tent. The desire is palpable, a living, breathing thing that threatens to consume us all.

"Do you think ..." I hesitate, my voice barely audible as I struggle to articulate my thoughts. "Do you think we should ... I mean, can we ..."

"We should take everything at your pace. Whatever you feel comfortable with," Remy suggests gently, picking up on my unspoken question. "You're going through a difficult time right now, Jocelyn. You're going to go through a whole range of emotions, and I don't want regret to be one of them."

"You're right," I choke out, sniffling. "I wish we would've brought Rolls with us. I could really use him right now."

Vox tugs me into his arms, helping calm the deep ache in my chest. I turn to face him, breathing in his comforting scent.

"I'll keep you warm," he says softly, his fingers playing with the strands of my hair.

I nod, feeling grateful for their presence. Their unexpected appearance in my life has thrown me off balance, but it's undeniably what I need right now. They understand me in a way that Alex never could. They know my deepest fears and desires, and they're not afraid to explore them with me, even when the words are difficult to articulate —they just seem to know.

Vox's grip tightens around my neck, as if his fingers were a chain of fire that seared into my skin. The heat radiating from him is dizzying, and I can't help but be drawn to the intensity of his gaze. His lips are like a magnet, drawing me closer until we are almost touching.

I close my eyes in anticipation of his kiss, feeling my heartbeat in my throat. His lips collide with mine in an explosion of fiery passion. I gasp, overwhelmed by the sensations coursing through me. His touch is urgent, pulling me closer until I feel my soul being consumed by him. Our tongues entwine in a desperate embrace, each of us searching for something that only the other can provide. I'm lost in a sea of blissful desire, drowning in the warmth and tenderness of his kiss.

Niko's hands slide down my back as he presses closer to me, his lips moving to the sensitive skin of my neck. I let out a soft moan, my body arching into his touch. He bites down gently on my skin, sending a flash of pain and pleasure through me, but doesn't break skin.

I want him to.

Remy moves closer and settles between my thighs. His fingers are like fire on my skin as they dance their way down my stomach, slipping beneath the waistband of my clothes and seeking out hidden pleasure spots. My breath catches in my throat at his touch, and I'm powerless against the overwhelming desire coursing through me. The heat radiating from him is almost unbearable, drawing me towards him like a moth to a flame.

My body is on fire as his fingers dip inside me, the slow and deliberate strokes making my skin tingle with anticipation. I'm shuddering under his touch, waves of pleasure radiating through me in electrifying jolts.

I can feel Niko's hot breath against my ear, his deep and sensual voice sending currents of desire down my spine. "We've wanted you for so long," he growls, his warm chuckle reverberating across my neck. "All this time wanting to spread these beautiful thighs apart. Tell me Joss, is this what you yearned for?"

I bite my lip to keep from screaming as Remy continues his tormenting touch, sending shocks up my spine with every stroke of his fingers. He shimmies up my body with deliberate movements, and before I know it his lips are just a breath away from mine. My heart hammers in my chest as he slides out of me and I plead desperately for more, my voice a low moan that breaks the silence. "Please," I beg, desperate. "I was so close."

"These are in the way," Vox growls, ripping my pants clean off me, and cool air meets my skin. "And I'm going to die if I don't taste this pussy again."

I don't have a chance to gulp in a breath before his mouth is on me, his lips dragging across my wet folds. I buck my hips up, a cry escaping me as he finds that one perfect spot.

"Please," I whine, hardly aware of what I'm asking for. "I need to come."

"Oh yeah, we're gonna make you come so hard you'll forget your own damn name," Remy groans, sinking down to his knees next to us.

When Remy's lips meet mine, it's like a possession, like he's claiming me just as surely as Vox is claiming my pussy, and I can't get enough.

I moan into him, my breathing picking up as sweat begins to form on my brow despite the cold air.

Vox swirls his tongue around my clit before taking it between his lips, sucking it until I see spots in front of me from the pure pleasure of it.

A strangled cry rends my throat as I writhe in ecstasy, feeling the wave of ecstasy growing within me. His fingers plunge deep into me and his thumb circles mercilessly on my aching nub until I am brought to the very brink of orgasm. "That's it," he pants, urging me with his gaze. "Look at me, Joss." Somehow I force heavy lids open and my vision blurs as my body is overcome with an unimaginable intensity. I scream out as my body shudders uncontrollably, my fingers digging frantically into his raven hair.

He eases his fingers out of me as I come down from my high. "This greedy little pussy wants more, doesn't she?"

I lift my head, meeting his pale blue eyes and nodding before my head falls back to the pillow again.

"Tell us what you want," Remy commands. "Use your words."

"All of you," I breathe. "Make me forget."

～

Remy

GRABBING JOCELYN'S HANDS, I pin them over her head and settle between her thighs. Her eyes are heavy-lidded, beautiful pools of emerald begging me to sate her.

I'll fuck every last gods damned name out of her so she only remembers mine.

"Get behind her," I grunt, releasing her hands. She keeps them above her head, just like I taught her.

Using one hand, I undo my belt, whipping it out as Niko positions himself behind Jocelyn, cradling her between his thighs so she rests her head on his already shirtless chest.

I hand Vox my belt. "Her hands. Behind his head."

He takes the belt without question, and I watch as he loops it around Jocelyn's wrists, securing her hands behind Niko's head, so she's stretched out.

"What's your safe word, Jocelyn?" Niko whispers in her ear.

"Viking." She squirms, trying to rub her thighs together, but I'm between them.

I unzip my pants, sliding them down my ass until my cock springs free. Jocelyn's eyes dart to where it bobs against my abs, licking her lips in anticipation. I kick my jeans away and line myself up.

"And you're going to let Niko and Vox watch as I part this pussy with my cock?"

She arches her back, straining to get some kind of traction. When she can't, she grins down at me. "If you ever get around to it."

My head falls back, and a laugh comes from deep inside me as I surge forward, impaling her all the way.

"Fuck," I groan as a deep, keening moan passes Jocelyn's lips. "She's so fucking tight."

The flick of a blade sounds just before it's used to divest Jocelyn of her shirt and bra. Her breasts spill free, ready for Vox's eager hands.

"I'll buy you new ones." He chuckles as his mouth closes around a nipple, teasing it with his teeth.

My heart thrashes and my stomach lurches as I throw caution to the wind. Fuck the consequences. I'm desperate for her, almost frantic; I feel like I could breathe her in like oxygen, craving that sweet scent, just so I can feel alive again.

"What is she to you?" Niko mutters, taking hold of her thighs and spreading them wide for me and watching her gasp as Vox tugs on her nipple with his teeth. "Is she a friend? A lover? An obsession?"

I reach down and wrap my hand around my base, keeping myself imprisoned so that I don't explode after just a few moments inside of her heavenly body.

"All of it."

Her flesh rosy-pink from her orgasm, she fingers the belt that binds her to him. Her skin glistens with sweat. Despite my best efforts, I can't resist the urge to lean forward and lap up some of it from her belly.

Her eyes are still on me, and her mouth tips into a smirk, even as her breathing quickens. "Prove it. Mark my skin." Her words end on a moan as I drag my pelvis against her clit.

My chest tightens. She's asking me to brand her as my own, but instead of elation, I feel dread. Because finally admitting it means I won't be able to pretend anymore that she's mine. That I can't actually keep her, no matter how much I want to sink my teeth into her flesh and prove to her just how perfect she is for me.

She doesn't know what she's asking. Oh, but she feels it. This craving to be dominated, owned, and marked? It's fae nature.

Knowing that makes my cock twitch with renewed urgency. Grinding against her, I let the head slip through her soft flesh again, coating myself in her juices. Drawing one of her nipples into my mouth, I bite down on it just a little before soothing it with my tongue. Just a little more pressure, and I'd sink my canines in, and she'd be mine.

Forever.

"More," she whispers. A whimper escapes her lips as I bite down a bit harder. "Please."

"You're going to be the death of me." A wicked smile crosses my face as I pull out of her.

I have to give myself some space before I do something unforgivable. Communicating this with Vox silently, he and I make the seamless transition of switching places.

"Undo her hands," he commands as he strips.

Her eyes never leave Vox, and her tongue sweeps across her bottom lip as he strokes himself. Vox's body is lean and muscular, covered with a taut skin that ripples with each movement. The golden rings around his eyes catch the light and reflect it back, like glowing embers.

We barely have to use magic to warm the tent anymore, our combined heat enough to keep us comfortable.

Arousal perfumes the air, and every breath I take drowns me in it. This is what I want—forever.

CHAPTER FOURTEEN

VOX

The round orbs of Jocelyn's breasts heave with each pant. She watches me drag my thumb over the head of my cock, and I want her pretty little mouth around me, swirling around my shaft as she brings me to my knees.

But I'm doing this for her.

I grab her ankles and drag her off Niko's lap, earning me a little squeak of surprise. Gripping my base, I glide my cock through her folds, groaning as her wetness coats me.

"Please," she begs. "I need you, Vox," she whimpers.

Five little words is all it takes to have me driving into her, sheathing myself in her slick heat. The first thrust sends a pleasured gap from Jocelyn's lips, and I swear I could come just from the sound.

"Fuck," I groan. The tight enclosure of her pussy is better than any drug. "So fucking good."

She tosses her head back and presses forward against me, trying to control the pace. But I know her, just as I know the face I see in the mirror. She wants me to take control. To own every ounce of flesh she can offer me.

Leaning back, I pull her onto my lap, gripping her hips so she milks my cock. Her arms fasten around my neck and her lips meet mine. She tastes like sex and sweat and what I've been chasing since the beginning of time.

I love her.

She's mine.

Whether she knows it or not, fuck the consequences, she doesn't need a mating bite to own me. No amount of magic will erase the truth from our hearts, nor do I need the marks on our skin to spell out exactly who I am.

I'm hers.

Sliding my hand between us, I find the little nub that brings Jocelyn so much pleasure.

She cries into my mouth, the sound ending in my name on her lips. Her pussy clenches and her insides pulsate, squeezing my cock, and not a force on this earth or the next could stop me from spilling my seed deep into her. The tremors of her orgasm pull me under, and I'm fucking drowning in my future mate.

Whatever it takes, I'll have her. If we have to run away, that's exactly what we'll do.

As soon as her limbs go weak, I ease her down onto the blanket beneath us, watching as my come dribbles out of her pussy. Collecting it with my finger, I shove it back inside, right where it belongs.

Niko

"YOU WANT MORE?" I purr, watching as her attention swings to me.

She nods, looking up at me through long lashes. "Please."

I grab her hips, flipping her onto her stomach in one smooth motion. "Use your safeword if you need it." I yank her back until she's on her knees and I shove into her.

The place where I'm supposed to tear her in two feels like the best home I've ever had. The tightness of the fit, the warmth of her body surrounding my cock.

And then she turns to look at me over her shoulder. "Niko," she begs. "Don't hold back."

That's all the permission I need. "Fuck." The word is hoarse on my lips, sliding deep from my chest. I surge forward, setting a punishing rhythm as my hand reaches around her hip to toy with her clit.

"You like them watching me fuck this pretty little pussy, don't you?" I grit.

Her only response is a moan as I strum her just right.

My hips rock against her, and just when I think I could do this all night, Jocelyn's hand covers her sex, squeezing my dick as she tries to milk the come right out of me.

"Is that my come you want?" I chuckle. "Ask for it nicely."

"Please, Niko," she gasps. Reaching up, she fists my hair, using it to tug me closer so I'm draped over her body. "Fill me. I want to feel your come dripping out of me when you're done."

"Damn straight." My hand cracks her ass, and I fuck her harder. My balls draw up against my body as I feel my orgasm take hold.

I come on a roar, my own release triggering hers as I grab Jocelyn by the hips, pulling her onto my chest as my orgasm fires long and hard, pumping my release deep into her body until I'm panting.

Remy

"Don't think for a minute I've forgotten you want to be chased," I whisper in her ear, my voice low and seductive.

Her entire body seems to awaken at my words. A slow grin spreads across her face as she sits up, her green eyes alight with anticipation. She reaches for my shirt and slips it on, the oversized garment falling just below her thighs, providing a teasing glimpse of her bare legs. Donning only the shirt and her snow boots, she's a captivating sight, radiating an irresistible allure.

She casts one last look my way, mischief dancing in her eyes, just as she unzips the tent and takes off into the woods.

It calls to the beast in me, listening to her footsteps crunch in the snow. From here, I hear her breath, and I shoot one last glance at the guys before I bolt out of the tent after her.

The woods are quiet, and it doesn't take but a second to see which way she went. She's a flash of red, darting through the trees from the shirt on her back.

The primal hunger within me stirs, awakened by the exhilarating chase. As I follow Jocelyn through the woods, the sound of her footsteps crunching in the snow sends a shiver down my spine. The mixture of fear and excitement in her voice as she lets out a playful shriek only fuels my desire to pursue her.

With each bound, I draw closer, the cold air biting at my skin as I push myself to keep up with her nimble movements. The vibrant red of the shirt she wears only serves to make her stand out amongst the snow-covered branches, and I can't help but marvel at her grace and agility.

As we continue deeper into the forest, the world around us fades away, replaced by the thrill of the hunt and the anticipation of our inevitable reunion. My heart pounds in my chest, a wild rhythm echoing in my ears.

Jocelyn's laughter floats back to me, her joy infectious, calling to the beast that lies within.

I glance back one last time at our friends, their faces a mix of excitement and approval, before returning my focus to the woman I'm chasing. I can feel the connection between us growing stronger, the energy of the chase binding us together in a way words cannot express.

As we dart through the trees, the snow crunching beneath our feet, the primal force that has awakened within me guides me, driving me forward. This hunt, this moment shared between us, transcends the mundane, tapping into something ancient and powerful. And I know, without a doubt, that we both crave this connection, this unbridled passion, as we embrace the wildness within ourselves.

My muscles coil and flex as I prepare to make my move, closing the distance between us. I can almost taste her sweet scent on the crisp winter air, tantalizing and intoxicating. The anticipation builds, a delicious tension mounting with each heartbeat.

Jocelyn dares to glance back at me, her green eyes filled with challenge, and I can't help but respond with a predatory grin. Our gazes lock, and something unspoken passes between us, a silent acknowledgement of the dance we've been sharing.

With a final surge of strength, I close the gap, my hand reaching out to claim her. Jocelyn squeals in delight, a blend of excitement and surrender, as my arms encircle her waist, pulling her close. Our bodies collide, crashing to the forest floor, and the warmth we share in that embrace banishes the chill of the winter air.

I bury my face in her blonde hair, inhaling her scent, and savor the victory of our primal game. Her laughter, tinged with exhilaration, mingles with my own, creating a melody that resonates through the forest.

As we lay there, entwined beneath the sheltering branches, I couldn't stop my beast if I tried.

Shredding my shirt off of her, I bury myself in her heat in a single thrust. The sensations of our bodies moving together stir within me a yearning I thought was dormant.

But this isn't just two bodies fucking in the woods. It is so much more.

This is a primal rutting, every bit as equally necessary and vital as the hunt that spurred us. I strive to possess every inch of her mind, body, and soul. I want her to need no one else but me. I'm not just filling her pussy; I am devouring every inch of her being. She is my prey, my woman, my claim.

Jocelyn seems to recognize it just as I do, baring her neck to me, begging me to make this permanent. She doesn't know why she feels this pull, this insatiable need to mark and be marked, but her glamoured, human-like nails still sink into my skin, anchoring me to her.

"Please," she whispers, but she doesn't know what she's begging for.

Doesn't know it can't be undone.

Just a little tease to sate her. As my hips drive into her, my canines elongate and I nibble at her skin.

Her hand threads through my hair, clinging me to her throat, keeping me from retreating, and sliding my teeth into her flesh. The sweetest ambrosia spills on my tongue, and I feel my pupils blow, my chest warm, and my beast sigh.

At last, it breathes.

Jocelyn moans, but she doesn't realize what's happening.

"Oh, god," she whispers as her body spasms around me. "Yes."

Out of pure instinct, my cock spills into her depths, filling her with my seed.

I realize the truth of the connection we've forged. This chase has awakened a deeper bond between us, a primal desire that transcends reason and logic. In that moment, I swear to protect and cherish this fierce, beautiful woman who has ignited the beast within me, for she is now an indelible part of my very soul.

Vox

NIKO and I sprint through the woods, my heart pounding wildly in my chest as dread rises like a sickening wave.

We skid to a halt, our bodies trembling from exertion as we cling to nearby trees for balance. Jocelyn and Remy are intertwined in their embrace, her glamoured human-like teeth sinking into his shoulder and her nails digging deep into his skin as his fangs pierce her neck.

Grief and horror surge through me like an oncoming tsunami of emotion.

We're too late. Too fucking late.

And she has no idea what's happened, other than she'll feel an inexplicable desire to be with Remy and love him until the end of time.

When they disentangle, and Remy helps her to his feet, he looks at her with a deep sense of devotion. But when his eyes meet mine, guilt stirs in their depths.

What's done is done.

She'll be exhausted now, and when she wakes tomorrow, we'll take her to the waterfall for her birthday and tell her about magic.

Show her exactly what she is, who she's meant to be, and deal with the consequences of the fall out that's sure to come from Remy taking her as a mate.

~

Jocelyn

THE NIGHT DEEPENS, and as I drift off to sleep, nestled in the embrace of Niko, Remy, and Vox, my thoughts are plagued with uncertainty. I know I need to make a decision about where my life will lead next, to find the courage to change my life and seize my own happiness. But the weight of that choice feels impossibly heavy, pressing down on me even as I find solace in the arms of these extraordinary men.

Remy awakened something in me, and I'm still trying to put my finger on it. I can't walk away from him. From this. From us. I crave him like I crave the air in my lungs.

The scent of pine and damp earth mixes with the unique fragrances of each of them, creating an intoxicating blend that lulls me into a restless slumber. As I teeter on the edge of sleep, my dreams begin to take shape, weaving together the threads of my past and the possibilities of my future.

In this liminal space, I confront my fears and desires, searching for the strength to make the choices that lie ahead. I am torn between the life I've known and the unknown possibilities that beckon from the shadows. And as the night envelops me in its embrace, I know that, come morning, I will have to face my new reality, whatever it may be.

I wake to the sound of birdsong and the first light of dawn filtering through the thin walls of our tent. The air is chilly, but the warmth of Niko, Remy, and Vox surrounds me, making it difficult to leave the cocoon of their embrace. As carefully as I can, I disentangle myself from their limbs and slip on my clothes, boots and jacket, doing my best not to disturb their sleep.

Casting a glance at Remy, my heart squeezes in my chest at the sight. His arm is above his head, and his mouth is slightly ajar as a soft snore passes between his lips. If I could find my phone, I'd snap a picture.

The morning is quiet, the forest still shaking off the remnants of night. I step out of the tent, the cold air biting at my cheeks as I take a deep breath, inhaling the scents of pine, damp earth, and the lingering traces of last night's campfire. The snow crunches softly beneath my boots as I make my way further into the woods, looking for a secluded spot to take care of my morning necessities.

The ground is uneven beneath my feet, a mixture of roots and rocks hidden beneath a thick blanket of glittering snow and fallen leaves. As I round a bend, I find a suitable spot to relieve myself.

Without warning, the air around me seems to shift, an eerie silence falling over the woods. My senses go on high alert, and I feel a shiver of unease run down my spine. Before I can react, a figure materializes out of thin air, his presence as unsettling as the silence that precedes him.

My heart thrashes in my chest as I scramble to my feet, terror flooding through me. This is my land, 600 acres of it—no one should be here. The man standing before me is undeniably the most attractive man I've ever laid my eyes upon, but there's something calculating about him, an otherworldly gleam in his eyes.

"Who are you?" I stammer, my voice shaking. "What's happening?"

He tilts his head, studying me with a half-smile. "My name is Socrates. And as for what's happening, well, that's a bit more complicated. But first," He steps closer, "Happy Birthday."

I try to back away, but my legs feel like they're made of jelly. "Am I hallucinating? Is this some kind of nightmare?"

He chuckles, a surprising warmth in the sound. "No, Jocelyn. You're not dreaming, and you're not hallucinating. But you've been deceived by those closest to you."

I frown, fear and confusion swirling in my chest. "What do you mean?" *Did Alex cheat on me?*

Socrates takes a step closer, his eyes locked on mine. "I can show you the truth, help you understand what's been hidden from you. But first, you need to trust me."

Before I can utter a word, the world around me shifts abruptly, plunging me into darkness. Panic surges through me, and just as I'm about to be consumed by it, a brilliant light explodes before my eyes.

In an instant, my surroundings transform, leaving me dazed and disoriented. The air, once crisp and cool, is now heavy and warm, infused with the scent of saltwater that envelops me like a gentle embrace. The rhythmic crashing of waves, a lulling soundtrack, fills my ears, drawing me in and creating an almost hypnotic effect. As I stand there, still trying to process this abrupt shift, I become acutely aware that I'm now standing within the confines of a lavish beach estate.

My eyes widen as I take in the grandeur around me; intricately carved pillars stretch toward the sky, supporting an elegant structure with an open design that invites the outside in. The sumptuous fabrics that drape the plush outdoor furniture beckon me to sink into their embrace, providing an air of both luxury and comfort. The colors surrounding me are vivid and alive; the sky, a breathtaking canvas painted with warm oranges, pinks, and purples, is mirrored by the glassy surface of the calm water as the sun dips below the horizon.

I feel the heat of the fine white sand radiating through the soles of my winter boots, a stark contrast to the snowy forest I was in just moments ago. I stand at the center of a U-shaped home. Towering palm trees and lush tropical plants frame the estate, providing a sense of seclusion, as though I've stumbled upon a hidden paradise.

My heart races, and I struggle to catch my breath, my body tingling with a mixture of awe and disbelief. The intensity of the sensations I'm experiencing in this enchanted setting is unlike anything I've ever known. As I absorb the beauty of this place, time seems to slow, drawing out each moment and making it feel as though I've stepped into another world entirely—one where the impossible becomes reality, and the line between dreams and waking life blurs.

With each beat of my heart, I become more captivated by this magical oasis, my mind racing in a futile attempt to make sense of the sudden, otherworldly transition. Yet, despite my confusion, I can't help but feel a strange sense of belonging in this ethereal realm, as if I've finally discovered a long-lost piece of my soul.

I've got to be dreaming.

"What the fuck?" I spin around in disbelief as I try to take in my new surroundings.

My eyes lock onto Socrates, and without a second thought, I bolt in the opposite direction. I sprint through an open breezeway that leads to the beach, my heart pounding in my chest as I desperately search for an escape. My winter boots sink into the sand, and I scream for help, hoping that someone, anyone, will hear me.

When I reach the water's edge, I skid to a stop, the crystal-clear waves lapping at my feet. Frantically, my eyes dart in every direction, searching for a way off this seemingly deserted island. But my heart plummets as I take in the sight before me.

I'm stranded on a narrow strip of land, entirely encircled by a vast, unforgiving ocean. There's no sign of civilization, no boats, or other islands in sight. Just this luxurious villa on this tiny, isolated islet.

A sense of utter despair washes over me, and I struggle to hold back the tears threatening to spill down my cheeks. What has happened? How did I get here? And most importantly, how do I escape this nightmare?

As I approach the villa, I see Socrates standing by the door, a welcoming smile on his face. It's obvious he was waiting for me to realize there's nowhere to run. I force myself to take a deep breath, swallowing my fear and anger as I prepare to confront him.

"Welcome back, Jocelyn," Socrates says, his tone warm and inviting. "I hope you've seen that there's no need to run. I'm here to help you, not harm you."

I look at him skeptically, not quite believing his words. "Fine," I say, trying to keep my voice steady. "Let's talk. But I want answers. And don't think for a second that I'll be trusting you after you kidnapped me." That's what you're supposed to say to kidnappers, no matter how attractive you find them.

Especially when you find them attractive.

Socrates nods, his eyes softening with understanding. "Of course, Jocelyn. I'll give you answers. But first, let's go inside. We have much to discuss, and I'd rather do it in a comfortable setting."

Reluctantly, I follow him into the villa, my mind racing with questions and doubts. I'm filled with an uneasy curiosity and an urgent need to understand why I've been brought to this enchanting yet unfamiliar place. With each step I take, the desire to unravel the mystery of my presence—and this stranger who evokes an inexplicable sense of familiarity—grows stronger.

We enter the villa, and Socrates leads me to a spacious living area. The room is furnished with plush couches, vibrant artwork, and a large, panoramic window that offers an incredible view of the ocean. It's a beautiful setting, but I can't shake the feeling of unease that clings to me, especially as the heat of the place gets to me with my many layers on.

"Please, have a seat." Socrates gestures to one of the couches. I hesitantly sit down, still feeling like this is all some kind of bizarre dream.

Socrates takes a seat across from me and looks at me intently. "I understand you're feeling confused and disoriented, Jocelyn. That's natural, given the circumstances. But I assure you, I'm here to help you and provide answers."

I shake my head, unwilling to accept what he's saying. "This is all too crazy to be real. It has to be a dream or a hallucination."

Socrates raises an eyebrow, but his voice remains calm. "I understand your skepticism, but I assure you, this is very real."

Desperate to prove this is all a dream, I stand up, kick off my boots, and peel off my coat, revealing my winter gear. "See? This doesn't make sense! I was just in the snow, and now I'm in some tropical paradise? Dreams are weird like that."

Socrates watches me with a mixture of amusement and patience. "Jocelyn, I used a form of magic called sifting to bring you here. It's a form of teleportation, if you will. The world you know is only a fraction of what exists."

I scoff, crossing my arms over my chest. "Magic? Really? And I suppose you're going to tell me I have magic too?"

Socrates nods solemnly. "Yes, actually. You're a fae, Jocelyn, just like me. Your magic has been suppressed, but it's there, waiting to be unlocked."

The thought of magic and fae being real is so absurd. There must be another way to prove this is a dream. A crazy, impulsive idea comes to mind, and I find myself laughing at the absurdity of it all. I close the distance between Socrates and me, grabbing his face and pressing my lips against his in a sudden, wild kiss, amused by my own reckless actions.

At first, he's caught off guard, but then his hands come up to frame my face as he kisses me back, his lips soft and surprisingly warm. We share a slow, lingering kiss, the kind that makes you feel like time is standing still. Like I'm right where I belong, and the feeling it evokes makes me want to weep.

When I finally pull away, blinking the fog from my mind away, I search his eyes for any sign that this is just a dream, that my actions have somehow changed the course of this bizarre experience. "There, I kissed you! Dreams are full of random, crazy things, right? So, any moment now, I'll wake up."

A slow grin spreads across Socrates' face, and a mischievous glint appears in his eyes. "Well, Jocelyn, if that was your attempt to prove this isn't real, I must say I'm quite impressed." He takes a step closer to me, his voice taking on a flirtatious edge. "And I wouldn't mind if you continued trying to convince yourself that way."

I blush, feeling heat rise to my cheeks. "That's not what I meant," I stammer, trying to regain my composure. "And your ears are kind of weird."

They're pointy.

Socrates chuckles and raises a hand, making a small flower appear out of thin air. "You think this is a dream, right? Well, let me indulge your imagination a little." He hands me the flower, the magic of its creation casting a mesmerizing spell over me.

I can't help but be captivated by the beauty of the flower and the way he created it. For a moment, I almost believe that it's not a dream.

But the idea of accepting that magic exists is too terrifying, so I cling to the notion that this is just a figment of my imagination.

As if he can read my thoughts, Socrates leans in and whispers, "What do you have to lose, Jocelyn? If this is a dream, you can do anything you want, and I won't hold it against you."

Believing I'm still in a dream, I feel an odd sense of liberation. It's not Alex that I miss, but Remy, Vox, and Niko. And this is yet another fantasy my mind has spun.

Encouraged by his words, I decide to seize the moment, casting aside any lingering guilt. I reach for him and pull him into a deeper, more passionate kiss, and the desire I feel for this enigmatic man in what I believe to be a dream is intoxicating.

As we break apart, Socrates looks at me intently, a smoldering fire in his eyes. "Jocelyn, it's your birthday," he breathes, his voice husky, "if this is a dream, you should enjoy every moment of it."

He leans in, his lips hovering just above mine, teasing me with the promise of another kiss. His hand reaches up, gently caressing my cheek, and the warmth of his touch sends a shiver down my spine.

"Maybe this dream could be enjoyable for both of us," he suggests, his eyes locked on mine, a seductive smile playing on his lips.

I can't help but be drawn to him, the magnetic pull between us undeniable. My heart races, and I feel an unfamiliar mix of excitement and apprehension. If this is a dream, I have nothing to lose by giving in to this stranger who has captured my attention so completely.

But in the back of my mind, doubt lingers. If this is real, if magic exists, and if Socrates is someone I should be wary of, I can't let my guard down completely. I've only just met this man. And as much as I crave the affection he offers, I need answers.

"I'll indulge in this dream," I say, my voice barely above a whisper, "but you have to promise me something."

Socrates raises an eyebrow, intrigued. "And what might that be?"

"You answer my questions, honestly and completely. Then, if I still believe this is a dream, I'll ... consider your offer."

A slow smile spreads across Socrates' face, and he nods in agreement. "Deal. I promise to answer all your questions, Jocelyn. But first, let's make sure you're comfortable. We have a lot to discuss, and I want you to be at ease."

I nod hesitantly, still not entirely convinced that this isn't a dream. But if it's not, I have to find out more about this world, about my place in it, and about the man who brought me here. I can't deny the pull I feel toward him, but I'm also wary of trusting someone who kidnapped me.

Socrates leads me further into a bedroom, gesturing towards a closet. "You can put on something a little more suited for the weather here." He grins.

I pull on a simple, purple sundress made of light fabric, and it hugs my figure just right.

I join Socrates back in the living room, and he gives me a tour of the place. As we walk through the house, I marvel at the beauty of the architecture and its surroundings, a stark contrast to the snow-covered wilderness I had left behind. He seems to notice my appreciation, and a smug grin tugs at the corner of his lips.

"Since you think this is a dream," he says, amusement dancing in his eyes, "is there anything else you'd like me to do? Any magic tricks or feats that might convince you?"

I raise an eyebrow, considering his offer. "Alright, make that vase," I point to an intricately designed vase on a nearby table, "float in mid-air."

With a flick of his wrist, the vase rises from the table and hovers effortlessly in the air. I gasp, a mixture of disbelief and awe washing over me. Socrates chuckles at my reaction, and with another flick, the vase returns to its original position.

"Anything else?" he asks, the playfulness in his voice evident.

I pause for a moment, an idea forming in my mind. "Can you create a fireball in your hand?"

Socrates smirks and extends his palm, conjuring a ball of fire that flickers and dances in the air above his hand. I stare, transfixed, as he extinguishes the flame with a casual wave.

Despite my lingering doubts, I can't help but feel a sense of exhilaration at witnessing these displays of magic. Socrates seems to enjoy my wonder, and for a moment, the tension between us fades, replaced by a growing connection.

As we continue to explore the villa, Socrates shows me more of his magical abilities, each feat more impressive than the last. And though I remain cautious, I can't deny the attraction I feel towards him or the way his presence seems to ignite a fire within me.

At one point, we find ourselves standing on a balcony overlooking the turquoise ocean, the sun setting on the horizon, casting a warm glow over everything. The scene is breathtaking, and I let out a contented sigh.

Socrates leans against the railing, watching me with a tender smile. "You're starting to see the beauty in this world, Jocelyn," he says softly. "And I hope, in time, you'll see that I'm not the enemy."

I glance at him, uncertainty still lingering in my heart. But as I look into his eyes, I see the sincerity there, and I find myself wanting to believe him. For now, I'll keep my guard up, but I can't ignore the pull I feel towards this enigmatic man who has changed my life forever.

In the back of my mind, a nagging worry about the three men I left in the woods persists, making me feel torn between the desire to understand my current situation and the responsibility I have towards them. Perhaps this dream is my subconscious' way of helping me to rest and makes sense of all the changes in my life. So for now, I focus on unraveling the mysteries that surround me, hoping that, in time, all the pieces will fall into place.

CHAPTER FIFTEEN

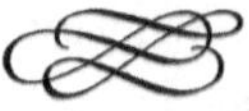

NIKO

I wake to the faint sound of distant voices, and something feels off. The birdsong and morning light filtering through the tent seem a little too quiet, as if something is missing. My heart races as I realize that Jocelyn is no longer nestled in the warmth of our embrace.

Panicked, I gently shake Remy and Vox awake, trying not to let my fear get the better of me. "Jocelyn's gone," I whisper urgently, and their eyes snap open, immediately alert.

We scramble out of the tent, our senses heightened as we listen carefully to the faint voices we hear. Jocelyn's voice cuts off abruptly, and a sense of dread washes over us. We exchange worried glances, knowing that something is wrong—something beyond our control.

Without another word, we fan out, searching for any sign of Jocelyn. The forest is eerily silent, as if it's holding its breath, waiting for us to uncover its secret. I can't shake the feeling that we're running out of time, that every second we spend searching is a second that Jocelyn is slipping further away from us.

The cold morning air bites at our skin as we move swiftly through the trees, trying to follow the fading trail of Jocelyn's scent. Frustration and anger bubble up inside me as we fail to find any concrete leads. I can't help but blame myself for not being more aware of our surroundings. For not keeping her safe.

As we move through the woods, I find myself cursing our carelessness. We should have been more vigilant, should have seen the signs that danger was lurking nearby. But we were too caught up in our own emotions, too focused on our bond with Jocelyn to recognize the threat that was closing in.

Remy, Vox, and I communicate silently through our fae bond, coordinating our search efforts and sharing any information we come across. But with each passing moment, the sickening feeling in the pit of my stomach only grows stronger.

Casting my magic wide, I search for any sign of her, but only sense wolves, rabbits, squirrels, and other tiny creatures. No other humans.

Which means there are magical forces at play. And if we have to go back to the gods and tell them Jocelyn is missing? They'd make sure we'll never get to see her again, even if she is found.

Hours seem to pass as we scour the forest for any trace of our missing charge. The weight of our failure presses down on us, and I can't help but wonder if we'll ever find Jocelyn again, or if she's been lost to us forever.

The sun climbs higher in the sky, casting dappled shadows on the forest floor, and still, we find no sign of her. But we refuse to give up, knowing that we'll do whatever it takes to bring Jocelyn home—even if it means facing the darkest corners of our own fears.

Jocelyn

OUR EXPLORATION of the villa continues, with Socrates showing off more of his magical abilities. The more I witness his power, the more I'm drawn to him. And yet, I can't shake the feeling that I should be cautious. This is all too surreal, and part of me still clings to the belief that it's just a dream.

As we enter a room filled with lush greenery and exotic flowers, I can't help but marvel at the enchanting beauty surrounding me. The air is perfumed with a blend of sweet fragrances, and the vibrant colors of the blossoms are a feast for the eyes. Socrates watches me, his expression soft and filled with tenderness.

"Do you like it?" he asks, his voice gentle.

"It's breathtaking," I admit, my gaze wandering over the stunning flora. "I've never seen anything like it."

He steps closer, the warmth of his body radiating toward me. "I created this room just for you, Jocelyn. It's a place for you to find solace, to escape the world outside, and to simply be."

I turn to face him, my heart fluttering in my chest. "You did this ... for me?"

Socrates nods, his eyes never leaving mine. "Everything I do, I do for you."

The sincerity in his words leaves me speechless. I can't help but be drawn to him, to the man who has turned my world upside down and yet offers me a sanctuary. As our eyes lock, I feel a magnetic pull, a connection that grows stronger with every passing moment.

Tentatively, I reach out and touch his hand. The warmth of his skin sends a jolt through me, and I shiver involuntarily. Socrates' eyes flicker to our entwined fingers, and he gently squeezes my hand in response.

"Jocelyn," he murmurs, "I know this is all overwhelming, but please trust that I'm here for you, to guide and protect you. And to show you the truth of who you really are."

I swallow hard, uncertainty gnawing at me. But as I look into his eyes, I see a glimmer of hope. If this dream truly represents my subconscious trying to resolve my feelings about Alex and the watchers, then maybe Socrates holds the key to the answers I seek, guiding me through this strange new world towards clarity and understanding.

For now, I'll allow myself to be drawn to him, to explore the mysteries he promises to reveal. But I'll remain cautious, always on guard, until I know for certain who I can trust.

And as we stand hand in hand amidst the captivating beauty of the garden, I can't help but feel that the path I've chosen is leading me towards something much greater than I could ever have imagined.

Socrates seems to sense my uncertainty and leads me to a cozy corner of the garden where a plush, oversized loveseat rests among the flowers. He gestures for me to sit, and I hesitantly lower myself onto the cushions, unable to resist the allure of the magical space he's created.

He sits beside me, his body close enough that I can feel the heat radiating from him. "You can relax here, Jocelyn. You're safe with me. Let me take care of you."

I study him for a moment, then decide that since I still believe this is all just a dream, I can indulge a little. "Alright," I say softly, allowing myself to lean into him. His arm wraps around me, pulling me closer, and the warmth and strength of his embrace sends a shiver down my spine. "Where exactly is *here*?"

"The fae realm of Bedlam." Socrates gently brushes a stray strand of hair from my face, his touch electrifying. "You're so incredibly beautiful," he murmurs, his voice filled with reverence.

In this dream-like state, I let my inhibitions slip away, reveling in the attention he's giving me. "Thank you," I whisper, blushing under his gaze.

He smiles, and his eyes seem to dance with a thousand unspoken emotions. "I could spend an eternity just admiring you, Jocelyn. You're a treasure, and I feel unbelievably fortunate to have found you."

My heart flutters at his words, and despite my lingering doubts, I can't help but be drawn to him. We sit like that for what feels like hours, wrapped in each other's arms, basking in the tranquility of the garden. Time seems to lose all meaning, and I find myself wanting to stay in this moment forever.

As the air begins to cool, Socrates leans in, his lips brushing against my ear. "I wish I could make this moment last an eternity," he whispers. "But there's so much more I want to show you, so many wonders you've yet to discover."

I pull back to look into his eyes, my curiosity piqued. "What do you mean?"

Socrates grins, a mischievous glint in his eyes. "There are countless magical realms, each more wondrous than the last, and I want to explore them all with you, Jocelyn. I want you to experience the full extent of your power and potential."

In that moment, the idea of adventuring through magical realms with Socrates by my side is undeniably enticing, and I find myself wanting to believe that this dream could become my reality. For now, I'll let myself be carried away by his promises and enjoy the connection we share, even if it's only fleeting. And when I wake up, I'll carry the memory of this enchanting encounter with me, a reminder of the limitless possibilities that exist within the realm of dreams.

I chew on my lower lip, mulling over the words Socrates had just spoken. The idea of having such an immense decision before me is overwhelming. But there's something that doesn't quite make sense to me.

"Why are you giving me an option?" I ask, curiosity getting the better of me. "If I'm supposed to be a part of the fae world, why do I get a choice to stay in the human one?"

Socrates hesitates for a moment, as if weighing his words carefully. "The fae gods didn't want to give you a choice, because you have a destiny to fulfill in our world. However, I couldn't stand by and let them force you into a life you may not want, especially after being raised in the human realm."

"A choice about what?"

"Magic. The council that governs fae guardians bound you. You've been without it your whole life. If you'd grown up in the fae realm, you would've been using it for decades now. When we're without, it can really mess with our emotions."

My heart misses a beat. My emotions have been all over the place for so long now, and I couldn't work out why. "Why didn't your council want me to have magic again?"

"For five hundred years, fae children were rare. Everyone wanted them, and kidnappings were at an all-time high in the rare chance a baby was born in any of the fae realms. Their families would move to

Earth until the fae child reached maturity, then they'd go back to the fae realms when kidnapping was no longer a threat."

He looks into my eyes, his expression softening at what he sees there. "I believe that you should have the opportunity to make an informed decision, to choose the path that feels right to you. I will gladly follow you to the ends of any realm and protect you. You should know that I will always be by your side, regardless of your choice. It's why I tried to unbind your magic the night the fae guardians left you in my care a little over a month ago."

"Why'd they do that?"

"To get permission to reveal themselves to you as part of this 'save your marriage' charade." He pauses, seeming to choose his words carefully. "Rolls was so excited to see me. I brought him a pocket full of game meat, but when you started having nightmares, he kept barking to try to wake you, so I had to muzzle him. I'm sorry. He probably feels so betrayed."

I sit up. "You what?"

"I used a spell to induce nightmares, which can often cause strong enough emotions to release the bind on your magic. The others arrived before it could do its job, and I had to take off before the others caught me. I'm so sorry."

"Oh," I whisper. As I consider Socrates' words, I remember the magic I've seen him perform and a thought occurs to me. "Can you ... remove the bind on my magic?" I ask hesitantly, not entirely sure if it's possible or even a good idea.

Socrates smiles warmly, his eyes lighting up at the suggestion. "There's nothing I'd love more. Before I do it ... you need to know that it's probably going to be difficult to control for a long time."

I nod, accepting the warning, and Socrates extends his hand towards me.

CHAPTER SIXTEEN

SOCRATES

The flickering candlelight bathes Jocelyn's face in a soft, amber hue, her cascading blonde hair a shining waterfall framing her heart-shaped face. Emerald eyes, alive with anticipation and uncertainty, peer up at me, and the profound responsibility of guiding her through this pivotal moment in her life grips me.

I've wanted this moment for so long.

Bound to her by an intense connection that neither of us yet fully understands, the knowledge of our intertwined fates whispers to me, forging a fierce protectiveness and affection. I'm prepared to venture into the grayest of moral grounds to ensure her safety and happiness. I've toed that line more than I care to admit when it comes to her, but I'd do worse. I want her to unravel the truth about her heritage and our bond in her own time, and for now, that means delicately treading a respectful line.

With a wave of my hand and a murmur of a spell, the surroundings morph before our eyes. Sifting her from the garden to our bedroom, I bring the outdoors inside. The room transforms into a serene, sacred space filled with lush greenery and a soft, warm glow that envelops us. The air, scented with the calming fragrances of jasmine and sandalwood, embraces us like a comforting caress.

I guide Jocelyn to the plush cushion at the room's center, coaxing her to lie down. The gravity of the situation feels heavy in my chest, and I'm determined to ensure she grasps the significance of the choice before her.

"Before we begin, Jocelyn, I must know that you genuinely want this," I say, my voice soft yet insistent, my eyes probing hers for any trace of doubt. Whatever she wants, she can have, because her joy is all that matters to me. "Releasing your magic is a monumental step, and once taken, there's no turning back."

Taking a steadying breath, the resolve in her gaze gleams like polished steel. "I understand. And yes, I want this. I want to know who I am."

A wave of relief courses through me. Having magic puts her at risk, and—

He'll come for her.

But I'm ready for him when he does. I'd die a million painful ways, endure countless torture before I'd let him get her.

Kneeling beside Jocelyn, I trace a protective circle around her form with an intricate pattern of glowing symbols. The air within the circle hums with the resonance of the ancient power they hold. With each symbol etched, the energies converge, weaving a protective barrier designed to shield her during this momentous transition.

Once the circle is complete, I turn my attention to Jocelyn, my voice a gentle whisper. "When I release the bind on your magic, you may feel a rush of sensations, like a tidal wave of energy washing over you. Stay grounded and let yourself become one with the magic coursing through your veins."

She nods, her eyes reflecting a cocktail of determination and uncertainty. My heart swells with admiration for her courage, and I offer her a reassuring smile.

Taking a deep breath, I position my hands over her body, palms facing down, and begin reciting the incantation. The air crackles with power as my voice weaves the spell. As the final words leave my lips, I feel the binding spell on Jocelyn's magic break like brittle glass, releasing her true potential.

A gasp escapes her as a wave of magical energy floods her system. The glow of the symbols intensifies, reinforcing the protective circle around her. She writhes, caught in the maelstrom of her unleashed power. I remain at her side, a steadfast anchor amidst the storm.

Gradually, her convulsions subside, and her breath steadies. Her eyes flutter open, their once-vivid green now shimmering with a newfound radiance.

As Jocelyn gazes up at me, I feel the burgeoning strength of our bond, the pull of our fates drawing us closer. And while we've barely begun to unravel the intricate tapestry that binds us together, I know that whatever lies ahead, I'll protect her, guide her, and love her until the end of time.

Even if it kills me.

~

Jocelyn

As the tingling sensation in my fingertips intensifies and spreads throughout my body, it awakens a dormant power within me. This strange yet exhilarating energy surges, filling every fiber of my being. Eager to test my newfound abilities, I glance at Socrates, whose eyes brim with encouragement and reverence.

Convinced that I'm still dreaming, I'm unafraid of any potential consequences. As I explore this magical awakening, a newfound confidence takes root within me. The sensation of control over this mysterious energy fills me with wonder and excitement, leaving me eager to delve further into its depths.

Socrates watches me intently, his proud and approving gaze supporting me as I take my first steps into a world of magic and limitless potential.

I decide to start small, attempting to levitate a pillow from the couch. To my surprise, the pillow shoots across the room, slamming into a vase and shattering it into pieces. Socrates chuckles, fixing the vase with a wave of his hand and looking at me adoringly.

Encouraged by his support, I try again, this time focusing on a small glass on the table. I concentrate hard, willing it to rise gently into the air. Instead, the glass shatters, shards flying in all directions. Socrates quickly steps in, repairing the glass and shielding us from the debris with a protective barrier.

Despite the chaos I'm causing, Socrates remains patient and loving, watching me with reverence in his eyes as I continue my clumsy attempts at magic. Each time I inadvertently destroy something, he's right there to fix it, never once expressing frustration or disappointment.

What a welcome fucking reprieve from my husband.

As I grow bolder in my experimentation, the destruction only increases. I try to summon a gentle breeze, but instead create a whirlwind that scatters furniture and belongings throughout the room. I attempt to change the color of the walls, but instead, the paint begins to drip and slide off, leaving a messy puddle on the floor.

Yet through it all, Socrates remains by my side, helping me learn to control my powers while simultaneously repairing the damage I've caused. The more time we spend together, the more I find myself drawn to him, captivated by his unwavering kindness and patience.

As the day goes on, my control over my magic remains tenuous at best, but Socrates never falters in his support. In the midst of the chaos and destruction, I can't help but feel a sense of belonging and acceptance in his presence. And as the sun begins to set, bathing us in gentle light and splashing over the villa, I know that there is still so much more to learn and discover about my powers and this strange new dream world. With Socrates by my side, I'm willing to embrace the unknown and see where this journey takes me.

And I'm really not looking forward to waking from this.

Much as I long to be back with Remy, Vox and Niko, waking up means having to deal with my train wreck of a life. I'm not ready for that. Feeling exhausted from the day's excitement and destruction, I decide it's time for a shower. Since I still believe I'm dreaming, I don't care that Socrates is with me as I undress and step into the luxurious bathroom. He stands near the door, his gaze never leaving me, but there's a tenderness and wonder in his eyes that makes me feel cherished rather than objectified.

The warm water cascades over my body, washing away the stress and confusion of the day. Socrates remains nearby, occasionally offering to help me with my hair or to scrub my back, but he never crosses any boundaries I'm uncomfortable with. His presence is a constant comfort, even as I continue to believe this is all just an intricate dream.

Once I'm finished with my shower, I wrap myself in a plush towel and step out of the bathroom, finding Socrates waiting for me with a gentle smile. He leads me to the bedroom, where the bed is covered in soft, inviting linens. I slip under the covers, and he joins me.

As we lie in bed together, Socrates and I take the opportunity to get to know each other better. The bright glow of moonlight—there are several moons here—streaming through the window creates an intimate atmosphere, and I find myself opening up to him in ways I never expected.

"So, tell me more about yourself," I say, my fingers tracing absent-minded patterns on his chest. "What's it like being a Fae Guardian?"

Socrates' eyes soften with a distant look, as if recalling countless memories. "It's a great responsibility, but one that I take very seriously. I've been watching over Fae who were sent to the Earth realm for many years. I help guide and protect them, ensuring their safety and well-being."

"What brought you to me?" I ask, curiosity piqued.

A tender smile graces his lips. "You're special, Jocelyn. Special to me. But that's a story for another day."

I blush at his words, touched by the sincerity and affection in his voice. "What do you like to do for fun?" I ask, eager to learn more about him.

He chuckles. "I enjoy exploring the different realms, discovering new and interesting places. I also like to read and learn about the various cultures and histories of the fae worlds. But, if I'm honest, some of my favorite moments have been spent watching you grow and learn, witnessing the incredible person you've become."

Feeling a sense of trust and openness, I hesitantly share my dilemma. "I've been struggling with the whole situation with Alex and the others. I'm not sure what to do or what's best for me. And I can't help but feel a little apprehensive about leaving Remy, Niko, and Vox behind."

Socrates' brow furrows, and he reaches out to gently touch my arm. "Jocelyn, I believe the best thing for you would be to let go of Alex and stay here in Bedlam with me. We can build a life together, and I can help you embrace your true self and your fae heritage. As for Remy, Niko, and Vox, true friendships transcend realms, and I'm sure you'll find a way to maintain your connection with them."

His words send a warmth through my chest. Even though I'm still not entirely convinced this isn't a dream, there's something so comforting about having someone who genuinely cares about me and has been watching over me for all these years.

We talk late into the night, our laughter mingling with shared stories, and I find myself feeling more connected to Socrates than I ever thought possible. When his gaze lingers on my lips and he leans in to kiss me, desire and affection flooding his eyes, I don't hesitate to meet him halfway.

Our lips meet in a gentle kiss, the passion growing with each passing moment. As we break apart for air, Socrates looks down at me with a hunger in his eyes that leaves no doubt as to what he wants next.

My heart races in my chest as he cups my face with a tenderness that nearly sends me to tears. His lips find mine again, kissing me with a renewed intensity that sets my body ablaze. Our hands roam over each other's bodies, exploring every inch as if we've been longing for this moment for an eternity.

I feel his arousal pressing against me as he deepens the kiss, his tongue seeking entrance into my mouth. I part my lips, inviting him in, and our tongues dance together in a fiery passion. Socrates pulls me closer to him, his hands trailing down my back and gripping my hips with a fierce possessiveness. I moan into his mouth, unable to resist the raw desire that courses through my veins.

Breaking our kiss, he trails hot lips down my neck, his hands pulling down the straps of my nightgown. I gasp as the cool air hits my skin, but the sensation is quickly replaced with warmth as his mouth finds my breast. He sucks and nibbles at the sensitive flesh until I'm writhing beneath him, unable to control the moans escaping my lips.

I reach down to stroke him through his pants, feeling his hardness strain against the fabric.

He growls low in his throat, and it's the hottest thing I've ever heard. His fingertips find the hem of my nightgown, sliding it upward until I'm bare beneath him. His mouth trails kisses down my torso, stopping at my navel to tease it with his tongue. I arch my back, my hands threading through his hair as he continues his path southward.

Socrates doesn't hesitate as he buries his face between my legs, his tongue finding my most sensitive spot with ease. I cry out in pleasure, the sensations overwhelming me as he licks and nibbles at my clit with his tongue.

His arms circle my waist, and he hoists me up so my thighs rest on his shoulders before he falls back onto the bed, and I'm straddled over his face. Afraid of suffocating him, I hover just over him, but he growls, yanking my hips so he bears all my weight.

My hips rock into his face, and my back arches as he increases the pressure and strokes my clit with his tongue. His fae magic caresses my breasts as he grips my thighs.

I cry out, the sensations too much to bear as I come hard, unable to control the quaking of my body and the sensation of hot wetness pooling between my thighs.

Socrates pulls me back so I'm lying across his chest, his hand stroking my stomach. He chuckles, "For more than a decade, I've wanted to taste you."

A grin tugs at my lips as he sits up, sliding me into his lap. I work to unbutton his shirt, revealing a chest full of golden tattoos that shimmer in the pale light of the room.

My fingers trace the hard planes of his muscles, following the intricate pattern on his skin. When I reach his belt, he sucks in a breath.

I smirk. "Are you nervous?"

"Maybe I have a little performance anxiety." He grins down at me as I press my lips to his lower abs, feeling them contract under me.

"Why do I have a hard time believing that?" I whisper against his stomach, my tongue teasing the soft skin just above his belt.

His hands tangle in my hair. "You're playing with fire, Jocelyn."

"Am I?" I look up at him, my fingers working to undo the belt from its loop.

He helps me push his pants off, and I take in the sight of his erection, wanting nothing more than to taste his beautiful cock. I slide off of him and onto the bed, taking him in my mouth, engulfing him completely.

A curse and a prayer leave his lips, and his hands tangle in my hair as my tongue explores his thick, heavy erection.

I work my way down, pulling him out of my mouth with a pop. "You're so warm," I whisper, pressing soft kisses to his thighs.

Magic radiates off of him, the air is charged with his power, and I want nothing more than to worship him as it brushes with my own. The sensation is so foreign to me.

I cup his balls, feeling their weight in my hand and then my tongue is on him, teasing his flesh as I lap at him, tasting him and absorbing his power.

I pull his cock out and then slip it back into my mouth, my teeth grazing his shaft as he groans, "Oh, fuck."

I hollow out my cheeks, and his hand tightens on my hair as he pulls me off him.

"Your throat is beautiful, but it's your pussy that needs my come. I can smell the perfume of your desire in the air."

"You can smell my desire?" Embarrassment floods my cheeks.

"Yes," he purrs. "Sweeter than any drug."

"Can you taste it?" I whisper.

He groans, pulling me up to him, "Are you trying to kill me?"

"I want you to come inside of me, and then I want to taste you, like this." I crawl up his lap until I'm seated in it. Bringing my mouth to his, he devours me, as though I'm the very blood in his veins and he needs me to live.

His lips find my jaw, then my neck, settling on my pulse. I arch my back, urging him on, but he only groans against my chest, his hands stilling.

"Jocelyn. Fuck, I ..." He pants. "You have no idea how long I've wanted this. Wanted you. I mean, I still do, and will until the end of time. But if we have sex right now, there's no going back."

"Going back?" I pull back so I can look into his eyes. "What do you mean?"

I wouldn't mind seeing how this fantasy plays out. Perhaps this is what my whole life couldn't have been like if I hadn't married Alex.

"This?" he gestures between us. "Means everything to me. And until it does for you, I can't in good conscience sleep with you. You'd never forgive me."

"I'm not a virgin, Socrates." I chuckle. "That ship sailed years ago. My husband and I used to have sex just about every single night." Sometimes several times a day.

And I had sex with Remy, Niko, and Vox.

Agony flashes across his face. "I know," he whispers, twining his fingers with mine. Meeting his eyes, I witness an eternity of heartache flash in them as he continues speaking. "Five-thousand-one-hundred-ninety-three days you've been married. But you lost your virginity the night of your sorority initiation six-thousand-eight-hundred-and-one days ago. You've had ten lovers since, having had sex four-thousand-two-hundred-sixty-two times, and oral s—"

"How do you know all of this?" I laugh.

"Because I felt each one."

I suppose this is my dreamscape, so he's really a figment of my own imagination, so of course he felt it all. "I'm sorry." I press my forehead to his. "We don't have to, but I want you to know I really, really want to."

Though I've only known him a short period of time, I feel like I've known this man my whole life. Having sex with him doesn't feel like a choice because it isn't. I crave it with everything I am.

As though I might die if I don't.

He stills, searching my eyes. "Jocelyn," he starts, but I interrupt him.

"If you want me, then you need to take me, Socrates."

I don't have to tell him again. He wraps me in his arms and lays me onto the bed, his lips pressing reverent kisses to jaw.

His breath stirs against my neck, and he whispers, "Jocelyn?"

"Yeah?"

"I need to apologize now, because I'm about to fuck you like I hate you, but that couldn't be furthest from the truth."

I don't have time to respond, because he's plunging into me in a single thrust, his cock filling me so completely, it borders the edge of pain and pleasure. I gasp, my body adjusting to his size. His lips crash against mine as he devours me, our tongues dancing as I match him stroke for stroke.

He ravages me, my body his playground as he pounds into me, our bodies slapping together. I grip his shoulders, clawing his back as I match his intensity. His roars of pleasure mingle with mine and soon the air is filled with the sound of us making love—so raw and passionate that it robs the breath from my lungs.

My pleasure builds until I'm on the brink of orgasm, but Socrates isn't ready to let go yet. He slows down and teases me with slow, shallow strokes that send a wave of pleasure radiating through my entire body until I'm screaming out his name, begging for more.

The urge to bite, to lay claim, consumes me until it's the only desire in my body. When he throws his head back in pleasure, I surge forward, sinking my teeth into his flesh. The taste of his blood fills my mouth, and I'm surprised to find it's sweet; not a coppery taste, but like honey as it coats my tongue.

Warmth fills my chest, a living thing blooming from within as Socrates finds the vein at my neck. I feel no pain, only unimaginable pleasure as he drives himself deep inside me one last time before collapsing beside me, our bodies still buzzing with ecstasy.

We lay tangled together in bed for what feels like an eternity before Socrates gazes at me tenderly, brushing a strand of hair from my face and pressing a gentle kiss to my forehead. "You okay?" he asks softly, and I can only nod—words failing me in this moment.

Resting my head on his chest, I breathe in his soothing scent. I'm at peace in his arms, and the feel of our magic twining together feels so right as I drift off to sleep.

~

WHEN I WAKE the next morning, I'm surprised to find myself still in the luxurious beach villa, Socrates sleeping peacefully beside me. The realization that I might not be dreaming after all begins to dawn on me, and a mix of excitement and apprehension fills my chest.

I miss Vox, Niko, and Remy. Rolls, too, though I'm surprised I don't miss Alex. Probably because I've spent so long feeling so neglected, he's taught me how to live without him this entire time.

If this is real … it might be a chance at a better life. Socrates is the kindest soul I've ever encountered, and my soul yearns for his like it does for Remy. But who am I kidding, though?

He's a dream. A figment of my imagination. It's not like he can be mine in real life.

And yet … he feels real, and the idea of him being made up in my head sends a flare of panic through me, just as the idea of this being real scares me.

What do you do if your dream guy turns out to be real?

I feel myself start to panic, but Socrates seems to sense it—he rolls over and catches my face in his hands. His striking blue eyes have flecks of gold that seem to sparkle in the rays of the sun streaming through the windows. His touch makes me feel grounded again, and when he brings his lips to mine, I can't help but melt into him.

As we pull away, Socrates brushes his thumb over my cheek. "Are you okay?"

"I don't know," I admit, snuggling closer to him. "I'm confused."

None of this makes sense. "If I'm allegedly fae, why am I still on Earth? Why didn't my parents take me back to ... the fae realm?"

How did I not see they were fae? They were great parents, but they spend a lot of time traveling to far reaches of the globe. Is that how they do it without being missed?

Socrates hesitates, pain flashing across his features. "I didn't want to tell you like this." He runs a hand through his raven hair before gripping it in his fist.

"What?" I demand, my heart pounding in my chest, suddenly feeling a tight knot in my stomach.

He takes a deep breath, his eyes filled with sorrow. "Your Earth parents aren't fae. And I don't know how else to tell you this, Jocelyn, so I'm just going to say it, but your biological mom—your fae mom— was killed when you were very small."

"What?" A wave of shock and grief washes over me, and my heart feels like it's being squeezed. "Why? When?" I manage to choke out, tears threatening to spill over. If this is real, I would know this— someone would have told me. Wouldn't they?

"Your Earth parents aren't your real parents, Jocelyn. King Valtorious, the ruler of the realm you're from, is a controlling king and ordered all children brought to him to raise. When your mother fled to the Earth realm with you just after your birth, he had his people hunt her."

Images of my childhood and the people I thought were my parents flood my mind. Their warm smiles, the times we spent together as a family, the love they showered upon me. The revelation makes my heart ache even more.

I'm *adopted*?

"Fae guardians don't get assigned to just any fae child. They're assigned to orphans at risk, Jocelyn."

"So fae guardians raised me?" The thought of being raised by magical beings while unaware of my true heritage raises the hair on my arms.

"No, fae guardians placed you into a loving home, altering both your memories and those of your mortal family so there's no suspicion. You see, Jocelyn, fae children grow at an accelerated rate compared to humans. We can reach full physical maturity in just a couple years," Socrates explains gently, gauging my reaction.

My eyes widen in disbelief. "So, my parents have only known me as an adult? They don't have true memories of raising me as a child?"

He nods solemnly. "Yes, that's correct. The guardians took great care to ensure your safety and to preserve the illusion of a normal human life, even though it meant altering the memories of those who cared for you."

I shake my head, trying to absorb all this information. It feels like I'm trapped in the most elaborate dream I've ever concocted. "But why am I not back in the fae realm, then? I'm no longer under threat, right?" I ask, seeking reassurance.

Socrates hesitates for a moment, his expression turning solemn. "That's ... not entirely true. You see, you're not just any fae, Jocelyn. You have a unique and powerful destiny that many in the fae realms believe you're meant to fulfill. King Valtorious still wants you under his control, and there are others who would use you for their own purposes."

I stare at him, disbelief and fear warring within me. "So, I'm still in danger?"

He nods, his eyes filled with concern. "Yes, but that's why I'm here, to protect you and ensure your safety. I've been doing everything in my power to keep you hidden and safe."

"But why haven't we returned to the fae realms if I'm still in danger?" I ask, trying to make sense of it all.

"You're in Bedlam now." Socrates takes a deep breath before continuing. "I wanted to give you a choice. You have a right to decide your own path, whether that means embracing your destiny in the fae realms or remaining on Earth. The other fae guardians and the council may not agree, but I believe you deserve that freedom."

His words touch my heart, and I can see the love and devotion in his eyes. Despite my lingering doubts and confusion, I find myself wanting to trust him and lean on him for support.

"But what if I choose to remain on Earth?" I ask. "Wouldn't that put everyone around me in danger?"

Socrates shakes his head. "I'll do everything in my power to ensure the safety of those you care about. If you choose to stay on Earth, I'll remain by your side, protecting you and your loved ones. If you decide to stay in the fae realms, then I will stand beside you as you face whatever challenges come your way."

As I take in his words, I feel a sense of comfort and reassurance settle into my bones. This may be the most bizarre dream I've ever had, but there's something undeniably real about the connection I share with Socrates. Whatever the truth of my situation, I know that I can rely on him to be there for me at least in this dreamscape, and that's a feeling I'm not ready to let go of just yet.

CHAPTER SEVENTEEN

VOX

An eerie silence hangs heavy in the air, wrapping itself around me like a shroud. Jocelyn is gone, vanished without a trace, and a cold dread coils in my gut. It's our duty to keep her safe, and yet, we've failed her.

Even calling myself her guardian feels like a disservice to what she really is to me. To us. We've had other charges over the years, all we've never felt anything other than duty for.

It would've been heartbreaking to lose one. But to lose Jocelyn? The woman who's managed to worm herself under my skin, burrow right into my heart?

That's soul crushing.

An agonizing defeat.

Remy, Niko, and I left the camp, and now stand in the center of Jocelyn's abandoned room, our eyes scanning every corner as if the answers we seek might suddenly materialize. The walls, once a testament to her vibrant spirit, now feel hollow and lifeless. The kidnapper, we suspect, is likely someone—or something—wielding magic, and the possibility that they could be fae leaves a bitter taste on my tongue. I can't believe Socrates would risk everything to take her ... but we can't ignore the possibility that another guardian would risk the wrath of the council to be with her.

We did.

Alex is in New York—we sifted there to check—and a scan of his computer proves he's been in meetings all day and attended the work lunch as scheduled. No cheating, just an asshole married to his work.

Remy's voice is strained with concern as he speaks, his emerald eyes filled with a steely resolve. "We need to find her, and fast. There's no telling what could be happening to her right now." He's trying to put up a strong front, but I see the trembling of his hands, and the panic in the way his chest expands with every quick inhale as he tries to suck in air. He's barely hanging on.

Niko nods, his dark, cropped hair glinting in the soft pitch of the room's lights. "Even if it means losing her, we need to tell the Council soon in case they need to intervene. I don't want to risk her life."

I clench my fists, my agreement absolute. "We'll find her, whatever it takes."

It would kill me never to see her again. But to exist in a universe in which she doesn't? The thought of it cleaves my chest in two.

We sift back to their property up north and divide our efforts, focusing on our individual magical strengths. Remy, as her mate, searches for any lingering trace of Jocelyn's essence. His connection to her runs deep, and if there's even a faint hint of her presence, he'll be able to track her down.

Niko, who has spent years cultivating an extensive network of informants, gets to work contacting them for any information about unusual magical occurrences or sightings of Jocelyn. These infor-mants range from supernatural beings like shifters, witches, and other fae to humans with a keen eye for the magical world.

Some of them are shopkeepers who deal in magical artifacts, while others are travelers who have seen things beyond the veil. Over time, Niko has built a web of connections that stretches far and wide, ensuring that he's always well-informed about the comings and goings in the world of magic. He reaches out to them all, desperate for any scrap of information that could lead them to Jocelyn.

As for me, I hone in on my expertise in magical detection, trying to sense any residual magic that might lead us to her. My abilities allow me to pick up on the faintest traces of magical energy, like breadcrumbs scattered across the fabric of reality. If Jocelyn's kidnapper used magic to take her, there should be some evidence of it—and I'm determined to find it.

Together, the three of us work tirelessly, pooling our skills and resources in the hope of finding Jocelyn before it's too late.

Hours bleed into one another as we relentlessly pursue any hint of Jocelyn's whereabouts. When we regroup in the living room of our safe house, a place hidden deep within a dense forest near Jocelyn's house, our findings are frustratingly inconclusive. This safe house was built by us as a contingency plan, in case Jocelyn ever needed a quick escape. A portal in the basement allows for rapid transportation to and from the house.

Remy has discovered a faint trail of Jocelyn's essence, but it's elusive and ever-changing, making it nearly impossible to determine her location, making us suspect an anti-detection spell is at play. Niko's contacts have heard whispers of a powerful fae spotted in the area, yet nothing concrete. My own attempts to detect residual magic have led me to several potential leads, but nothing definitive.

Still, we refuse to yield. The three of us exchange glances, each of us vowing to bring Jocelyn home.

"We'll keep searching," I say, my voice thick. "We'll find her, and we'll bring her back."

Remy and Niko nod, their eyes alight with unwavering resolve. We may not have all the answers yet, but we won't rest until Jocelyn is safe once more.

As our search continues, I worry about what Jocelyn must be enduring. We've always been there to shield her from harm, but now she's alone, facing untold dangers. The thought ignites a fierce protectiveness within me, and I silently swear that once we find her, I'll never let her out of my sight again.

Crashing to the snow, I hang my head. "We must consider the possibility he's found her."

"Fuck," Niko mutters.

Remy picks up a snow-covered rock and chucks it into the forest. "Or could it be that Socrates has had her this whole time?" he questions, reflecting on the earlier suspicion we had about her potential kidnapper.

"I think I'd rather Socrates has her than she be stuck with that monster." My voice comes out haunted.

Niko helps me to my feet. "If there's a possibility he's found her, we need to check."

KING VALTORIOUS' castle looms over the city of Lynsandria, a dark, foreboding structure that seems to swallow the light. It's situated at the heart of Romarie, a once-thriving city now reduced to a shadow of its former self under the tyrannical rule of the power-hungry king. The streets are a labyrinth of cobblestone alleys and towering buildings, now worn and crumbling from years of neglect.

From what I've learned, Valtorious is ruthless, keeping a harem of powerful fae concubines to reproduce for him so he can siphon their magic. The brides and their children are nothing more than pawns in his twisted game, their lives consumed by his insatiable hunger for power. Among his numerous offspring, Jocelyn stands out as a potential heir due to her unique blend of magical talents inherited from both her parents. The king believes that Jocelyn's rare abilities would make her a formidable asset in his quest for domination.

He's a monster.

However, there is an ancient prophecy that foretells if Valtorious can capture Jocelyn before she turns forty, he can exploit her powers to strengthen his rule. Conversely, if she manages to evade him until she reaches the age of forty, she will possess the strength and knowledge to defeat him and end his oppressive reign. This adds urgency to Valtorious' pursuit of Jocelyn and further raises the stakes of her fight for freedom.

The thought of Jocelyn being trapped within those cold, unforgiving walls leaves a gnawing pit of dread in my stomach. If she's back there, it means she's at the mercy of a king who cares for nothing but his own wicked desires.

The three of us exchange worried glances, our faces a mix of determination and dread. We can't ignore the possibility, no matter how much we wish to. Jocelyn's safety is our priority, and if that means confronting the horrors of Romarie and Valtorious himself, so be it.

We set off toward the city, our steps heavy with the weight of the task ahead. As the castle comes into view, I steel myself for what we might find. After a recent problem with Aggonid, the ruler of the fae underworld, King Valtorious has set up powerful wards around the castle, preventing anyone from simply sifting in or out. These wards force us to approach on foot, stealthily navigating our way through the city and its defenses. The challenge of bypassing the wards only serves to remind us of the danger Jocelyn faces and the lengths we'll have to go to in order to save her.

If he's hurt her ... I'll flay him. Strip the meat from his bones, and then piss on his husk.

We cast an invisibility spell over ourselves, the gossamer threads of magic weaving around our forms, masking us from view. As much as I long to storm the castle and demand Jocelyn's return, we must tread cautiously. Alerting Valtorious to our presence would only serve to place her in greater peril.

As we draw closer to the castle, I try to focus on our mission, but the concern for Jocelyn's well-being gnaws at the edges of my thoughts. I love her, and the notion of her in the clutches of such a vile creature sends a wave of fury through me.

We traverse the castle's shadowed halls, our steps as silent as whispers, our senses heightened to an almost unbearable degree. Every distant sound, each subtle flicker of movement, sets our nerves on edge. We stand prepared to face any challenge, confront any foe, in our relentless pursuit to find Jocelyn.

The grand hallway we pass through is adorned with tarnished chandeliers, their dim glow splashing eerie shadows upon the walls.

Once-majestic tapestries depicting scenes of war and seduction now hang in tatters, reflecting the decay that has seeped into the heart of this place. As we venture further into the castle, we find ourselves navigating a maze of twisting corridors lined with grotesque statues and faded murals. The once-gleaming marble floors are chipped and stained, their polished surfaces worn by the passage of countless footsteps.

Descending into the depths of the castle, we enter the dungeon, where the dank air chokes our lungs as we search each cell for any sign of Jocelyn. The cold, damp walls seem to close in around us, their rough stone surfaces bearing witness to the horrors inflicted upon those who have been held captive here.

As we move cautiously through the castle, I spot Valtorious entering a dimly lit room. His tall, imposing frame is clad in dark, regal clothing, his broad shoulders emphasized by the rich fabric. A heavy crown sits upon his head, his jet-black hair cascading in waves to his shoulders. His tan skin, flawless and ageless like that of all fae, might have been attractive if not for the wickedness that radiates from him, marring his features.

Motioning for Niko and Remy to follow, we approach cautiously, taking care not to alert anyone to our presence. We peer into the room, our eyes quickly adjusting to the darkness, and witness the depths of Valtorious' malevolence firsthand.

Inside, a group of children huddles together, their faces etched with a mix of terror and exhaustion. Valtorious stands before them, his towering frame casting a dark shadow across the floor. A cruel sneer curls his lips as he berates them for some perceived failure. His voice is cold and sharp, the words cutting through the air like a dagger.

One of the children, a young, red-headed girl with trembling hands, steps forward hesitantly, attempting to explain their situation. Her voice wavers, choked with fear, but her resolve to speak her truth is apparent. Valtorious listens for a moment, his eyes narrowing, before he erupts with rage.

In an instant, his hand shoots out, gripping the young girl's arm with bruising force. She gasps, her eyes wide with terror as she tries to pull away from his grasp. I stalk forward to intercept as the other children cower in fear, watching helplessly as their companion suffers at Valtorious' hands. The scene unfolding before us makes my blood boil, my heart aching for the pain inflicted on these innocent children.

Before I step out of the shadows, he releases the girl, who crumples to the ground, her arm red and throbbing with pain. Valtorious turns to address the rest of the children, his eyes filled with malice. "Let this be a lesson to all of you," he hisses. "I will not tolerate failure or insubordination. If you cannot perform your duties to my satisfaction, you will suffer the consequences."

As the scene unfolds before us, it's becoming increasingly difficult for Niko, Remy, and me to remain mere spectators. We exchange conflicted glances, struggling to balance our mission's secrecy with the instinct to intervene and protect the innocent.

Valtorious storms out of the room, leaving the children in a terrified huddle, and we know we can't just stand by and let this injustice continue.

Once we're certain Valtorious is far enough away, we materialize, our invisibility wearing off. The children gasp, their eyes wide with shock and fear at our sudden appearance. I hold my hands up, palms out, in a gesture of peace. "We're not here to harm you," I say softly, trying to reassure them. "We're here to help."

The children exchange wary glances, uncertainty etched across their faces. After a moment of hesitation, the oldest child, a girl with black waves, speaks up. "Who are you? And what do you want?"

"My name is Vox, and these are my friends, Niko and Remy. We've come to this castle on a mission, and we couldn't just ignore what Valtorious did to you," I explain, my voice gentle as I crouch so I'm at their level. "We want to help you escape this place and take you somewhere safe."

The children's eyes widen in surprise and hope. The thought of leaving this nightmarish existence behind sparks a newfound courage within them. They whisper among themselves before the girl speaks again. "If you can really help us, we'll trust you. But where will you take us?"

"We'll take you to Bedlam," I say, a reassuring smile tugging at my lips. "It's a sanctuary for people like you who need protection. You'll be safe there, I promise. Their high king and queen are kind people with several of their own children."

The kids, their resolve strengthened by the hope we offer, agree to follow us. As we navigate the castle's maze-like corridors, we carefully avoid detection, the weight of our responsibility to these children only adding to our purpose.

Once we've reached a secluded spot within the castle grounds, Remy opens a portal to Bedlam. As the shimmering gateway materializes before us, the children marvel at the magic, their expressions a mix of awe and trepidation. As minors, their magic probably hasn't come in yet. And if they're prisoners, they probably aren't around a lot of people who use it, aside from it being used against them.

"Go on," I encourage, my voice quiet. "You'll be safe there, and you'll find others who have escaped similar fates. Trust us."

One by one, the children step through the portal, their gazes filled with gratitude and hope for a brighter future. As the last child disappears into the swirling vortex, we share a moment of quiet triumph. Our mission to find Jocelyn is still paramount, but our detour has brought a small measure of justice to the lives of these innocent children.

With renewed determination, we continue our search for Jocelyn, more driven than ever to protect her from the monstrous force that is Valtorious.

We spy on unsuspecting servants as they gossip in dimly lit corners, our ears straining for any whisper of Jocelyn's name. We listen intently to the hushed conversations, our desperation mounting as we find no trace of her.

As we scour the castle, the sinking realization that she's not here dawns upon us. Relief mingles with frustration and worry, creating a tempest of emotions within me. If Jocelyn isn't in Romarie, where could she be? Niko's informant said he saw Socrates—alone—just before we left. Could they have been wrong?

Niko swears under his breath, his knuckles turning ghostly white as he clenches his fists. "We've wasted precious time searching this fucking place. But thank the fates she isn't here."

Remy nods, his jaw clenched as he struggles to maintain composure, the strain of Jocelyn's absence etched into every line of his face. "Given that we already know he's assembled a group to interfere with her fate, Socrates is our most viable lead. Let's track him down and see if he has any knowledge of her whereabouts." The desperation in his voice is unmistakable, revealing a man barely hanging on by a thread, driven by the need to find his mate.

My heart aches with the weight of Jocelyn's absence, lost and alone in a world far beyond her understanding. In that moment, I make a silent vow to myself that I will do everything in my power to bring her home, no matter the cost.

Though the thought that Socrates may have unbound her magic, allowing her to use it freely, fills me with dread. If she's using her magic, it's only a matter of time before King Valtorious senses it. As his blood, she is a beacon for him, a prize he will stop at nothing to claim for himself.

Moreover, Socrates's actions seem uncharacteristic of a fae guardian who has only watched over Jocelyn for a mere two weeks at most throughout her adult lifetime. I struggle to comprehend why he'd want to kidnap her, but with every other possibility exhausted, he appears more and more like the prime suspect. Despite our awareness of this potential threat, I can't help but worry about the consequences of him actually going rogue, acting on his own accord instead of following the shared mission of protecting Jocelyn. If he's taken her without our knowledge or consent, it's even more crucial that we find her before it's too late.

With every moment that passes, the pressure to find Jocelyn grows as we comb through Bedlam. We scour the scholarly halls of Academia, the vibrant streets of Rexuna, and the majestic landscapes of

Draconum. We venture to Sundahlia, the tropical haven where many fae and witches from Earth find solace, and then to the storm-ridden Convectus, the mysterious Tristique Islands, the haunting shadows of Occasus, and even the dangerous shores of Penn Island, where Bedlam Penitentiary looms menacingly.

Vox and Niko exchange tense glances as we press on, each continent presenting its own challenges. Each of us knows the consequences of failure, the danger that awaits Jocelyn if we can't find her in time, and the unsettling possibility that Socrates may not have her best interests at heart.

As we continue our search, I find myself growing more frustrated with each dead end we encounter. But we cannot give up. We must find her, for her sake and our own.

It's a race against the clock, and the stakes have never been higher. With Jocelyn being the most powerful heir according to prophecy, her significance in maintaining the balance of power in the realms is immense. King Valtorious will stop at nothing to control her and her magic, and he has shown no mercy to heirs who dared to defy him in the past.

He sent the last one to an early grave.

We can't stand by and allow his absolute domination over the magical world.

As we forge ahead, driven by love and desperation, I can only hope that our efforts will be enough to save her from the darkness that threatens her and to protect her from those whose intentions may not be as pure as our own—including Socrates.

My throat tightens at the thought of him. Could he be in cahoots with the king?

Remy

MY HEART RACES as we search the shadowy corridors of yet another castle—this time in Bedlam—rumored to be an old haunting ground of Socrates, the cold, damp walls seem to close in on us. I notice the faintest tremble in my hands, a visceral reminder of the grief I once experienced when I lost my parents. When I was too late. That pain had been unbearable, nearly shattering me, but it had also awakened my ancient powers as a fae guardian.

Now, as we search for my mate, a sense of dread builds within me that's far more intense than anything I've ever experienced. Every creak and groan of the castle echoes the growing unease in my chest, reminding me of the overwhelming sorrow that once gripped my heart. Losing Jocelyn, the one person meant to be my true partner, would be far more devastating than any past loss.

Niko's face is pale, his lips pressed into a tight line. I know he shares my worry, as does Vox. We all care deeply for Jocelyn, but for me, her absence feels like a gaping void, an emptiness that threatens to consume me whole.

I try to keep my focus on our task, searching every hidden corner and listening intently for any whisper of his or her name. But the false information we'd been given about Socrates not having her haunts me, feeding the dread that coils in the pit of my stomach. I can't help but imagine the devastation losing Jocelyn would bring—not only to me, but also to the realms and everyone we care about.

As we continue our desperate search, I notice my breaths coming in shallow, uneven gasps. I pause for a moment, leaning against a wall for support. My vision blurs, and the memories of my past loss bleed into the present, making the pain of Jocelyn's absence even more unbearable. Is this what a panic attack feels like? As though my chest is being cleaved in two? I force myself to take a deep, steadying breath, trying to push back the tidal wave of despair that threatens to drown me.

I think about the consequences we might face if we fail to find Jocelyn, and a cold dread runs down my spine. I could never live with my failure.

Because I can't live without her.

But as the seconds turn into minutes, and the minutes into hours, hopelessness continues to gnaw at my resolve. I grit my teeth and clench my fists, forcing myself to keep moving, to keep searching. We must find Jocelyn—for her sake, for our sake, and for the sake of all we hold dear. We cannot let the shadows of the past destroy our future.

CHAPTER EIGHTEEN

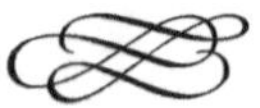

JOCELYN

The sun hangs low in the sky, spilling its hue, like molten honey, over the island. I pull on my swimsuit and head down to the beach, the warm, white sand sinking beneath my feet as I walk. The crystal blue ocean beckons, its waves crashing against the shore, and I can't resist its call. The tension of the past few days has been building, and I need an escape, even if it's just for a little while.

I wade into the water, the cool waves lapping at my legs as I swim further out. The salty spray stings my eyes, but I continue, feeling the water grow colder and deeper.

As I swim further from the shore, I feel an inexplicable connection to Socrates, the mysterious man who has captivated me since I first laid eyes on him. I can't deny the pull I feel towards him, despite the strangeness of the situation. There's something about him that has me questioning everything I thought I knew about my life and myself.

Suddenly, the water around me shimmers and changes, as if a veil has been lifted. My heartbeat quickens, my senses sharpening as I realize I've crossed some invisible boundary. Panic rises within me. What have I done? How did I manage to wander so far from the safety of the island? I feel exposed, vulnerable, as if I've unwittingly revealed myself to the world.

Quickly, I turn and swim back toward the island, my heart pounding in my chest. The water shimmers once more, and I know I've crossed back over the boundary. I need to tell Socrates about my experience—perhaps he can make sense of it.

As I reach the shore, I race across the sand, my feet sinking into its warmth. I find Socrates near the edge of the beach, his eyes filled with concern as he takes in my frantic state.

"Socrates," I gasp, struggling to catch my breath. "I crossed some kind of boundary in the water. I don't know what it means, but I felt like I was exposed, like I'd revealed something I shouldn't have."

He furrows his brow, his expression darkening. "Jocelyn, that boundary is a protective shroud I placed around the island to keep us hidden. By crossing it, you may have alerted others to our presence."

Just as he finishes speaking, the sky darkens, and a deafening roar echoes through the air. I look up to see Remy, Vox, and Niko, powerful wings carrying them through the stormy sky. Their faces are etched with worry and urgency.

Is all of this ... real?

As they land on the beach, an overwhelming blend of relief, confusion, and hurt surges through me. The sight of Remy, with whom I share an inexplicable bond, and his companions with powerful wings unfurled makes it all too real, solidifying the truth I've been shielded from my whole life. Remy's wings are a striking blend of gold and copper hues, the feathers glinting in the sunlight, while Vox's wings are an iridescent silver that seems to shimmer and shift with every movement. Niko's wings are an elegant deep indigo, like the midnight sky dotted with stars.

The realization that I've been lied to for so long leaves me reeling, my emotions at war within me. The connection I feel for Remy is strong and undeniable, but so is the pull I feel toward Socrates, the mysterious man whose connection to me remains unknown. Fear grips my heart at the thought that my actions might have alerted King Valtorious to my presence, putting all of us in grave danger.

Remy speaks first, his voice heavy with urgency. "Jocelyn, you must come with us. Crossing that boundary has alerted us to your presence, but it may have alerted others as well." The panic on their faces intensifies the knot of unease growing in the pit of my stomach. I stand there, torn between the comfort of Socrates's presence and the powerful connection and protection Remy, Vox, and Niko offer, while grappling with the truth that has turned my world upside down.

"What do you mean?" I ask, my voice shaking.

"Did Socrates tell you who we really are?" Remy approaches, hand outstretched, but I shrink back from him, and into Socrates' arms.

"Did he explain how you lied to me? Yes," I whisper, the hurt in my voice evident.

Agony flashes across Remy's face, and I feel it in my chest.

"We've been keeping an eye on you for your protection. Everything we did, we did because your life is at risk." Vox gestures to Remy and Niko before pointing to where I'd been swimming. "But now you've crossed the boundary, others may know you're here. Others like King Valtorious."

My heart thrashes as I process their words, feeling a mix of betrayal and fear. Socrates has been honest with me from the beginning, while the others have been keeping secrets. Yet, with danger looming, I know I need to trust *someone* if we're to face the challenges ahead.

As I stand on the beach, I can sense the tension between Socrates and the guardians. They regard each other with suspicion and distrust. Remy, Vox, and Niko clearly believe Socrates is a threat, having kidnapped me and taken me away from them. But from what I've experienced with Socrates, he only wanted me to know the truth about my identity and keep me safe.

Socrates, on the other hand, doesn't seem to view the guardians as enemies. He's wary, but his focus is on protecting me.

"What are you doing with her, Socrates?" Remy demands, his voice filled with anger and concern. "You took her from us without any explanation."

Socrates remains calm, his gaze never leaving mine. "I did what I thought was necessary to protect her and reveal the truth about her heritage. She doesn't deserve to be lied to."

"It's our job! *Your* job! Or did you forget that?" Remy's face hardens. "We've been protecting her. That's our duty. You know we had our reasons for keeping the truth from her, and now you've put her in danger."

I feel torn, caught between the men I feel an undeniable connection to and Socrates, who has shown me nothing but kindness and honesty. I don't understand why they're at odds with each other, but I need to know the truth.

"Please," I say, my voice trembling. "Can someone explain to me what's going on? Why is everyone keeping secrets from me?"

Socrates looks at me, his eyes filled with empathy. "Jocelyn, there are forces at play that neither you nor the guardians fully understand. I've been trying to protect you, but it seems there's someone who wants to use you for their own gain."

The guardians exchange glances, clearly uneasy about the situation. Niko speaks up, his voice cautious. "Socrates, if what you're saying is true, then we might be on the same side. But we need to know more. We can't just blindly trust you."

Socrates nods, understanding their concerns. "I realize that. But time is running out, and we must act quickly if we're to keep Jocelyn safe."

As the tension mounts, I'm left with a million questions, too few answers, and a growing sense of dread. What will happen now that everyone knows I've crossed the boundary, revealing my location not only to the guardians but potentially to King Valtorious as well? Can the guardians and Socrates find a way to work together to protect me, or will their mistrust drive them further apart?

And what will become of me, caught in the middle of this web of secrets and lies?

As I stand there, struggling to comprehend everything that's happening, a sudden, powerful gust of wind sweeps across the beach. The air crackles with energy, and a strange, foreboding sensation washes over me. I can see the fear and uncertainty on the faces of the guardians and even Socrates.

The beach, once a serene paradise, now churns with an undercurrent of dread. The sand appears to dance with the wind, creating a disorienting scene, as shadows creep from the corners of my vision. In that instant, the world shifts, and a group of sinister figures emerges on the beach, their twisted forms like a living nightmare.

Seeing them tugs at a memory locked deep inside me. Scenes of my early childhood come rushing back—my birth mother, a beautiful, ethereal woman with pointy ears and hair as white as bone, carrying me in her arms as we flee through the woods in the earth realm. She was desperate to protect me, her eyes filled with fear and resolve. Her love for me was unwavering, even as the monsters pursued us relentlessly. She knew that they were sent by King Valtorious to capture me, and she was willing to risk everything to keep me safe.

The monstrous figures on the beach are eerily familiar, their grotesque appearances etched into my earliest memories. They have black, gnarled skin, like burnt bark, and twisted limbs that bend and contort in unnatural ways. Their eyes are empty, black voids that seem to swallow the light around them, and their mouths are filled with jagged, razor-sharp teeth.

As these memories flood my mind, a mixture of fear and rage takes hold of me. My birth mother had sacrificed everything to keep me away from these monsters, and now they were here to finish what they'd started so many years ago.

The sinister creatures snarl and hiss as they approach, their twisted bodies moving with a horrifying grace. Socrates, Remy, Vox, and Niko form a protective circle around me, their faces set with steely resolve.

With a sudden surge of energy, my newfound magic ignites within me, fueled by my intense emotions. The raw power thrums through my veins, empowering me as I step forward, ready to face the monsters that had haunted my past.

"Enough," I say, my voice steady and unwavering. "I will not let you take me, and I will not let you hurt those I love."

As the monsters charge, we brace ourselves, prepared to fight for our lives and the future of the realms. And as the creatures press in around us, we know that our fate, intertwined and bound by love and destiny, will change the course of history forever.

Whether or not I'm ready for it.

WILL Jocelyn and her fae guardians be able to overcome the monstrous forces sent by King Valtorious? Even if they do, can they evade his grasp for another three years, until it's safe for Jocelyn to reclaim her rightful place as ruler? And what will the council have to say about the intimate bond forged between Jocelyn and her guardians, a breach of the longstanding Edict of Separation? **Discover the answers in Fae Guardians (Fae Gods Book Two).** And if you want more from the realm of Bedlam or Romarie, I suggest you start with **Bedlam Moon (Bedlam Moon Trilogy, Book One).** Wonder what your fae order would be? **Take the quiz on my author site.**

ACKNOWLEDGMENTS

Dearest readers,

Your unwavering support and encouragement have been a constant source of inspiration throughout this journey. Your enthusiasm for my characters and their worlds keeps me going even on the toughest writing days. Thank you for being the best fans a writer could ask for (I've created a new group just for you, too).

To my family, thank you for putting up with my unpredictable writing schedule and my constant stream of "what if" questions. Your unwavering love and support have kept me grounded even when my characters were spiraling out of control.

I'd like to extend a special thank you to Jess, my brilliant editor and partner in crime. Your insight and guidance have been invaluable to me, and I feel so fortunate to have you in my corner. You truly are a wizard, and I can't imagine embarking on this journey without you.

I also want to acknowledge the talented professionals who helped bring this book to life, from the cover designer to the proofreader to the marketing team. Your hard work and dedication have not gone unnoticed.

Last but not least, a shout-out to my writing group, whose feedback and support have been instrumental in shaping this story. And to my mentors and teachers, who have helped me develop my craft over the years – thank you for believing in me and pushing me to be my best.

XOXO,
Kathy

ABOUT THE AUTHOR

As a blood descendant of literary greats like Jane Austen and Emily Dickinson, and from a long line of artists and creators, #1 bestselling author Kathy Haan believes that the secret to telling a great story is living one. The second youngest, in a massive horde of children between her parents, she did her best to gain attention and kept everyone entertained with jokes and wild stories.

She lives a life of adventure with her hunky husband, three children, and Great Pyrenees in the Midwest, United States. While this is her fourth series, you might've seen her work in Forbes or US News, where she's a regular contributor. Or, in Notoriety Network's 12x international award-winning documentary, #SHEROproject.

CHAPTER ONE

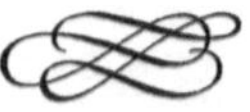

BEDLAM MOON (BOOK ONE, BEDLAM MOON TRILOGY)

Time is a funny thing. The worst moment of my life is so fresh in my memory, but twenty-six years is an entire lifetime to be away from her. I was eight years old when she vanished. Long enough to remember her, but not long enough to hang on to the details.

There's a sign outside the entrance to the long, overgrown driveway that leads to the cabin. It reads, *"NO TRE3PA33ING"* with inverted S's. Below the sign is a little alien ship attacking Earth, although I'm not sure how ominous any would-be trespassers think it is.

I turn my Jeep off the main logging road and drive down the gravel entrance, which snakes around giant pine trees and wildflowers. Weeds grow amongst the rocks, cracking them apart and taking their place. After the last set of evergreens, the vegetation thins out, and the driveway opens up into a clearing in front of the cabin. The old place sits on a hill overlooking a small pond that ripples in the early summer breeze.

My hands shake involuntarily as I pull the Jeep next to the cedar log cabin. The old beams of sunlight stream through the branches of the pines and oaks, creating an oasis of light in a patchwork of darkness. I place the vehicle in park and shut off the engine. *So many years.* I slide my trembling hands under my thighs in an attempt to steady them and lean against the headrest before closing my eyes.

I thought I'd never come back here again, let alone find the place, but somehow my heart knew the way. The police tape around the weather-warped porch has faded to a warm, soft yellow color reminiscent of a baby chick.

This is where I last saw Mom.

She went out to catch breakfast at the little bluegill-stocked pond on our property. She hadn't returned by the time I woke up, so I went to look for her. The fish was good that time of year, and she wanted to fry up a batch of fresh fish cakes for dinner that night. Her fishing pole and tackle box sat next to her chair, but she wasn't there. They never found my mom, and with no dad around, they sent me to foster care.

Now I'm back at the place where my entire world fell apart.

But there's a bud of hope blooming in my chest when I open my eyes and turn my gaze to the small brown package, still untouched, sitting on my front passenger seat.

Whenever I'm traveling the world, my best friend Hannah receives mail for me and lets me know what bills I have. When she got this package, she forwarded it to the concierge at the Minneapolis airport so I could fly back from the Amazon and see if this leads me to more clues at the cabin.

When I relax my hands and slow my breathing, I reach for the box and place the parcel on my lap. After taking a few deep breaths—like my former therapist taught me—I use the Jeep key to pierce the packing tape Hannah placed around it. I pull out the white slip of paper and worry my lip while reading the scrawling print.

Lana,

I'm sorry I didn't send this to you sooner. This was in your mother's things, and Annabelle would want you to have it now.

Love,

D

The handwriting is unfamiliar. I set the mysterious letter on my seat and unfold the cream-colored tissue paper at the bottom of the box. Nestled within it is the key that Hannah told me about. The new key in my hand is strange; its handle a deep, dark metal with a pattern of blue and red gemstones embedded in the surface, too many to count. It almost seems to vibrate with energy, ricocheting through my limbs.

Not an ordinary key, indeed.

I turn it over in my hand and trace the intricate details with my finger. Tilting my head back against the headrest, I vaguely remember my mom having a similar key, but this isn't hers.

I remember little about hers, other than its weight and the pearly sheen that glimmered in the light. When I had friends over, we'd spark our imaginations, dreaming up stories of how her key could open any door in any house. Mom wasn't too keen on my fascination with it and would insist I be gentle with it.

Now, I have a similar key of my own, but who sent it? An array of small, vibrant blue and red gems adorns the entire handle. There are far too many to count, and I have a strange suspicion these might not be ordinary gems.

Palming the key in my hand, I grab my backpack from the floor of the passenger seat and toss the letter, box, and tissue paper inside. Stepping out of the Jeep, my gaze lands on the aged humble abode I spent every summer in during my youth. After twenty-six years of neglect, the wood is weathering, and a pang of guilt hits my stomach that I haven't been back to look after the place.

I grip the police tape and ball it up before shoving it into my jacket pocket, cursing as thunder cracks in the distance. I look up. The sky is blue, but along the horizon, storm clouds threaten to drop a lot of rain.

I cup my hand over my eyes as I peer into the glass on the wooden door. Inside the cabin everything is just as it was when I left it; in the kitchen is an oak table where my mom and I would roll out dough for biscuits. One of the legs is a little shorter than the others and makes a wobbling sound when you rest your elbows on it. Part of me thought Mom did that on purpose so I wouldn't.

Standing back from the door again, I eye the keyhole, slightly larger than a dime. The door is a dark green, with a large brass knob in the center. I've come too far not to try it.

I position the key against the hole, not sure if it will fit. The key feels warm and tingles in my hand. What is happening?

A black barrel sprouts from the bottom of the keyhole and darts around like an insect. It starts to spin faster and faster, like a drill bit, the sound of metal sliding against metal. Just as quickly as it began, it stops, exhaling a puff of smoke and leaving a hole large enough for me to fit my pinky finger through. I glance around the property in disbelief, wondering how someone pulled such an elaborate prank on me. And *why*?

At first, the key doesn't look like it will fit. I push on it anyway, and the bit shrinks and slides into the keyhole perfectly. I turn the key, and it rotates smoothly in my hand as the door unlocks. I push the door open, and it creaks with almost three years of disuse.

No ordinary key, indeed, I think again before placing it in my jacket pocket.

With my hand on the doorknob, I step over the threshold and close the rustic, wooden door behind me as I take in my familiar surroundings. It's like stepping into a time capsule: the worn pine floorboards, the fieldstone fireplace with lopsided cinder blocks for hearthstones, and the red and purple oval rug made from old t-shirts draped in front of it. On particularly chilly nights, I'd fall asleep on the rug while playing with my dolls. By morning, my mom had scooped me up and placed me in bed.

I glance over at the kitchen. The old oak table that had been covered in so much spilled food and craft projects as a child is still here, and the cabinet with glass doors is still above it. Inside there are all my old school photos, ribbons, and medals.

I step over to my rocking chair and stare at the ashes in the hearth, long cold, as a melancholic ache crushes my chest. In front of the fireplace is my white stuffed gorilla I named Kongo after watching it in theaters. Thinking back on it, I was far too young to see it, but Mom let me anyway. She'd given this to me when I got my tonsils and adenoids taken out. It kept me company through many late-night bedtime stories, where she'd read me R.L. Stine books until I was old enough to read them myself. All of my Barbie dolls are still stacked next to it in an unceremonious heap.

The cabin isn't huge but it's big enough for two people; a tiny kitchen, a Queen-sized bed, a twin-sized bed, and a couple of rocking chairs placed in front of the fireplace along the opposite wall.

The entire property is off-grid, and there are still a few logs in the holder next to the fireplace, but I will need to gather some more firewood if I plan on being comfortable tonight. This far North, thunderstorms can often welcome evenings just on this side of cold. After bringing in the rest of my bags and the supplies, I look for the ax we kept here for chopping wood and I find it in our tall cabinet in the kitchen.

Walking outside, a dark gray rain jacket on, and new hiking boots squeaking on the soggy overgrown path that wraps around the cabin, I make a mental note to clean the leaves off it in the morning.

In the shed I find protective glasses and a splitting wedge, which will make my job a lot easier. With the storm headed this way, I don't have much time to get the job done. I'm happy to find a felled black walnut tree nearby. Mom always hated them, and not because they dropped huge green husks that fell from them and clogged up our push mower.

I spend forty-five minutes chopping wood, resting on my knees every thirty seconds. It's the same thing I do when I travel so people don't see me huffing and puffing while climbing the hills of Riomaggiore. Only then, I turn around and snap pictures so it looks like I'm meaning to stop, and not just out of breath.

So, I might be a little more than out of shape.

The sky darkens until it's difficult to tell when one log splits into two, and that's when I give myself permission to stop. The first of the raindrops hit my cheeks, helping cool my overheated skin. Exhaustion takes over me after the back-breaking labor and carrying the split logs into the cabin to nestle in the wood holder next to the fireplace. I contemplate heading straight to bed, but a rumble in my stomach warns me otherwise.

I didn't know how hungry I was until I smell the smoky, spiced scent that now tickles my nostrils. I follow the odor around the side of the cabin, straining to find the source of the smell. And then I whip my head up when I hear the crunch of gravel out front.

As I approach the front of the cabin, I spy a tall, shadowy figure stalking up the driveway, and I freeze mid-stride. Ice bubbling to the surface of my blood, I stand still, like a deer caught in the sights of a predator, more afraid than I've ever been. I'm in the middle of nowhere, and the fading light of day, coupled with the storm right near us, gives the area an ominous feel.

Who on Earth is here?

"I'm sorry for frightening you, *Sahira*." He has an accent that I can't quite place, and his voice is like liquid honey.

"Who … who are you?" I fumble to turn on the flashlight on my phone.

I point the beam of light at the figure, slowly closing the gap between us. In front of me is a man built like a granite mountain, and I glance around for any sign of another person.

The second I determine he's alone, my eyes lock onto him, drinking in every detail as if my life depended on it—and it might— his jet-black hair resting across his forehead, terra cotta skin, and dark eyelashes that frame striking blue eyes, like gemstones caught in the light of the setting sun.

He appears to be in his early thirties, his complexion flawless enough to pass for a professional model on any magazine cover. Paired with his tailored suit, so at odds with the Northern woods, he appears as though someone plucked him from the pages and deposited him in my path.

My heart thrashes in my chest at the intensity radiating from his gaze. Raw emotion flashes across his face, as though I were the answer to every question, prayer, and hope he's ever had. I feel undressed in front of him, like my soul is laid bare before him and he cradles it carefully in his hands. I'm overpowered by a flood of emotions so powerful I can barely breathe.

I should be afraid and curse myself for leaving my ax by the chopping block. Instead, I continue to freeze where I'm at, staring far longer than is acceptable for a first encounter.

The man standing before me is more than just beautiful. He's exquisite. My mouth hangs open slightly as I take in his well-defined arms hidden underneath his tight two-piece suit, his lean waist, and the way his strong legs take root in the ground below him. He must be well over six feet, and his broad shoulders hold a confidence I don't feel right now.

My eyes travel to his face. He has a dark, sun-drenched look to him that makes me think he's from the Middle East, although his blue eyes suggest I might not understand what the hell I'm talking about.

Is he an investigator? Did Hannah let them know about the box I received?

The corners of his mouth curl up, revealing a brilliant straight set of teeth, radiating kindness. Like a warm embrace, I'm overcome with a feeling of peace, one I don't fully understand. How could his smile be so captivating and comforting? Was it the soft twinkle in his eye or the slight curve of his lips? I'm aware I should be afraid, but instead, I feel a strange sense of safety, especially as the intensity in his eyes fades.

I angle my body toward the man on the driveway, giving a little wave as I push my long, tangled hair behind my ears. My rain jacket hangs open, and that's when I notice my oversized t-shirt and black leggings are covered in dust and small bits of wood. I desperately need a shower and my muscles ache from chopping wood. I should run for the ax, not get lost in this stranger's eyes.

"I'm Osgood Finlandian, but you can call me Oz. I own a cabin down the road and thought I'd check out the place after I drove by and saw tire tracks leading here. No one's been here in a good twenty-five years, so I wanted to make sure people weren't breaking in."

Twenty-five years? While true, the man in front of me can't be over thirty-five or forty. I don't recall any other kids living nearby when I was little. Unless you count the occasional family staying at the campgrounds between here and the entrance to the forest.

"Thanks for looking in on the place. I'm Lana Chapman-Sawyer. This is my cabin, but I haven't been here since I was a kid." I'm still wary of the stranger in front of me.

"Ah, okay." He runs a hand through his thick, jaw-length hair. "You're the woman whose mom disappeared here ... I'm sorry."

And there it is—the inevitable moment when people remember the scared little girl whose mom vanished. My stomach flip-flops at the idea that this beautiful stranger knows about the absolute worst event of my entire life. It broke me, and I've spent the rest of my life trying to find the pieces again.

"Yeah." I absentmindedly toe gravel at my feet. "I was eight when she disappeared. I'm back to piece together what might have happened to her." No sense in hiding the story; he already knows it.

Everyone did.

"Would you like some help? My family has owned a lot of this forest for several centuries, and I don't think there's another person alive who can navigate these woods better than I do."

I think about that for a moment, digesting Oz's offer, and consider the odds. Investigators spent years trying to figure out what happened to Mom, to no avail, so I could use the help. Besides, despite being startled when Oz first arrived, I believe I can trust this man. My intuition has never steered me wrong before.

"Actually, that would be great. Thank you. Uh ... I'd invite you in, but I haven't settled in yet, and I'm still trying to find my bearings." Glancing at the storm, I wince. The nice thing would be to invite him in, especially as the rain picks up, but I'm still hesitant.

While I don't have a lot of belongings, my stuff litters the table and both of the beds. I'm also very certain that the bra I'd taken off and flung across the room as soon as I got in the cabin is on full display somewhere on the floor. With that realization, I throw my arms over my chest and zip my jacket.

Oz averts his eyes. "Not a problem, Lana. Would you like to come over to my place, and we can map out a game plan? I've got a hot shower. You can freshen up while I make us something to eat. You've had a long day from the looks of it."

Ouch. Was he admitting I look like shit? Despite my embarrassment over my disheveled state, the idea of being close to him stirs up something inside me.

"I'd kill for a hot shower, thank you. Let me grab a few things really quick." I start walking away but hesitate, turning back to meet his gaze. "Just wait here, okay?"

He inclines his head, and I pivot on one leg before bolting up the creaking porch steps to the cabin, taking them two at a time. Adrenaline courses through me as I slip on the top step, and in a horrifying second, I stumble. My arms stretch outward, desperate for something to grab onto, but instead of the unforgiving ground, my hands meet those of a stranger. He catches me as I trip, his muscled arms holding me steady. His skin is cold, but his touch sears through me like fire, blazing a path through my chest before pooling low in my belly.

Oz helps right me, and I dust myself off. He saves my dignity and doesn't say a word. Mortified, I run into the cabin to grab my stuff, and after shutting the door, I shrink down against it.

Well, that was freaking embarrassing.

I collect myself against the door, but then I remember Oz is still waiting outside for me, so I dart across the room, grabbing clean clothes and some toiletries. I pause my hand over my makeup bag and consider whether I should bother putting on makeup after I shower. He's seen me at my worst, and it is late in the evening. I don't want him thinking that I'm trying to impress him.

I mean, I *am* trying to impress him, but I don't want him actually *knowing* that.

Who am I kidding? Of course I'm going to put makeup on. Sure, he's probably not interested, but I can always bring my best self, right?

Maybe this man likes thick chicks, and we'll spend the evening rutting in the woods.

A wicked grin crosses my face, and I grab the makeup bag and toss it in my backpack. *Careful, Oz; I'm a man-eater when I have my hair and makeup done.* With that thought still on my mind, I exit the cabin, locking the door behind me.

A grin spreads across Oz's face, and his two eyebrows rise in unison. "All set?"

The air between us is perfumed sweet with a hint of spice and vanilla, so I take a deep breath through my nose before I respond. Perhaps it's the wildflowers at the side of the house.

I give him a nod, and we start down the long driveway. Now that I'm side-by-side with Oz, a breeze sends another aroma up my nose of Earth and elemental, which is likely the storm that seems to be holding out on us. I can't help but take a deep breath to inhale more.

As the leaves and gravel crunch beneath our feet, I gaze down at Oz's leather shoes. Why is he dressed so nicely out here? They're huge and had to have cost more than my entire outfit combined.

"Size fifteen." Oz quirks an eyebrow at me.

I glance down at my boots. "I thought I had big feet."

He smirks. "Where were you before you came back to the cabin?"

Do I explain that after my adoptive parents died, I had an early mid-life crisis and sold everything I owned so I could escape and travel the world? That, since then, I've traveled through much of Europe, Central, and South America, hitching rides on boats and buses and clinging to the sides of trucks? I'm not sure if he's ready for that level of crazy yet. Instead, I tell him about South America.

"I was traveling in Colombia for a bit, and I stayed near Leticia in the Amazon Rainforest, right off the Amazon River."

"I spent a lot of time in that area, so I'm familiar with the Amazon. ¿Habla Español?"

"No. I took Spanish, but I remember little. Are you fluent?"

"I speak a few languages, and I've done a lot of traveling. I have business dealings all over the world."

As a free-spirited person, I feel even more inadequate learning those things about Oz, and I can only imagine what he thinks of me now. The gal who got an MBA only to give up a lucrative corporate job in pursuit of adventure.

The rain starts, and I pull my hood up. Oz plucks a black umbrella out of the inside pocket of his coat. We continue small talk and walk another half mile, wedged together under his umbrella until we reach the entrance to his cabin's driveway. He starts up the pavement, and I follow suit, but there's no cabin in view at all, although I spy light through the trees. My nerves stir a little.

"It's about a quarter-mile walk. Are you going to be alright?" He eyes my obviously brand-new, never-been-scuffed-before hiking boots.

I tell him to press on, although my heels are chafing.

Eventually, the "cabin" comes into view. The only word that comes close to describing this place is "compound." His definition of cabin and my definition of cabin differ wildly. His definition is grand, mine simple; he focuses on what you can see, I on what you cannot but feel.

The jack pine trees standing between me and the lodge-like building are so tall that I can't see their canopy in the dark. Each window of the place is at least twenty feet high, and a single door—just as big—sits at the front.

It's beautiful, and it fits him. Though, the idea of Oz living here, alone, in this seclusion doesn't make sense to me. Where are his friends? His family? If anything, it stirs a deep sadness in my chest.

Is he alone, too?

Embarrassed, Oz admits he got a little carried away when designing the place.

His cabin is resplendent in forest green with warm wooden beams. I step back and crane my neck to take it all in. The wood is stained a deep oak color, and the roof is made of cedar, which softens the security lights that filter through the trees. Scents of dirt and moss tickle my nose.

I can't breathe, can't think of anything but the big, lonely home in front of me. Yes, it's warm and inviting, but are the halls hollow and free of the pitter patter of little feet? Do the walls hold a lifetime of memories, or secrets of sorrow, too?

The wooden front door and the window frames, even the roof beams look as if they've been whittled by hand. Understanding dawns on me now. Each and every square inch of this place is meticulously crafted, with a heart and an artisan's soul. Details I'd been too naïve to notice now come alive. From the driveway, this place is foreboding and a little cold. But up close? At the heart of it?

This is Oz.

My feet carry me up the stairs, and my heart places me somewhere I never thought I'd be again—home.

Wait, *home?* I shake my head. What the hell is wrong with me? I don't know this man, nor have I ever been inside his home. And I definitely didn't know this place sat right next door until today.

He holds the door open. "After you."

As I step inside, a cool gust of wind rushes through the side of my hair, billowing it back. Oz steps around me and takes my jacket from me, and places it in a closet near the front door. A glow of firelight warms the cold moisture off the marble floor as I step in.

I am at his *house.* This is a *big* house, but I can feel the warmth from the decor, which echoes sentiments of an old world gone by. A vintage chandelier, its beaded chain dripping with crystals, hangs from the vaulted ceiling and casts light upon the entry. All around the walls hang artwork, its curator one with a unique eye for the past and how it could inform the present.

My eye catches a painting across the foyer, and I step closer to capture a better look at the artwork. The painting is of a curvy woman, dressed in nothing but a sheer blanket draped around her ample bosom and tiny waist. My face heats at the signature in the bottom right corner of the canvas—*O. Finlandian,* painted in big loopy swoops.

He painted this woman, stroke by stroke, with such passion she seems to come alive under his brush.

Lucky girl. I pull at my filthy shirt, feeling like an intruder in my dirty clothes, and ask Oz to show me to the bathroom so I can shower.

He walks me past the expansive kitchen, where I inhale the smells of baking bread, up the wooden stairs, and down to the bathroom at the end of the hallway. It has a standalone, deep jetted tub along one wall and a marble-tiled walk-in shower along the other.

Oz flicks on the towel warmer and sets a very fluffy bath sheet along the top bar. "Do you want a towel for your hair, too?"

He must spend a lot of time around long-haired women, but probably not enough time around curly-haired ones. "No thanks. Because I have curly hair, I usually wrap it in a t-shirt to dry."

At that, he inclines his head, leaves the room, and returns with one of his t-shirts.

"Oh, you don't have to … "

"I insist." He extends his arm towards me, the t-shirt clutched in his hand.

I reluctantly take his shirt from him and set it on top of the towel, giving my thanks. He leaves the room, and I lock the door.

Foolish to be here, in a stranger's house using their shower, but let's not push it by leaving the door unlocked. I won't make it easier for him to murder me.

After undressing, I pick up his shirt, hold it up to my face, and inhale deeply. *It was him earlier;* that intoxicating aroma of earth, vanilla, spice, and an elemental sort of scent reminding me of thunderstorms.

My mind races with a million questions. What kind of crazy am I, drawn to a stranger like this? I want to trust him, but at the same time, he has that irresistible charm that all the women in true crime documentaries fall for. Still, he has a lovely Burberry-scented body and a face that could make even an angel cry.

Or sin.

Those pants of his hug his sculpted thighs so tightly, and I'd be a fool to not be attracted to him. I wonder if he's as into me as I am him?

Gods help me.

Read the **Bedlam Moon Trilogy**, starting with Bedlam Moon (book one) for the full story. It follows the story of Lana and her paramours and features tropes like found family, one bed in an inn, hidden powers, captive romance, evil cults, and a time traveling witch hellbent on making things difficult for them all.

ALSO BY KATHY HAAN

<u>Bedlam Moon Trilogy (Complete)</u>

Lana sets out to find the truth about her past, and when a hot vampire begins to unravel it for her, she's caught up in the web of an evil cult, prophecies, and curses. All while falling for the King of Vampires and his royal court. This is a why choose romance.

Bedlam Moon (Book One)

Tales of Bedlam (Book Two)

Wicked Bedlam (Book Three)

<u>Fae Academia Series (Incomplete, 8 planned)</u>

A spin-off of the Bedlam Moon Trilogy, we follow Lana's daughter, Rose, while she attends a magical university. The summer before college is perfect until the family begins to receive threats, and Rose ends up getting into a different college from her twin brother and her boyfriend. A male roommate, his hot friends, and a sexy professor all find themselves eager to win her affection. This is a why choose romance.

Bedlam Academy (Book One)

Arcane Scholar (Book Two)

Forbidden Rose (Book Three, ETA Q4 2023)

<u>Aggonid's Realm Series (Incomplete)</u>

A Realm of Fire and Ash (Book One)

A Realm of Dreams and Shadows (Book Two, ETA Q4 2023)

When the commander of an elite group of phoenixes ends up dead for real, she tries to convince the fae devil there's been a huge mistake. Can she convince him to let her go before he snags her heart? This is an enemies to lovers why choose romance.

~

<u>Fae Gods (Incomplete)</u>

Fae Gods (April 2023)

Fae Guardians (TBA)

They watched their charge her entire life, completely invisible to her and only intervening when necessary. When they get fed up with her miserable marriage, Jocelyn's fae god watchers decide to help. After all, no fae of royal lineage deserves to be left to wilt away on Earth. They devise a plan to reveal their true selves to her, calling themselves the Marriage Doctors. But what happens when, during the course of their live-in lessons, the infallible gods fall for their off-limits charge? This is a why choose romance.

~

<u>Bedlam Penitentiary (Incomplete)</u>

Bedlam Penitentiary (TBA)

At the most ruthless prison in the fae realm, you're either at the top of the magical food chain, or you've got to form alliances with those with the most power. Because at a prison where you must expend your magic or you'll die, it's a no man's land full of dangerous criminals. This is a why choose romance.